BEYOND CHANCE

KARICE BOLTON

DEDICATION

A huge thank you to the readers of the Beyond Love Series. You've made this series come alive, and I can't thank you enough for spreading the word about Brandy, Gabby, and Lily. Thank you also to my amazing husband and mother. Your support means everything.

ACKNOWLEDGMENTS

I want to say a simple thank you to Amazon, iBook, Barnes & Noble, and all of the other avenues available for the indie publishing world. It allows the art of storytelling to continue to flourish in unexpected ways!

Thank you also to:

Cover artist: Phatpuppy
Photography (couple): Teresa Yeh
Photography (background): Jon Bolton
Typography: BB Designs
Female model: Anya Kod
Male model: Steve Alario
Makeup/Hair artist: Nadya Rutman
Translated Poem: Baudelaire, Charles. Fleurs du mal. "Reversibility". Trans. William Aggeler, The Flowers of Evil (Fresno, CA: Academy Library Guild, 1954)

BOOKS BY KARICE BOLTON

BEYOND LOVE SERIES
BEYOND CONTROL
BEYOND DOUBT
BEYOND REASON
BEYOND INTENT
BEYOND CHANCE
BEYOND PROMISE
BEYOND the MISTLETOE

ISLAND COUNTY SERIES
FINDING LOVE IN FORGOTTEN COVE
LOVE REDONE IN HIDDEN HARBOR
TANGLED LOVE ON PELICAN POINT
FOREVER LOVE ON FIREWEED ISLAND
TEMPTING LOVE ON HOLLY LANE
CHANCE AT LOVE ON MYSTIC BAY
IRRESISTIBLE LOVE AT SILVER FALLS

LUKE FLETCHER SERIES
HIDDEN SINS
BURIED SINS
REDEMPTION
MIA

V MAFIA SERIES
BLAKE
DEVIN
JAXSON

MORE BOOKS BY KARICE BOLTON

THE WITCH AVENUE SERIES
LONELY SOULS
ALTERED SOULS
RELEASED SOULS
SHATTERED SOULS

THE WATCHERS TRILOGY
AWAKENING
LEGIONS
CATACLYSM
TAKEN NOVELLA (A Watchers Prequel)

THE CAMP

AFTERWORLD SERIES
RecruitZ
AlibiZ
UprisingZ

KARICE BOLTON

Chapter One

I dipped a freshly picked strawberry into a bowl of whipped cream and took a bite. The sweet juice and cream exploded in my mouth, and I let out a little moan of delight. I knew they had strawberries in Paris, but they wouldn't be as delicious as the ones in Washington. June strawberries in Washington were the best. Glancing around the kitchen, I leaned against the granite counter and dipped another strawberry. The sound of boxes being taped up down the hallway pushed an odd mix of emotions through me. I was excited to be going to Paris in a few weeks, but I was already missing the friends and life I'd be leaving behind.

Aaron was leaving in the morning to get things settled before I flew over, and that made my plight even worse. It had sounded like a great idea when he first mentioned it, but being without Aaron for three weeks was going to be awful. It's not like we hadn't spent time apart since we'd become a couple, but truth be told it wasn't this much time. And it wasn't like I wouldn't survive without him, but I knew I'd miss him like crazy, and I wasn't a fan of self-imposed torture. Everything about him always left me wanting more—whether it was his dashing smile or the brooding look he'd get when his imagination wandered to us—and the thought of being without either was excruciating. I let out a sigh at the thought and convinced myself it was time for a shower. It was starting to get chilly in only my camisole and boy shorts, and I hadn't planned on getting sidetracked by berries.

A strawberry stem fell to the floor, and I bent over to grab it. A sharp pain shot down my leg that took my breath away. I snatched the stem from the tile and shut my eyes as I tried to shake off the pain. Recovery had been a long process, and at times, it felt like I'd never completely be rid of the pain.

I slowly rose, tossing the stem in the sink, and let the pain work its way out. When it felt like the kinks had mostly left my leg, I opened my eyes to see Aaron watching me from the hall. There was something so intoxicating about his presence. His dark eyes held an intelligent spark that cut most off at their knees, but for me that spark enticed me to unwrap him and find out who he was. And so far it had been a fun adventure. Aaron arched a brow, accentuating his chiseled cheekbones and soft, pouty lips, which provided the perfect balance between hard and soft. Dressed in a pair of loose-fitting pajama bottoms that hung below his waist, the man was without a shirt, which rocked my stability a little too much.

"You okay? I heard a grimace."

I drew in a breath and nodded. Aaron seemed to be more in tune with my body than I was. It always amazed me how he knew when I was hurting, when I needed him. I felt a slight twinge at the thought of being without him even for a few weeks. To most it might sound a little ridiculous, but this was how our relationship worked. We were best friends, and we enjoyed one another's company. So shoot us.

"I didn't realize I'd made a noise. It was just a muscle twinge or something. No biggie." I smiled and took a bite of the strawberry I was still holding in my hand.

"Doubt it was nothing," he said, taking a few steps toward me. "Anymore strawberries in that bowl?"

He let me off the hook and for that I was grateful. I hated focusing on my injuries and prolonged recovery. I didn't want that to define me.

"A few." I picked an extra large berry out of the bowl and dipped it into the cream. "If you want it, you better come and get it."

His mouth inched up in a wickedly, deliciously

grin, and his expression intensified as his eyes filled with want.

"Is that so?" he asked.

I nodded and held the strawberry in front of me. "You better hurry or the whipped cream will melt and fall off."

His gaze held mine as he slowly walked through the kitchen and shook his head. "It's going to be damn near impossible to stay put in Paris while you're over here."

"We can always Skype and Face Time," I offered, feigning innocence.

He took a bite of the strawberry, and I finished it off before tossing the stem in the sink.

"That's not gonna cut it, babe." He stood in front of me, his eyes piercing as his stare captured mine. His fingers traced along my bare shoulder and up my neck, sending prickles along my exposed skin. I was at a loss for words as I stared into this gorgeous man's eyes. It was hard to believe how close I'd come to losing him and how much he'd given up for me.

"So what do you propose we do about it?" I asked, sliding my arms around his waist.

He tilted my chin with his hand and grinned, bringing his lips only inches from mine.

"I have so many things planned," he growled, as his mouth touched mine.

His lips tasted like strawberries as his kisses deepened and my body surrendered to his. Desire moved lithely through my blood as if he was a drug, and I needed my next fix. Feeling the heat of his mouth as his tongue dipped and teased with every passing moment created a fierce amount of longing and desperation. I didn't want to be away from him for more than a second, let alone three weeks.

Aaron's hands slid down to my waist, and he raised me up and gently placed me on the counter. Wrapping my legs around his waist, my body shuddered as he lifted my camisole over my head, tossing it on the floor. His lips left mine and slowly worked down my neck, shoulders, and breasts. I let out a moan as he cupped my breasts with his hands, slowly taking me into his mouth.

My hands ran through his hair as I threw my head back in ecstasy with every slight pull and tug his mouth delighted me with. The feelings inside of me exploded in an endless need for Aaron as I tightened my legs around his waist. Slowly releasing his mouth from my flesh made me insane with yearning as he brought his searing gaze back to mine. I slid my fingers around his waistband and pushed it down slowly. His eyes became more heated and wicked as my fingers scraped along his bare flesh.

"You drive me insane," he murmured, brushing his lips along the crook of my neck.

I cherished those words as both our bodies begged for more. He kicked his pajamas off the rest of the way and slid me off the counter, carrying me to the large couch in the family room. Placing me down gently, he sealed his mouth to mine with a soft and unexpected hum of delight as he hovered over me. I ran my hands down his stomach and felt his arousal as our kisses deepened. Cupping my face in his hands as if claiming me made my longing soar to a new level. The heat of his kisses turned demanding as the realization of his departure lingered between us. Propping himself with one arm, he slid his other hand down my belly and over my boy shorts. His fingers slid down to my thigh, along the edge of the fabric, causing my body to shudder with anticipation.

Unable to tear my gaze away from him, my eyes pleaded with him for more, but he only shook his head as he continued to tease and watch my body respond to him. Seeing his gaze canvas my body as if I were one of his sculptures destroyed my self-control, but I knew I was at his mercy.

His gaze tore away from mine as he brushed his mouth along my belly and moved lower. Using one hand, he slowly pushed my boy shorts down, and I shifted to move them the rest of the way. Aaron's gaze was heated as he brought his eyes back to mine. My breath faltered with anticipation as he bit his lip and slid his finger inside me. I ached for more as he watched my body answer to him as he scattered kisses along my belly. His hands followed right behind his mouth as I twisted my fingers in his hair, pulling him up to me. Feeling the warmth of his skin press up against mine created an aching hunger to feel all of him.

"I love you, Aaron Sullivan," I whispered, as my hands reached down to guide him. Without hesitation, he moved in between my legs and my world began to spin.

"You are my everything, Brandy," he murmured, his mouth next to my earlobe. "I love you."

A low rumble of untamed desire erupted between us as our worlds collided into one many times over before his departure. It had to be the best farewell in history.

CHAPTER TWO

"*I'*m going to miss you like crazy," Lily said, nearly running into a waitress as she bolted toward our table with her arms flung out. Gabby snickered and shook her head as Lily nearly strangled me with me a hug.

"It's not like I'm going to Paris for the rest of my life," I said, gently unwrapping Lily's arms from around my neck so I could swallow. "It's only for the summer."

"You're not gonna want to come home. I know it. Who would? I mean it's Paris," Lily said, as she slid into the booth next to Gabby.

"She's right," Gabby said, before taking a sip of her vanilla milkshake. "It's a dream of a city and the food..."

"Friends and family are what makes a home

and happiness, not location. Besides, I'm already getting homesick, and I haven't even left yet." I shifted the paper napkin out from under my silverware and glanced at Lily who was eyeing Gabby's milkshake. That girl could eat.

We had decided to meet at Carol's Diner for dinner tonight to say our farewells. The plan was to eat, gossip, and then run off to watch Ayden's fight so I could say my goodbyes to my brothers. Ever since I'd found out about Ayden's hobby, I'd been uneasy about keeping it from my parents, but I respected my brothers' wishes. We all knew what would happen if my dad found out, and it was best not to let that happen. Plus, the one fight I'd seen was pretty telling when Ayden laid his opponent out flat.

"I forgot when Aaron actually left for Paris. How long has he been there?" Gabby asked, as Lily flagged down the waitress.

I held in a sigh. "He's been there for three weeks. The pictures of the place we're staying look pretty sensational. It's near a ton of galleries and bookstores. It's completely furnished. He says he's already gained five pounds and had to stop eating crepes every morning."

Gabby chuckled. "Sounds like Aaron to be worried about that."

"I'm sure he's already added a few more crunches to his routine to compensate. I highly doubt he's willing to give up the crepes."

"Yeah. Probably not."

"What district is it in?" Lily asked.

"The sixth, I think he said. I have no idea what

that means in terms of location. The maps online tell me nothing."

Our server came over, and Lily placed an order for a milkshake, along with several appetizers for us to split. She was a woman on a mission and apparently very hungry. Lily turned her attention back to Gabby and then to me and smiled. "That's a really nice area to stay in. I love the first and sixth arrondissements. Great access to all the must-sees and the places are really posh."

"Posh?" I teased. "That sounds like me all the way." I gestured toward my body, which was covered in a pair of leggings and a sheer ivory top with a camisole underneath. My hair was scooped into a clip and if I remembered to even dab mascara on my lashes, I'd be surprised. Come to think of it, did I even shower this morning? I'd been so busy packing, I can't remember. I showered so late last night that had to count for something, right? Probably not. "Do I need to wear my wannabe-attorney clothes over there?"

Lily rolled her eyes. "You know what I mean. You'll love it. But I have to say..." her voice trailed off.

"What?" I steadied my gaze on Lily.

"The thing I'm going to love most about this whole thing is when we get to come for our visit. Can you imagine the three of us in Paris together? They're not going to know what to make of us," Lily laughed.

"Just promise me one thing," Gabby begged.

"What's that?" I asked.

"Don't do the cliché thing and start smoking. No matter what."

I smiled and nodded. It was impossible not to love Gabby. She was the perfect mother for us all. "I promise I would never dream of doing it. Promise."

"She's got a point," Lily chided in. "Everywhere you go, people are smoking. I think there are more people who do than don't."

Gabby grimaced and caught my attention. "Anyway, what time do you want me to take you to the airport?" she asked.

"I think I'd like to get there around nine in the morning, if that's okay."

"Totally."

I'd spent weeks getting ready for this trip and had already shipped the bigger items over. I'd run all our last minute errands over the past week. I changed our mailing address to a post office box that my family could check for us; I left a spare set of keys with Jason and Gabby; I gave Jackie a list of things to take care of for us; and I sent all of my registration papers to school again. I hadn't fully decided if I was going to attend in the fall, but I wanted to proceed as if I would be going.

Lily's milkshake was delivered, and she began sucking on the straw like she hadn't eaten in a week.

"So this will be it for awhile. All three of us out to dinner in Seattle…" Gabby mused. "Better soak it up." She flashed an evil grin as she dealt

11

another guilt trip.

"I bet you won't even know I'm missing. It's only a few months. Between Katie and the bakery, you'll be so busy you won't even know I'm gone."

"Nice try," she retorted.

"How's Katie doing?" Lily asked, turning in the booth to face Gabby.

"She's amazing. Absolutely amazing. I keep thinking that we've got it too good. She's adjusted so well and Jason is in love. I mean there are moments when I'll walk into the kitchen, and he's got her on the counter talking to her like she's his best bud. Granted her vocabulary isn't there yet, but that doesn't seem to faze Jason as he plots their next big adventure."

"That's so cute," Lily gushed. "You've got a good guy."

"I don't think you're doing so bad yourself," I teased. "My brother's not so shabby."

"Very true." Lily arched a brow and let out a sigh. "He's the one."

"The one?" I asked, thrilled to hear Lily talk about love, let alone dream about it.

"I know. I know. I never believed in all that soul mate stuff, but how else can I explain it?"

"It's true. There are so many different personalities in the world that when two people are not only attracted to each other, but are also compatible, it seems like it has to be divine intervention," Gabby agreed.

"And persistence," I interjected. "For those of

us who aren't always that willing to see what's directly in front of us... persistence by the man is always fortunate."

"To divine intervention and persistence," Lily said, raising her almost-empty milkshake glass for a toast.

We did our toast and placed the glasses back on the table as the server delivered our appetizers. By the looks of things, this would also be our dinner. I grabbed a nacho and took a bite, crunching into heaven.

"Do you think Ayden's going to stop fighting soon?" I asked, my eyes narrowing on Lily. "I've heard just one more fight over and over again, and I'm not sure what to make of it."

Lily nodded, wiping her mouth. "I bought it the first few times, but I don't anymore. I think the truth is that he loves fighting. There's an intensity about him when he gets in the zone. I honestly don't see him quitting anytime soon."

"I worry about him," I confessed, and Gabby nodded in agreement.

"I know," Lily said, glancing at Gabby and then at me. "I worry about him too, and I know Mason does as well."

She knew my brothers well, and it made me feel better about leaving. Granted they were my older brothers, but I still worried about them, and it was nice to think that someone would be watching over them while I was in Paris.

"I think you're right about that," I acknowledged. "Mason would never forgive himself if something happened to Ayden, and he hadn't been there to stop it."

"Let's not get all serious. This is your fun night before you leave. It's bad enough we're not having any drinks to celebrate."

"It was your idea," I pointed out, grinning.

She took a bite off a mozzarella stick and shrugged. "Touché."

"Well, I think it's fantastic that you'll be spending the summer in the city of love." Gabby smiled. "It seems like a dream. To have my brother's sculptures appearing in a gallery in Paris... I'm so proud of him, and I know my parents are too."

I nodded, knowing the amount of pressure that Aaron was putting on himself to make this opening a success, and it worried me. I wasn't exactly sure what it would take for him feel like he'd accomplished what he'd wanted, but I prayed that it would happen. He was putting so much of himself into these pieces that the thought of someone not liking them made my heart actually hurt. I couldn't imagine creating something and then putting it into the world only to be torn apart. I shuddered at the thought and redirected my attention.

"The sketches he's been working on for the sculptures are insane. I can't even imagine what they'll look like when he's finished. He's meeting with the curator tomorrow. She's really excited, and she says the gallery owner is too."

"Do you know much about her?" Lily asked.

I knew exactly what she was getting at and chose to ignore it.

I shook my head. "Not much. I'm excited to meet her though." I glanced down at the platters of appetizers and noticed most of them were almost empty. Gabby's gaze fell to the platters, and she smiled wryly before turning her attention to Lily.

"Is Ayden not feeding you while you two are at work?" Gabby asked.

Lily blushed and pushed away her plate. "I didn't eat anything today and then had a grueling workout. And since when did you become the food police?"

Gabby chuckled. "Just want to make sure Brandy's brother's feeding you. That's all."

The server arrived and glanced at the mostly empty platters.

"Can we get the rest to go?" Lily asked, handing the server a credit card without even waiting for the bill.

"Absolutely," the server responded, grabbing the platters off the table.

"Should we head over to the match?" I asked, glancing at the time on my phone.

"Probably," Gabby said.

"I'll bring your check," the server said.

"Thank you," I replied, getting a small knot in the pit of my stomach as I thought about the upcoming fight. No matter how I tried to fool myself it didn't work. What person in their right mind wanted to see their brother possibly get the shit kicked out of them?

"You look a little green," Gabby said.

"I think I—"

"Not you. Lily," Gabby said.

Lily stood up quickly, and she didn't look well. She spun around and rushed toward the bathroom.

"I'll go after her. You grab her food." Gabby dashed after Lily, and I waited for the leftovers. The server handed me the plastic bag and the credit card and receipt.

"Thanks," I responded, hoping the server would leave so I could sign for Lily and be done with it.

My phone buzzed and I saw a text from Aaron come over. My heart almost bounced out of my chest with glee. I'd missed him so much since he went over there, and I couldn't wait to see him.

Hey beautiful. I just woke up and wanted to tell you how much I love you. I haven't been able to keep you out of my mind. I can't wait to see you tomorrow. I've missed you so much, and I've got a little surprise for you...

My heart flipped, and I couldn't erase the smile that had magically plastered itself on my lips. Quickly texting him back, I felt the excitement of getting to see him again run through my veins. I was finally allowing myself to come out of the haze that I'd put myself in the last few weeks.

I can't wait to see you. I can't believe I'll be in Paris living with my artist boyfriend in a little over a day. Love you and don't forget about me.

He replied quickly.

You are unforgettable.

I sent him a heart and felt the warmth of his love flow through me. This was exactly what I needed. My assailant's trial was about to begin and I needed to be somewhere else. I'd been haunted by the accident and the nightmares never seemed to subside. I needed a fresh start in a new place until the trial was over and even then all I could do was hope that he'd be convicted.

I couldn't think of a more fun somewhere else to be. I spotted Lily and Gabby near the exit. Hopefully Lily wasn't so green. I snatched the credit card and leftovers and walked toward them.

"Feeling better?" I asked Lily.

She nodded. "Yeah. I didn't get sick. I just felt gross."

"Well, you look a lot better," I offered.

"And you look extremely dopey," Gabby snickered.

"I do not," I said, smiling.

"Yeah. You do," Lily agreed.

"I just got a text from Aaron."

"And he does that to you long-distance?" Lily smirked. "That's pretty impressive."

"No more impressive than what I've witnessed with you and Ayden." I opened the door and Lily and Gabby marched through it, with me following only a few steps behind.

"I'll take Lily since she got sick," Gabby said.

"I didn't get sick. I only felt a little queasy. I'm fine now and I'm driving myself. Besides. Ayden and Mason are taking one car and Ayden can drive us home after the fight. I promise I feel fine."

I grabbed my keys out of my purse and saw Gabby tuck in the annoyance behind her expression, but there was no arguing with Lily, especially since she was already opening her car door and sliding inside.

"See ya there," I said, walking to my car.

This was it. My last night in Seattle before I headed off to Paris. I slid into the seat of my car and glanced at the pile of unopened mail sitting on the passenger seat. A grey envelope caught my eye, and I picked it up quickly not recognizing the sender. I slid my finger along the seam as dread sizzled under my skin. I glanced around the parking lot and neither of the girls had left yet so I had time to check out what was tucked in the envelope. it was probably just a sneaky piece of junk mail. Companies were getting trickier every day.

With a quick tug on the document and an unfolding of the tri-fold paper, a claustrophobic sensation almost suffocated me as I stared at the writing. How could this be? He was in prison, awaiting his trial. Bail had been denied by the judge. There was no way he was out, and the prison checks all outgoing mail. My hands began shaking as I read the words slowly, and the nightmares threatened to overtake me.

Have a nice time in Paris.

How would Derek Bourot know that I was leaving for Paris? My hand moved down my leg; my fingers running along my leggings as the scars from the surgeries heated with my touch. I attempted to steady my breathing and tucked the paper back inside the envelope before tossing it on the seat. I backed my car out of the parking spot and followed Gabby and Lily to the match. I didn't have time for this. I would be gone soon and could leave this nightmare behind. I needed to leave it all behind.

CHAPTER THREE

*T*he warehouse was packed with fans. Tonight's fight was bigger than the last one I'd attended. It seemed like underground fighting was getting more popular by the minute, which I'm sure increased Mason and Ayden's take and added another reason why Ayden wouldn't be hurrying to leave the gig. Not that he needed extra cash, but easy money was easy money. I sighed and followed Gabby and Lily up the stairs to where Ayden and the other guys were getting ready. A man was standing guard at the door and took a step forward, blocking us from entry.

"I'm Ayden's sister and this is his girlfriend. He should be expecting us."

The guy nodded and took a step away from the door, letting us inside. The hallway was narrow and the linoleum floor dingy.

"This is so crazy," Gabby whispered.

"Tell me about it," I replied, trying to push away the anxiety from the letter. I was here for my brothers and didn't need to complicate the night. "We didn't have that greeting last time."

"Things must be more serious," Gabby said.

We turned the corner and spotted the guys. Ayden was already dressed for the fight and Mason was leaning against a table, talking to Jason.

"Lookin' good," I said, smiling at Ayden.

"Looking like a winner, I hope." Ayden's grin fell the moment his eyes connected with mine.

"What's going on?" he asked.

I looked over at Mason, and his eyes flashed to mine. His body stiffened as Ayden took a step forward. The halogen light flickered above, and the room felt stuffy and extremely warm. I didn't need Ayden worried about me as he was about to enter the ring.

"What do you mean?"

Ayden's stare stayed fixed on me.

"Just worried about leaving everything and everyone. Going to Paris for this long is a big deal, especially for me."

Ayden laughed. "A truer statement couldn't have been spoken. You'll love it over there, and it'll be your last hooray before law school. I bet this is the first time that you're going into a situation without a plan in place..." Ayden grinned and his brows arched up. "Am I right?"

I couldn't help but smile back. He was

absolutely right. I had no idea what to expect in Paris, and I had absolutely no idea what I was going to do over there. I was used to plans and routine and this was anything but.

"Don't sweat the small stuff," Ayden said, stretching toward the ceiling.

"I won't. You're right."

Gabby walked over to a chair near Jason and collapsed. "How did Katie do with Carla coming over to babysit?"

"Absolutely wonderful," Jason assured her. "It didn't hurt that Carla showed up with a teddy bear and a bag of popsicles."

"She certainly knows the way to someone's heart." Gabby closed her eyes as Jason placed a quick peck on her cheek, and I longed for Aaron. It wouldn't be long before I'd be in Paris, and all this nonsense could be put behind me. I knew I needed to pass on the information I received, but it wasn't ideal timing considering it was the night before I was set to leave on a plane.

Mason was far too quiet, and his eyes remained on me as Lily started speaking about eating too much at dinner.

"I know the feeling," I said, commiserating with her even though I'd barely eaten.

When Ayden was distracted with Jason, Mason walked over and pinned me in place with his gaze. He dropped his voice. "I know there's more going on than pre flight jitters. You need to tell me what's really on your mind."

Lily's smile dropped, and she watched me closely as I attempted to come up with another excuse only none came.

"Brandy, what's going on?" she whispered. "You didn't mention anything at dinner."

I glanced at Ayden and then back at Mason and Lily. "That's because it hadn't happened yet. Listen, I'll tell you both after Ayden's fight. I don't want to interfere or give anyone any reason to be distracted. Please..."

Mason nodded and Lily wandered over to Ayden.

"Is it about the trial?" he asked.

"Maybe. I don't really know the ramifications, but please, let's just drop it until after."

Mason nodded.

Ayden was hugging Lily as she gave him her little pep talk, and I glanced back at Mason, silently pleading with him to stay quiet.

"I hate to break up this little party," Mason said. "But I think it's that time."

Relieved that the attention had been taken away from me, I jogged over to Ayden and gave him a quick kiss on the cheek.

"Make it quick and painless," I teased.

"I'll do my best." He smirked and fist punched Jason and Mason before they left the room with Gabby and Lily right behind them.

"Good luck out there." I smiled and made my way out of the room to let Ayden have a few moments of quiet. Mason stood next to the door, waiting for Ayden, and Jason and the girls were down the hall, motioning for me to hurry up.

I stopped in front of Mason and held up my hand for the group to hang on.

"I'm going to miss you this summer," I said. "I wish you'd change your mind about coming over to Paris."

He shrugged and shook his head. "This is the busiest time of the year at dad's company. It wouldn't be right to leave him hanging like that."

I pretended to knock his jaw and laughed. "Who would've thought you'd be the responsible one."

"Hey, I resent that. I've always been the responsible one," he teased.

"The moment Ayden knocks his opponent flat, you better be prepared to let me know what's going on," Mason whispered.

"Promise. Now concentrate on pumping up our brother or whatever it is you do." I sprinted down the hall, leaving Ayden and Mason behind as we jogged down the stairs and pushed our way through the large crowd.

I scanned the crowd for any sign of the other fighter. I didn't know who or what I thought I was looking for, but I hoped to find someone who looked slow and sloppy.

The crowd began clapping, and I turned my attention back to the ring where the announcer was now stationed next to a female who was dressed in a white, string bikini.

"Is that Mason's girlfriend?" Lily teased.

"Beats me but probably." I grinned as I saw the ring girl parading around the mat, motioning for the crowd to get their volume up before they introduced the first fighter. Her red hair stretched down her back in ringlets, and her white bikini was strategically placed. One sneeze, and we'd have a serious wardrobe malfunction on our hands. It only took her one loop around the ring and the place was going nuts. The announcer introduced the first fighter, Maxwell Duncan, and the crowd turned into a mixture of boos and cheers.

My stomach became uneasy as he walked down the aisle. His body was oiled up, and his silver trunks hugged a very muscular form. He looked shorter than my brother, but he looked strong. I glanced at Jason who was nodding his head, assessing Maxwell.

"What do you think?" I hollered through the crowd noise.

"I think Ayden's got this hands down." Jason smiled and draped his arm over Gabby, drawing her into him.

"Me too," I said, watching Maxwell sneak between the ropes of the ring.

My brother's name was announced, and a loud roar surged through the building as Ayden began walking through the crowd with Mason right behind. Ayden looked like he'd already won the match. His concentration was solely on the ring and man in front of him as he made his way down the aisle. Ayden stepped between the ropes and into the ring. Mason gave him some last minute instructions as the first clang of the bell sounded.

The flutter of uneasiness had grown into full-blown panic. I wasn't cut out to watch my brother fight like this. Just one mistake was all it would take for my brother to be the one down on the mat.

The two men bobbed and weaved as they worked around the ring. Maxwell swung a jab and my brother ducked out of the way. Another swing from Maxwell missed my brother, but Ayden still didn't throw a punch. Lily was on her tippy toes even though there was no crowd in front of her. Her hands were clasped tightly as she stared intently at the ring. No matter what she said, watching Ayden made her as nervous as me. I turned my attention back to the fight just as Ayden landed a punch on Maxwell's cheek. The skin split open as Maxwell attempted to shake off my brother's punch. Maxwell ducked and landed a punch on my brother's ribs. Lily let out a gasp, but Ayden barely flinched from the contact. The ding of the bell signaled the end of the round, and I let out the breath I didn't even know I'd been holding in.

Ayden walked to the corner of the ring and Mason spoke to him as he wiped off sweat. I think Ayden was surprised that Maxwell managed to slip some contact in there. From what I'd heard and seen, my brother dodged the punches ninety-nine percent of the time. The next round began, and my brother's gaze penetrated straight through Maxwell as he effortlessly landed a punch into Maxwell's side. Spit flew out of the fighter's mouth, taking him off guard just enough for my brother to get in there again. Strategy was as much a part of winning as brut force, and my brother had both down pat.

I watched my brother's arm become the weapon of a victor as he looped over the shoulder of Maxwell. My brother's fist landed an overhead right punch into Maxwell's jaw, producing a spray of spit as his opponent's mouth dropped open; his entire head turning as his body flew to the ground. The look of triumph crept onto my brother's face as the match was called in his favor. It didn't take long for the crowd to go nuts as we all quickly exited. Mason led Ayden back up the stairs with Lily right behind, while the rest of us went to the parking lot.

Whether a person was into these fights or not, it was impossible not to get caught up in the whole excitement of everything. The exhilaration could be felt zapping through the air as spectators triumphed with their pick. My brother had obviously been the favorite.

"Wanna just meet at the place up the street?" Gabby asked.

"Sounds good to me." I climbed in my car and turned on the overhead light to look at the envelope once again. There were so many things about it that bothered me. I didn't even know what to be most concerned about: the fact that it had gotten through the prison screeners, or the possibility that it had never been mailed from behind the bars in the first place. Not to mention the content of the letter. How did he know I was going to Paris? I shoved the envelope into my purse and turned off the overhead light. I spotted

Lily, Ayden and Mason leaving the building and waited for them to pile into their cars. The trepidation flowing through my veins was exactly what I'd been running from ever since the accident. I'd done a really good job of hiding it from everyone, including myself, and now with this six-word sentence, my bubble was threatened, and my fear was that escaping clear across the globe wasn't enough.

Pulling behind Mason's car, I followed him in a trance of uncertainty to the place we were all meeting. It felt like I was on autopilot as I pulled into the lot and parked. I watched them all pile into the bar and gave myself a few extra minutes. I needed to calm myself down. I felt so alone without Aaron here. He'd been the one who helped me cope this entire time. It wasn't until he was gone that I realized how much support he'd lent over the last few months. I drew in a deep breath and glanced around the lot. Even though it was almost nine o'clock in the evening, the sun still hadn't set, which made me feel marginally safer. I swung open the door and made my way inside the bar.

Lily and Ayden were already huddled in a large booth in the far corner. Gabby and Jason were still standing at the edge of the booth gabbing, and I scoped the place for Mason, spotting him at the bar ordering a round of victory shots. I made my way toward my friends and brother and felt immensely better. No more being alone with my thoughts.

"Was that intense or what?" Lily said, shaking

her head. "He's certainly got that skill down." She looked up at Ayden admiringly, and he flashed a grin. There was nothing more satisfying than seeing Lily with Ayden. They were meant to be. There was no denying it.

I laughed and slid into the booth next to Lily. Gabby and Jason slid in across the table and I nodded. "He certainly does know how to get the job done."

"Now spill the beans, knucklehead. What are you hiding?" Ayden said, and Lily pressed her body to the back of the booth, looking somewhat like a robot, so that Ayden's gaze landed on mine.

I let out a sigh. "Mason already blabbed?" I asked.

"He didn't have to," Ayden said. "I could tell the moment I saw you. And by the way, I didn't buy your story."

"I didn't know I was that transparent."

Gabby chuckled and shook her head. "Seriously? We can read what's on your face before you ever open that mouth of yours."

I shot her a dirty look and grinned.

"I knew you were crushing on my brother from the beginning," she teased.

"You did not."

She flashed a wicked grin, and I couldn't help but laugh. I was so lucky to have such an amazing group of friends.

Mason walked over with a tray full of shots and placed them on the table. He snatched a chair from an empty table and spun it around, placing it at the head of the table, and took a seat.

"To victory," Mason said, as we all reached for a shot.

"To victory," we all sang back and slammed the shot.

The sourness trickled down my throat, and my lips puckered as I shook my head in protest. "No more of whatever that was."

I saw Ayden slam another shot and noticed Lily beaming as he chugged on her behalf.

Curious.

"Let's have it. What's going on?" Mason asked, as a round of waters arrived.

"Well, I picked up the mail today and didn't bother looking at it until right before the fight." I opened my purse and dug out the grey envelope. "This came to me. It looks like it's from Derek, but he's still behind bars awaiting the trial."

I flipped the envelope around and looked at the postmark.

"So it got through the screening at the prison?" Gabby asked.

I shook my head.

"The zip code doesn't match where he's at," I sighed.

"Maybe they take all the mail to a different sorting facility," Ayden replied.

"I hope so. The alternative isn't a pleasant thought." My body shuddered at the idea of another person connected with Derek on the outside. It was something that had occurred to me off and on, but I refused to go there.

"What was inside?" Mason asked.

I let out a deep breath and pressed my lips

together before speaking. It was like I was buying myself a few more seconds of peace before my brothers came unglued. "Have a nice time in Paris."

Lily gasped, and Gabby bumped her water glass, but Jason caught it before much liquid was spilled onto the table.

"How is that possible?" Ayden asked. His hands were fisted, and his body was completely tense as the information soaked into us all.

"I've been racking my brain and can't figure it out. I mean, it isn't a secret that Aaron's sculptures will be appearing in Paris, but I'd imagine it's only a select few who know about it. It's hard to believe that someone in prison would be running in the same circles."

"I don't like this one bit," Lily said, shaking her head. "Not one bit."

"I don't either, but I'm headed out of town, and hopefully this whole thing will blow over. I honestly don't have time for it."

"It's too late for that," Mason said. "You have to make time for it. You need to let the authorities know, and you need to let Aaron in on everything."

"It's not like I have to worry about this in Paris," I said, knowing that wasn't the case, but it made me feel better.

"You can't count on that," Ayden said. He cleared his throat and brought in a deep breath. "You really can't. I'd like to believe it's only Derek, but this has me worried. We need to let mom know about it."

I nodded, knowing he was right. Speaking with detectives wasn't how I wanted to spend my last night in Seattle, but it was the right thing to do.

"Well, I was hoping you guys would hand it over to the police for me, but I'm guessing..." I smiled.

Mason already had his cell in his hand. "Not gonna happen."

"Lily and I will stay with you tonight," Ayden replied. "We can take you to the airport tomorrow so Gabby doesn't have to run back and forth."

"I don't mind," Gabby said. Her voice was tipping on the verge of panic and my chest sank. This wasn't how I'd envisioned my bon voyage party.

"Nah. We got it," Lily said.

Gabby nodded and smiled, but the sadness in her eyes told me everything. She was as disturbed as I was about this development.

Mason was already on the phone with mom, and before I had a chance to take a breath, he shoved his phone in front of me. I twisted my lips in frustration and took the phone.

"Hey, mom."

"Honey, what's going on?"

"I got a letter in the mail that read have a nice time in Paris. I'm assuming it's from Derek, but I don't have time to deal with this. I'm leaving for Paris in the morning." Fear had now been replaced with anger, and my mom seemed to be feeling the same emotion. "But I know someone needs to see it."

"That creep will never see the light of day," my mother replied. "Listen, I'll call the prosecuting attorney and explain the situation. I'll call you back in a few minutes. My guess is that you'll have to meet with him and a detective tonight."

"That's fine. Just as long as I make my flight tomorrow, I'll meet with them whenever."

"Good. And Brandy put your brother back on the phone. I don't want you alone."

"Ayden already called dibs on spending the night," I half-chuckled.

"Great, but put Mason on."

"Okay. Love you, mom."

"Love you too. We'll get this taken care of, and you'll be able to enjoy the rest of your summer."

I knew there was more than she was telling me, but I honestly didn't care to know. I'd never been one to hide in the shadows or not deal with reality, but this one time, I was willing to bury my head in the sand until I arrived in Paris. I needed to feel safe and a faraway location was my only salvation at the moment.

"Thanks."

I handed the phone back to my brother and a chill crawled up my spine. I looked around the bar, but it didn't look as if anyone was paying attention to us. I definitely needed to leave the states. The paranoia was already settling in. The bar in the middle of the floor had several couples sitting at it, along with a few singles, but everyone looked completely content either watching the flat screen televisions or chatting it up with the bartenders.

"You doing okay?" Lily whispered.

I shook my head. "No. Not this time. I don't think I am."

CHAPTER FOUR

My phone buzzed and a tingle of delight pulsed through me at the thought of this new chapter in my life. I glanced down at my cell as the endless texts from Aaron flooded my screen from the flight over. The plane had just landed in Paris, and we were allowed to turn on our devices. Aaron had surprised me with a first class upgrade and the extra room was sensational. I pulled my bag out from under the seat in front of me, careful not to elbow the guy next to me. He'd been a perfect row companion for this flight. He didn't speak English so I didn't feel any sort of obligation for small chat.

I'd managed to meet with the authorities before I'd left Seattle, and they assured me they'd get to the bottom of things, but what made me feel the most at ease was walking through the terminal and onto this plane. Poor Aaron only got snippets of what was going on before I got on my flight, and my hunch was that my brothers and Gabby managed to worry him the rest of the time as I was blissfully unaware at thirty-five thousand feet.

But now, none of it mattered.

I was in Paris!

Paris!

The door of the plane opened, and everyone crowded into the aisle. Passengers lifted their bags out of the overhead bins, plopping them on the floor, and quickly rolled them down the aisle out to freedom. My heart literally sped up at the thought of getting to see Aaron. It had been far too long. The man next to me rolled his bag away as I hoisted my weekender bag onto his empty seat. I managed to pull my heavy carryon out of the overhead bin, and it landed with a thud behind me. I quickly brought up the handles and snatched up my other bag, hoisting it over my shoulder, as I wheeled myself out of the plane and onto the jet bridge.

I don't know what I expected when I reached the terminal, but it looked like every other airport I'd been in, except everything was in French. I'd planned on stopping at the restroom and touching up my makeup and hair, but I didn't care any longer. I just wanted to get to Aaron. I followed the signs with the arrows pointing toward the baggage claim, hoping I wouldn't get lost. I kept scanning the crowds around me, mostly hearing English, as I kept moving toward the baggage claim. I spotted a few BuY PARIS duty-free shops and my heart skipped a beat. Being in Paris didn't feel real. I guess I still had to wrap my head around the fact that I would be living in Paris. For several months, this city would be my home.

I glanced at the signs leading me to the correct baggage carousel. As I wheeled through the crowd of people, I heard his voice.

"Brandy, over here," Aaron's voice was like a lightning rod to my soul. I swear I could power the entire city off the excitement I was feeling.

I looked through the crowd and saw Aaron walking quickly toward me. His stride was so long, it took him only a few steps to reach me. He looked amazing. He was dressed in a pair of jeans and a black t-shirt, which showcased the tautness of his body. His dark hair was cut a little shorter and stubble traced along his jawline. To say he looked sensational was putting it mildly.

I jumped on my toes and released my suitcase, which dropped to the ground. He grabbed me in his arms and hugged me tightly, as he somehow kicked my suitcase in between us. Being in his embrace made all my worries drift away. This was where I belonged.

"You look gorgeous," he whispered. "Absolutely gorgeous."

His mouth curled slightly as he touched my cheek and drew my lips to his. It was like I hadn't a care in the world being in his arms. The warmth of his mouth, and the tenderness of his touch pulsed such pleasurable sensations through me that I almost lost my bearings. As I savored everything about Aaron, my fingers tangled through his hair, and our kisses deepened. The hustle and bustle of the airport stilled in our small corner of the world, and it didn't matter that I was in Paris. It only mattered that I was in the arms of the man I loved.

He took a step back, still holding me, and I looked into his dark eyes, smiling sheepishly as I glanced around the airport.

"That was a nice welcome," I whispered, wishing I was still tasting his lips.

"There's plenty more where that came from." He smirked, and the adorable grin that always got me in trouble rattled my insides. He picked up the suitcase and slipped his free hand into mine. "It finally feels like home now that you're here."

His statement swirled the emotions I'd already bottled up for him and all I wanted to do was get to the apartment and show him my appreciation.

"I'm so happy to be here," I whispered, looking into his eyes. "The last forty-eight hours didn't go as planned."

Aaron let out a sigh as we walked toward the carousel that had started moving baggage along the wide metal conveyer.

"No kidding. I still can't believe it. It just makes me so angry," he said, as we stood in front of the carousel. "I swear to God if he was in front of me I don't know what I'd do."

I flashed him a grin because I knew exactly what he'd do to him and it was flattering. "Me too. I thought I'd moved past it all."

He bit his lip and shook his head as his body rocked back and forth. "If we need to stay here longer, we can."

I shook my head. "Thanks. I don't know what to do or make of it."

He nodded. "I know and there's no rush."

Searching for my two bags, I nodded and watched the carousel intently. Catching a familiar gleam in Aaron's eyes, my stomach flip-flopped at the thought of being alone with him again. Three weeks had been far too long. If anything could help get my mind off things, it would be spending some quality time with him alone in an apartment in Paris. I was so busy daydreaming, I didn't even notice the first bag until he said something.

"Suitcase one," he said, reaching over and hauling the large, brown suitcase off the belt. It hit the floor with a thud as I spied the next suitcase rounding the corner.

"And suitcase two," I said, pointing.

He picked it off the carousel and positioned my carryon bag on top of one of the large suitcases, wrapping it with a strap.

"I can take one of those," I said.

"You've got enough to worry about. Just keep an eye on your purse and other bag. Keep them in front of you and zipped until we reach the car. There are a lot of greedy little hands willing to dig right into our bags and pockets."

"Seriously?" I asked.

"Seriously. I actually got to meet one of the friendly thieves as she was reaching her fingers into my pocket as I walked into the airport this afternoon." He shook his head and adjusted the bags before taking a step.

"She? No way. What did you do?"

"She ran away as soon as I grabbed for her hand, but from what everyone's told me, that's just how it is. It's even worse around the tourist traps and on the Metro."

"That's not exactly what I imagined." I followed him out of the airport and to a waiting car. The driver jumped out of the sedan and took the bags from Aaron, securing them in the trunk.

I looked around the busy terminal, hearing the honks of horns and yelling as I stepped inside the vehicle, which he'd filled with white roses.

Aaron followed behind. "Welcome to Paris."

My entire body warmed as I took a seat next to one of the large, wrapped bouquets. The air was filled with the glorious scent of roses, and the electricity charging between us was filled with hunger for one another.

"This is quite the welcome," I whispered, buckling in.

Aaron skirted a finger along my arm and leaned in as the driver got us on our way. "You look even more sensational than I remembered," Aaron murmured.

My entire body sprang to life as the spark between us renewed.

"You're not looking so bad yourself," I teased.

"Paris has been good to you."

He shrugged and sat back in the seat, taking my hand in his. "It's been interesting. I've been trying to get as much work done as I could before you got here so I wouldn't be completely buried when you arrived."

"You're here for work. That comes first," I said, nestling my head on his shoulder. It felt so good to be back in his arms.

"You come first," he corrected. "But I think I've got some great things planned for us. Unfortunately, tonight won't be one of them."

"What's going on tonight?" I asked.

"The owner of the gallery is holding a dinner that we've been invited to."

"That sounds fun."

"I know what would be more fun." He smiled and squeezed my hand.

"Who's to say we can't do both?" My brow arched, and he swept a kiss along my cheek giving a low chuckle in return.

I watched the scenery go by as we drove down the highway. Surprised by the amount of graffiti tagged on different buildings and walls, I pointed and Aaron laughed.

"For some reason, I assumed Paris was immune to graffiti artists," I said.

"Wait until you see it in the city. Nothing like seeing a beautiful masonry building with stepped terraces and red geraniums overflowing through the wrought iron, and then a huge tag right next to it."

I laughed. "Guess nowhere is immune."

Aaron wrapped his arm around my shoulders and brought me in closer. His breath feathered across my scalp, and I felt completely safe in his embrace. This was where I needed to be—far away from the craziness of the trial and the man behind the notes.

"So you don't mind about dinner tonight?" he asked. "It certainly wasn't what I'd planned."

"Not at all. I'd love to meet the brilliant man who recognized such talent. Meeting new people will be good. It'll take my mind off of everything going on."

Aaron let out a sigh. "Did you read any of your messages?"

"No. I just bolted off the plane to you. I didn't really want to know, and I doubt they found out anything anyway."

There was a restrained silence filling the car, and I knew that I was wrong. Really wrong. I wasn't certain that I wanted to hear what Aaron or anyone had to say about the matter. It was bad enough to be in an accident because someone hated me so much, but now it was like the evil would never go away. Never before had I fully understood the victim's side of things in law. It made me rethink what I wanted to study if I went back to school.

I glanced up at Aaron and saw the expression in his eyes. He needed to tell me, and I needed to listen. No matter what temporary fantasy I wanted to play with myself, it wasn't fair to the ones who loved me. They had to recover from the events as much as I did.

"Alright. Let me have it," I sighed.

"The letter wasn't sent from Derek Bourot."

My blood chilled with Aaron's statement.

"What do you mean? How is that possible?"

Aaron squeezed me closer. "He had a cousin he'd conned into sending it. They arrested him, but the detectives think there's more to this."

"Why's that? Are you sure they're not reading too much into it?"

Aaron bit his lip and glanced out the window. "They think we're dealing with a group of very unstable individuals. Derek is very persuasive, and there is far more involved than the detectives originally realized. Once they arrested his cousin, they learned more."

"How so?" My palms became slick with sweat. How could this turn from one psychopath to a family of them? That wasn't how things worked. Was it?

"He's very manipulative, and he apparently tapped into a couple of causes that allowed him to develop a following. The people who believed in him are very upset and feel he's being wrongly accused. They see Derek as the victim."

"They're fools," I muttered.

"Be that as it may, they're on the outside and think they're fighting for a cause. They feel that he was wrongly accused."

"You've got to be kidding me."

"I wish I was. There is good news out of this."

"What's that?"

"You received another letter, and this one was from Texas so that makes it a federal crime since it went across state lines."

"That's good news?"

"The FBI's involved now."

I drew in a deep breath as my head began to jumble with information. It felt like my world was coming down around me. The fact that there were people out in the world who believed Derek Bourot's lies scared me beyond belief. I knew what he was capable of, but I couldn't let my mind imagine what he could convince others to do.

"He's created quite an online presence and the following he has is cause for concern. He's using religion as the catapult for all this."

"What do you mean all this?"

Aaron took out his phone and went to his email. Scrolling through his inbox, Aaron pressed his lips together and handed me the phone.

"The investigators never found this information when they were searching his apartment. He was using an anonymizer and wiped his disc clean every time he logged onto the chat rooms."

"Chat rooms?" I asked, staring down at the screen.

To my horror, he had three hundred and seven followers. In the scheme of life that wasn't many, but that meant there were possibly three hundred and seven individuals who were willing to cause my family harm. I let out a shaky breath and began reading the sermons of Derek Bourot.

CHAPTER FIVE

*T*he city gave me chills. I'd never been somewhere that held this much beauty and history any direction I turned. Our car slowly made its way along the tiny streets, and I took everything in about the fantastical city that I'd be calling home. Aaron held my hand as I peered out the window absorbing the French baroque buildings with their pilasters and ornate detailing around the windows and doors. It was like I'd been whisked back to another time until the horns sounded from behind and placed me firmly back in the twenty-first century. This beauty was what I needed to focus on—not some creep behind bars back in the states.

"It's breathtaking," I whispered.

"I thought we could drive around before we

head to the apartment. Give you a flavor of the city."

I flashed him a smile and nodded before turning my gaze back to the streets of Paris. The sidewalks were bustling, and the buildings seemed almost alive with the ghosts of another time. Cafés marked every other opening with bakeries, bookstores, galleries, and floral shops in between. My heart skipped a beat as I saw the beauty of one florist spilling onto the sidewalk in a carpet of petals and an arch of fuchsia and white roses inviting patrons inside. The sidewalks seemed to belong to the businesses as much as they did to the city. A real dialogue between the city and the people was evident. There wasn't one café that didn't kiss the sidewalk with tables and chairs inviting patrons take a seat as they walked by.

As we sat at a light, I looked up to the building across the street and sat in quiet awe. The building was imposing in its beauty with uniquely perpendicular rooflines that almost looked like they disappeared into the sky with the way they sat on the building. The trapezoid shape allowed for a few dormer windows dotting the boxy mansard roof to invite the imagination to wander. Were there people in the attic? Was there a family down below claiming it? I immediately fell in love with this style of architecture. It was different from the baroque style only a few buildings before.

"Absolutely whimsical," I said, sliding back against Aaron once the car accelerated again.

"It is," Aaron agreed. "That's from the famed Second Empire. Good old Napoleon III wanted to glam up the city."

"Well, it worked."

As the car continued to carry us through the streets, my worries from back home slipped away. Not only did I feel a million miles from the fears that threatened my sanity, I felt invigorated and alive with hope. Hope was something I hadn't felt in a long time. I'd managed to let it slip away along with my dreams somewhere between the accident and recovery.

Being in a city that crackled with life made me realize how numb I'd become since the accident. The things I usually took pleasure in skidded away from me as my life looped in an uncontrolled game of chance. If it hadn't been for Aaron over these last several months, I didn't know where I'd be.

"You okay, baby?" Aaron whispered, running his hand along my leg.

I smiled and sank the back of my head into his shoulder. "I am now."

He kissed my head and slipped both arms around me as I settled into him. "We're close to our apartment. I think you'll like it. The view is sensational."

I let out a deep breath and allowed myself to enjoy these few minutes of peace before the night's activities.

"I'll try not to get you in trouble," I whispered.

"Trouble?" he asked. "What kind of trouble could you possibly get me in?"

I ran my hand along his thigh, and he let out a low groan as he leaned into the seat. "That's not playing fair, Brandy Rhodes."

"When have I ever?"

The car slowed, and I turned my attention to the building that our driver parked in front of, but rather than Aaron letting me go, he unbuckled our belts and slid me onto his lap. The driver exited the vehicle and Aaron exploited that opportunity. He slid his hand along my cheek and sealed his mouth over mine. The greed behind each kiss sent a feverish desire through me as his lips slowly parted from mine.

"Welcome home," he murmured, his lips still pressed against mine, muffling his words.

"It's good to be home," I whispered, offering one last kiss while the driver slammed the trunk.

Aaron let a little groan out, and I opened my eyes to see him smiling as he slid his hand to the door handle.

"Absence makes the heart grow stronger," I said, dropping my hand to his lap, noticing just how insane I must have made him. My job was done.

He grinned, and I scooted off his lap as he shoved the door open. I attempted to smooth over my clothes, but there was no point. We were going upstairs to our apartment. I stepped onto the sidewalk and was immediately hit with the sweet smell of butter and sugar. I scoped the area and saw a sign dangling from two small chains, La Crêperies Parfaites.

"That place will be the death of me," Aaron

said, standing next to me on the sidewalk. "And our apartment is right above it. Poor planning on my part."

"Excellent planning on your part," I laughed, my eyes falling to a red door tucked in between the café and a bookstore.

Ducking back into the car, I strapped my purse over my shoulder and grabbed the three large bouquets of roses and held them tightly as I glanced up at the cream-colored limestone building and noticed it was like the ones I'd admired along the way. Wrought iron cresting tipped the boxy roof, and dormered windows sprinkled the top of the building, along with several balconies overflowing in flowers.

Aaron paid the driver and took the bags from the sidewalk as I drew in another breath filled with the aroma of sugary goodness. Aaron managed to balance all the bags as I tried to keep up with his swift stride as he walked right to the red door.

"No way. This is the entrance to our apartment? It's so cute."

He nodded and leaned the luggage against the doorframe. Quickly pushing in a security code, the door buzzed open, and I immediately felt like it was Christmas morning as I stepped inside. The hallway was divine and filled with old-world charm. A line of brass post office boxes lined the right wall, and straight ahead were three marble steps, leading to a tiny elevator. Possibly the smallest elevator I'd ever seen.

"We might need to do two trips. The elevator's

a tight one," he said.

"You don't say," I teased, still taking in the lobby when I glanced up and saw a beautiful mural painted on the ceiling. An angel appeared pulling back a curtain of clouds to reveal a white horse drawing a carriage, which glistened in gold.

"Wow. Is there no surface left untouched?" I asked.

His eyes connected with mine, and I felt that familiar sensation run through me as he watched me carefully. "It's really nice to have you here. I never looked up."

"Are you serious? You didn't see that?" I smiled at the revelation.

He pressed his lips together and shook his head. "I didn't. You seem to point out the beauty in everything."

Whether that was true or not, I appreciated the compliment—especially with everything that had been going on recently that made me feel like negative Nancy. Aaron pressed the call button, and the elevator slowly hummed its way to our floor. He slid the large, brass gates to the side and slid the suitcases to the back wall and stepped forward. "I think there's enough room for you too."

I chuckled at the sight in front of me as Aaron stood as straight as he could, pressing himself to the side of the elevator.

"Maybe," I replied. "But a few roses might not make it."

I stepped into the tiny carriage and felt it

lower slightly. "Is there a weight limit?" I asked, glancing around for signage.

"Probably," Aaron said, attempting to maneuver around me as he reached for the brass gate to lock in place. "And with all the crepes I've been eating, I probably ensured that we just went over it."

Pressing my body as far into the carriage as I could go, I sucked in my stomach and squeezed the roses to my chest. The click of the gate locking into place, and the sound of the gears shifting meant liftoff had commenced, but we seemed to be going nowhere fast as the motor churned.

"Should I hop off?" I asked. "Is this normal?"

Aaron shook his head. "Believe it or not, the elevator sounds this promising every time I've used it."

"Are there stairs? You know in case there's a fire or something?" I asked, feeling the elevator finally begin to grind its way to the appropriate floor.

"There are. I usually use them. It's actually faster even though we're six floors up."

"Oh, I believe it," I chuckled, just as the elevator bounced into place.

We did the dance again as Aaron reached across my shoulders to unlatch the gate, and I was never more excited to get off an elevator as I was this second. I'd definitely be getting friendly with the stairs.

Aaron shoved the gate to the side and I stepped into the hallway, amazed at the sight.

The wide-planked wood floors were dull with wear but added a sense of history to the hallway. There were only two doors, one to the immediate left and one directly in front of us at the end of the hallway. I looked behind me as Aaron rolled the suitcases out of the elevator and I chuckled aloud realizing what little help I'd been.

"Sorry. I think I'm on Paris overload." I touched the plaster walls, shaking my head as I felt the roughness under my fingertips. "Imagine how many people have lived here and walked through these very halls."

Aaron flashed a huge smile and pointed toward the door at the end of the hallway. "Wait until you see inside."

Giddiness pulsed through me as he tossed a ring of keys toward me. I caught them with a jangle and started toward the door, analyzing all the odd shaped keys. "Even the keys are fanciful."

Arriving at the door, I saw four different shaped locks spaced inches apart. I propped my roses against the wall just when Aaron came up behind me, and my body trembled with the closeness.

"I'll show you which key goes with which lock." His deep, seductive voice made my knees weak, and I wasn't sure how we'd ever get to the dinner on time.

"You do that," I whispered, far more breathily than I anticipated.

He reached his arms around me and held my hands that were holding the keys. Maneuvering a large brass key with his fingers, he held our hands to the top lock.

"This one is the first lock you have to unlock or the others won't come undone. It's a pressure lock of sorts."

My body sank back into his as he clicked the lock open. Aaron pinched another key, this one small and silver, and brought it down to the lock below. "And this one fits in here just like that."

His breath feathered over my scalp, and my entire body trembled. How he made opening a door sexy, I'd never know.

"This is my favorite key. It looks a bit like a heart and unlocks this one." My hands were completely limp in his as he continued turning the lock, and all I could think about was those same fingers running along the curves of my body.

"Hurry up and open the last lock. I'll learn the keys later," I said.

He chuckled and lowered his chin next to my ear and whispered, "What's the hurry?" The deep timber of his voice did me in as his hips pressed into me. Whatever his plan, I was falling right into it.

The last click of the lock signaled my time to move, but I couldn't. Aaron removed his hands from mine as I still held the ring of keys. His fingers slowly caressed up my arms before moving my hair to the side. He brushed his lips behind my ear, and I let out a small moan as he pushed open the door to our Parisian apartment.

"Welcome home."

I drew in a breath and attempted to gather my bearings as I looked around the beautiful space in front of me. The apartment was flooded with light from the large, open windows. The sheer curtains blew gently from the breeze, and the bright white walls showed off the beautiful, architectural details.

I bent down and picked up the roses, glancing quickly behind me at Aaron who seemed to be gauging my reaction to our new surroundings. I stepped onto the tiled mosaic entry, only to be left more awestruck. An ornate, crystal chandelier hung in the center of the room. Blue Velvet couches were centered in the room and a chenille throw hung from a blanket rack. Worn wood floors began in the living area and ran into the other rooms. A pale grey rug anchored the room and surpassed my Parisian expectations with its exquisite pattern.

I looked up to see ornamental frieze detailing wrapped around the entire room, which made the entire space feel more regal and far more sophisticated than any apartment I'd ever lived in. I set my roses on the cherry table that ran along the wall and took another step forward as Aaron closed the door behind us, clicking each lock into place.

"This is beyond my expectations." I walked farther into the living room and saw an elaborate doorway leading into another large room and another beyond that.

"Through there is the dining room and then the sitting room. It's not that easy to find an apartment with abundant natural light, but we certainly lucked out. The flat is an L-shape so we get sun exposure from all sides at some point."

I followed Aaron through the living area, hearing the wood floors creak below with each step. When I entered the dining room, my jaw dropped at the silk taffeta curtains, which pooled into grey puddles on the wooden floors. This apartment really was gorgeous. Another chandelier hung over the table and several paintings hung on the wall.

"Check this out," Aaron said, walking toward the back wall. He pressed on a door that I'd completely overlooked, which was flush with the surrounding wall. The chair rails continued from the wall and across the door as if to disguise the opening. "This leads upstairs to the studio. I was told that's where the help used to live."

I walked quickly over to Aaron and popped my head into the opening. A dark hallway led to a wooden staircase. "So cool."

I turned to face Aaron who was grinning. "You think you'll be okay over here?"

"Okay? I think I'll be more than okay. Gabby and Lily said I wouldn't want to come back and I thought they were full of it. Now I'm not so sure." I slid a kiss across his cheek as he shut the door.

"That's what I wanted to hear." He walked me into the sitting room, where a chaise and small table were tucked in a corner. I turned to my right and saw the kitchen. It was small, but larger than I imagined. The whole flat was larger than I expected. To make the room appear larger, the cabinet doors were paneled in glass and soft grey tiles covered the back walls and floor.

"If we make our way through the kitchen, we'll find the two bedrooms. What I think was supposed to be the master suite, I left as the guest bedroom. It's bigger, but when you open the shutters you stare directly at a wall from the other building and it's pretty dark."

I nodded and followed him through the kitchen and into the bedroom. It was cozy, but I could understand why he chose it. The white shutters were open and the sheer curtains moved slightly with the breeze. The bed was centered in the room and covered with a large white duvet. Two chairs were positioned in front of the window, and I made my way over to look at the view of the bustling Parisian street below.

"I think this is the perfect room for us. You chose well, Mr. Sullivan." I flashed a grin and imagined myself waking up in the morning in such an idyllic setting. "I can't wait to bring the roses in and put them on this table." I spun around and Aaron was less than a foot away when I spotted a gorgeous, red dress hanging from the armoire. He followed my gaze and slid his arms around my waist.

"I thought you might like something new to wear to tonight's dinner. When I saw it in the boutique's window, I knew it was meant for you."

I brought my eyes to his and smiled as I attempted to push away the anxiety that was threatening to ruin this moment. When he mentioned dinner tonight, I assumed it was a normal dinner, but I should've known better. Nothing in Aaron's world was normal. If my family mentioned throwing a dinner for someone, pot roast was in the oven and mashed potatoes were on the stove. In his world, galas were the norm and cocktail parties the equivalent to our backyard barbeques.

"Everything okay?"

I nodded and smiled. "Sorry. I ...I didn't know it was that kind of dinner. I assumed it was something small and..."

"You'll do amazing," he interrupted, his thumb running along my cheek.

Going to events with Gabby should've prepared me for Aaron's lifestyle, but it didn't. I still felt like a fish out of water, and I had no idea why. Ever since the accident, I noticed my tendency to shy away from events. Well, not just events—people in general, and I kept hoping that putting myself out there would make it easier. It still hadn't.

"If you need to rest..."

I shook my head. "No way. And let my sexy man have fun in Paris without me? I don't think so."

He shot me a devilish grin and scooped me into his arms. Tonight would be full of new beginnings, and I couldn't wait to see what tomorrow held.

Chapter Six

A bowl filled with floating candles and white rose petals greeted partiers in the front foyer. Large bouquets anchored the doorway leading into a sitting room. A man dressed in a tuxedo offered flutes of champagne to the couple in front of us, and I glanced at Aaron who was taking in the scene. He looked to be in his element. Except for an occasional snippet of French, the party could have been held in Seattle.

"Merci," I said, as I took a flute of champagne from the tray.

"You're very welcome," the man said, giving me a wink.

So much for nailing my French.

I chuckled and took a tiny sip as Aaron led me into the sitting room where several small groups had assembled. Watching the guests sip champagne in between whispers and laughter reminded me so much of all the other parties I'd attended with Aaron. It was like there was a handbook on how to throw these kinds of gatherings and no one ever veered. A tiny seed of homesickness sprouted, and I had to push down the silly feelings as I thought back to my family's parties of streamers and confetti.

"The guest of honor," a man called from across the room with no hint of an accent.

The man's greeting was just the trick to pull me out of myself. His wide smile and sparkling eyes conveyed a chumminess that I hadn't expected. The older man made his way through the room, and Aaron slid his arm around my waist as I spotted a woman in her late twenties trailing behind the man. Maybe she was the man's daughter. There was a slight resemblance. He had blue eyes and so did she. Both of their jawlines were strong, and their expressions held determination. Her red hair was braided loosely and a diamond pendant dangled on her creamy skin. She was breathtaking. I was completely grateful to Aaron for picking out my dress as I watched this woman practically glide through the room. Dressed in a powder blue dress that streamed behind her with each step, I felt completely out of my league. Her eyes fastened on Aaron and that was when I figured it out. I was Aaron's surprise. She gave me a considering look as her eyes slowly trailed up and down my body, and I realized that my standing here must be quite the disappointment for her.

"Aaron, it's wonderful that you could come tonight," the man said as they shook hands. His eyes fell on me, and his smile deepened. "And who is this lovely woman?"

"This is my girlfriend, Brandy Rhodes. Brandy, this is Gregory Sennet and his daughter, Tracy."

"It's nice to meet you both." Before I had a chance to react, Tracy gave me two air kisses— one on each cheek—and her father did the same.

"We're really looking forward to Aaron's opening," Gregory said, nodding. "His pieces are quite soulful. It's unusual to capture such expression with metalwork."

Tracy nodded and continued to eye me. "Amazing indeed. I'm thrilled Elizabeth reached out to me about your work."

Aaron's body stiffened, and I caught a flicker of something behind his gaze.

"I am too," Gregory responded. "It's always exciting to introduce such talent to the world."

"Your ex-fiancée always had exquisite taste." Tracy smiled at Aaron and took a sip of her champagne as I attempted to stay upright with this revelation.

I watched a subtle change transform Tracy's face as she watched Aaron. It was a mixture of smugness and amusement, and I wasn't completely sure at whose expense.

My heart pounded, and my face flushed as I struggled to keep my confusion, anger and hurt in check. This wasn't the place to discuss such a gut-wrenching surprise. In fact, I didn't think anywhere in France would be an ideal locale to discuss finding out my boyfriend of almost a year, who also excelled at running away in life, had an ex-fiancée that he just so happened to forget to mention. I felt the fury ramp up my spine, and it felt eerily similar to the moment when I'd found out Aaron was headed to China without me. This communication thing had to improve.

I was all for ending things gracefully with an ex. In fact, I'd endured endless teasing from Gabby on the subject, but that didn't mean I had ex-fiancés and husbands hanging out in my closet of relationships past.

Even though the room was filled with air-conditioned air, I felt extremely hot as I puzzled over what else Aaron forgot to mention. Gregory was completely oblivious as guests surrounded our group, and he began introducing Aaron to everyone.

Aaron slid his arm from my waist and began greeting the waiting guests as I shuffled off to the side. I didn't feel much like plastering a Howdy Doody grin on my face so I retreated to the hors d'oeuvres table and stared at the escargots smothered in garlic butter. A shudder ran up my spine at the thought of having to plop one of those slippery suckers in my mouth. I preferred all my snails and slugs to slink along in our garden not on a dining table.

I let out a sigh and picked up a small plate as I eyed the rest of the spread. Besides the snails nothing screamed French to me until I landed on a beautifully presented platter of ham rolled around a cheese spread. A tiny card in front of the rolled meat dish read, Jambon Chevre. That sounded French enough to me as I placed a few pieces on my plate. I heard Aaron answering questions behind me, and my chest tightened. I knew I should be standing next to him, showing him support, but I needed a few minutes to collect my thoughts.

Weren't things supposed to be easier than this?

"It's so nice to see Aaron settling down," Tracy cooed as she came up behind me.

I'd already hit the elaborate crudité display when I heard her. I turned to greet her while still loading my plate with vegetables. Not realizing how many carrots I'd loaded onto my plate, one rolled off and hit the ground. I kicked it quickly under the long tablecloth and put the tongs down.

"I'm not sure that's completely possible." I smiled, stepping away from the table.

"How long have the two of you been an item?" Tracy asked, picking up a plate.

"About a year," I said, glancing behind me at Aaron, who was being bombarded by eager art collectors. Gregory and his daughter certainly were excellent at building the buzz.

"That's impressive." She placed two snails on her plate and flashed me a smile. "And you two are living together?"

Not that it was any of her business, but I found myself nodding.

"He's a wonderful man, but he's a man," Tracy said, her voice lowering. "Elizabeth understood certain things would never change."

Gripping my plate tight enough that it might shatter, my fingertips began to tingle.

"It's never a good idea to try to change someone," I said softly.

"She's here in Paris, you know. But she decided not to come tonight. She didn't want to be a distraction."

I nodded and smiled. "Very thoughtful of her."

"You didn't know about her, did you?" Her eyes narrowed on me.

"I...uh—"

Aaron came up behind me and interrupted the conversation that threatened my ability to maintain control. "You doing okay?" he asked, his hands gripping my hips.

I nodded and spun around to see him. "Better than ever."

We glanced at Tracy as she wandered off, leaving us standing in the middle of the bustling party.

"A fiancée?" I arched a brow and waited impatiently. I kept a smile plastered on my face so nothing looked as off as it felt. I prided myself on being fair and not one to rush to judgment but come on...never a mention?

"I can't argue with the obvious. I should've told you, but it meant so little to me I—" he stopped himself once he saw my horrified expression.

"How could being engaged mean nothing?"

He drew in a breath and glanced around the room before bringing his gaze back to mine. "I honestly didn't think I was engaged."

Another carrot tumbled off my plate, and I quickly bent down and picked it up. Looking for a place to put everything, I spotted a tray with a few empty plates. Since I'd lost my appetite, I walked my full plate to the tray and dumped it off. Aaron was right on my heels as I attempted to grasp what he was saying. How in the world could someone not know they were engaged?

I spun around to ask that very question right when a couple of guests introduced themselves to Aaron, and I lost him in the crowd once more. This wasn't the time or the place to discuss anything like this with Aaron, but with my best friend across the globe? Absolutely. I opened my clutch and pulled out my phone. Even though Aaron was doing his part at acting interested in everyone around him, I saw a worried look only a blink away and knew that whatever he had to tell me wasn't something that I'd want to hear. I quickly did the math in my head and felt better about calling Gabby. She was probably already at the bakery.

Wandering through the foyer with phone in hand, I began texting Gabby this nasty revelation. Still feeling quite stuffy, I trundled outside to get some fresh air. There was something about tonight that seemed almost surreal. Aaron and I had been through so much, and yet I suddenly felt like he was a stranger. I glanced up at the windows as I walked down the street and saw the back of Aaron as people continued to indulge him with attention. I let out a sigh and stopped walking so I could finish texting Gabby. I knew she didn't know about an ex-fiancée, but I thought I'd ask anyway.

It was early evening and the sidewalks were bustling. A line at the patisserie across the street wrapped around the side of the building, and the coffee shop patio was filled with customers sipping lattes and smoking. Maybe that would make me feel better—not a smoke—but my first Parisian latte. I looked both ways and crossed the street. There was no question I was overdressed for a cup of coffee, but I needed an escape and this seemed perfect.

I took a seat outside on the patio, and the waiter immediately appeared with a menu. Once he heard me squeeze a few French words out, he switched over to English, and it was as if a huge weight was lifted. He could understand me, and I could understand him. Now if only it was as easy with Aaron. Aaron was a complicated man, and it seemed as if the longer we were together, the more complex he became. I watched the waiter return back inside, and I let out a sigh as my phone buzzed.

Gabby texted her response, which was that she was horrified and had no idea, and asked if I needed to come home.

I almost laughed aloud when I realized I hadn't even thought about going back home. My reaction wasn't to run, yet hers had been and so was her brother's. Was that what happened with his fiancée? He ran?

My latte was delivered, and I ordered a brie sandwich before turning my attention back to texting Gabby. I relayed what little I knew and waited for a response. I didn't want to overthink things, but I was getting nervous.

I looked across the street and saw Aaron through the window. He was laughing and talking in a large group. I'd be lying to myself if I didn't admit I was a little puzzled. Did he even know I was gone? I let out a deep breath and picked up my large mug of frothy goodness and took a larger gulp than I intended, but it was so delicious. I'd never had a latte this creamy, and then it hit me, I was probably drinking whole milk. I took another sip, confirming my suspicion, and delighted in the cavalier attitude the French appeared to have toward fats. I watched as the crowd slightly dissipated around Aaron. He pulled his phone out of his suit jacket and began texting. Within seconds, my phone buzzed, and I couldn't help but soften slightly as the text came over asking where I went. So he didn't forget about me.

I let out a breath and texted Aaron as the waiter set my brie sandwich in front of me.

Look out the window.

Aaron slowly turned around, and I gave a quick wave before pointing to my sandwich. He smiled and texted back.

Not a fan of the escargot?

I texted quickly.

Not even on my worst day and this just might qualify.

His text came right over, and I glanced back down at the phone.

We need to talk. Whatever might be going through your head is probably not what actually happened. Promise me that you'll hear me out.

I looked up into the window and saw Aaron besieged with more admirers and let out a deep breath as he tucked his phone back in his pocket. Taking a bite of the sandwich, the creaminess of the brie melted in my mouth, and I wondered if I'd ever be able to eat a sandwich in America again. I also wondered why my feelings were so mixed about Aaron not revealing he'd been engaged. Wasn't I supposed to be furious? I didn't know who or what to blame, but the numbness wasn't new. I just hadn't expected to be numb in all types of situations.

Taking the last bite of the baguette, I slid my plate away and sipped down the rest of my latte. Leaving Aaron wasn't the right thing to do, but sometimes emotions didn't always play fair. Apparently the anger toward Derek I'd managed to hide from myself also seemed to effect my reactions to most everything else.

The waiter asked if anything else was needed and dropped off the check. I glanced at the total and put cash down before pushing away from the table and crossing the street. Food helped to put things in perspective. It always did. Making snap decisions on an empty stomach was always a terrible thing to do. Sage advice from my mother, who always felt any family crisis could be averted with a platter of fried chicken.

As I mulled over the Aaron issue, I almost ran right into a woman who was staring into the window of the home I was about to reenter. She was dressed in an emerald knit cocktail dress with a deep-v dipping down her back.

"Oh, sorry." I cringed when I realized I hadn't even attempted French, and I'd probably just perpetuated the myth that we were all rude. "Je suis désolé."

A feeble smile tipped the woman's lips and she shook her head. "I'm from the states as well." She barely turned her head from the window as she spoke.

I laughed and glanced inside. I saw Aaron using his hands to describe whatever it was he was talking about, and I knew where I belonged. Right next to him. "Thank goodness. My French is really rusty."

She hardly gave me a look as I climbed the steps and paused. "Are you coming inside?"

Her gaze was fixed on the window when her voice caught. "No. I just. I thought I knew someone inside."

I pushed away the feelings of worry that

started to steal my wits. The very wits I'd prided myself on for so long. The party I'd left was quite lively, and the energy could be felt by anyone who happened to steal a glance. I was certain that was all that was going on with the woman next to me.

She looked on intently, almost as if she was wishing herself inside, and that was when dread filled my entire body as I realized I was staring at Elizabeth, his ex-fiancée.

Chapter Seven

I had two options. I could continue on, open the door and go inside, or I could turn around and introduce myself. One option allowed me to ignore fate and the chance encounter standing behind me, and the other option forced me to face the truth that Aaron had been so good at hiding. As my hand rested on the door, I took a deep breath and knew which option I had to choose. I heard laughter from inside the building, and I almost chickened out. It would be so much easier to pretend this woman didn't exist.

But she did.

My heart threatened to break silently as I turned around slowly and walked down the steps to introduce myself. The woman looked startled as I stopped in front of her. I debated what to say, and I realized I had absolutely no idea as my smile slipped away. Her brown hair was in a pixie cut, and her dainty features only accentuated how large and beautiful her eyes were. She was quite pretty. It was hard for me to imagine Aaron being attracted to me after being with her, and I hated myself for thinking such a ridiculous thought.

"Is there something I can help you with?" she asked, finally disconnecting her gaze from the window and connecting with mine.

"Is your name Elizabeth?" My heart pounded so loudly in my ears I could barely hear my voice when I spoke.

Her blue eyes widened, and she bit her lip before speaking.

I glanced behind me and saw a couple walking up the steps to the party. I returned my attention back to the woman and drew in a breath.

"I am," she replied coolly, but her trembling hand slid down her dress.

A shiver ran through my body as I stared at Aaron's ex-fiancée. What had I thought I'd accomplish by introducing myself to her?

"Thank you for recommending Aaron for this exhibit. It's such an amazing opportunity. I'm sorry. I'm his girlfriend, Brandy." I stuck out my hand rather robotically and she politely shook it.

"I didn't really do anything. His work speaks for itself," she assured me. Her body relaxed slightly and mine tensed. "It's nice to finally meet the woman who tamed Aaron."

"I don't think there's ever any taming Aaron," I

laughed, but my voice was unexpectedly strained.

I glanced through the same window Elizabeth had been staring at and saw the back of the man we'd both loved.

"You have a point there," Elizabeth chuckled slightly. "But with everything he's been through, I'm surprised he's willing to finally settle down. I honestly didn't think it was in his DNA."

I wriggled my fingers in front of her. "I'm not sure it is." The color drained from my face when I realized what I'd just done. I didn't feel that way. It had to have been the champagne. I wasn't sure what was coming over me. This man had been by my side during my darkest days, and now I was dismissing the importance of everything because he didn't mention the woman standing in front of me.

"True." Her lips pressed together, and then her mouth broke into a smile. "But I can tell you, he's more in love with you than life itself."

Her words immediately warmed me, but it quickly turned to suspicion. She obviously still had feelings for Aaron so why was she being so nice?

"Well, thank you for that. I love him more than I thought possible. He's been…" my voice trailed off. Why was I talking to his ex-fiancée about how much I loved the very man she'd been staring at before I interrupted her?

Elizabeth folded her arms in front of her and took in a deep breath. "You didn't know about me, did you?"

I wasn't sure who I felt worse for, Elizabeth because Aaron never bothered to mention her, or me because Aaron never bothered to mention her.

"That's what I thought," she replied, without me replying.

Things had gone from awkward to uncomfortable, and I began regretting my decision to introduce myself. A breeze swept down the sidewalk and I shivered.

"Would you like to come inside?" I asked. "I'm sure Aaron would love to see you."

Elizabeth's expression turned to horror and she shook her head. "No. This is his night. I don't want to take away from that."

I felt lightheaded, but that didn't stop me from what I was about to ask. I glanced up and caught Tracy staring out the window. Aaron was no longer around, and my heart pounded at the thought of him coming across us. Sense was knocked to the curb, and I blurted out what had been eating me since I found out Aaron had been engaged.

"Is there a good reason why he never mentioned being engaged?"

"I don't know if it's a good reason, but there's definitely a reason; one that he really should tell you."

"What if he doesn't?" I asked.

"I think you already know the answer to that. Don't let him get away with dismissing this or—" she stopped herself.

She knew Aaron well. She understood his

ability to sweep things under the rug or run away, whichever was easiest for him. I'd hoped we'd broken the latter of the two, but I honestly didn't know.

Not realizing I'd been holding my breath, I exhaled slowly and nodded.

"Aaron was involved in something that changed him forever. He was a broken man, Brandy. You've somehow changed that. But it's not fair for you not to truly know the man he is. It might be easier for him, but it won't be easier for you. These things have a way of sneaking up on people, on couples."

"Tracy mentioned you and Aaron speak every day..."

Elizabeth rolled her eyes and looked genuinely annoyed. "Of course she did." She shook her head and her arms now hung at her side. "She's a good friend. A little too good. But to answer your question, we are in touch almost daily whether it's a text or a call."

It felt like I'd been punched in the gut and I became nauseous.

"I see." Wasn't I supposed to be Aaron's confidant? These two had some sort of shared history and somehow that was continuing to shape his future. To say I wasn't pleased was being kind, and I was no longer in a kind mood.

"We'll probably have to be in touch almost daily for many years." Her eyes connected with mine.

My heart dropped at the thought of what she was saying. Did Aaron have a child? Is that why they were in constant contact? That would be the end. I couldn't take someone not telling me something so important. My heart ached, and all I wanted to do was go back to the apartment and bury myself under the sheets. Her voice brought me out of my endless spiral of confusion, and I steadied my gaze on hers again.

"He invested in a business that I started and has been helping me grow it. The task has been difficult because I've been trying to break into a category that's pretty small. If it hadn't been for his guidance, my business never would've even made it off the ground."

My body and mind felt like it had been liberated from the ghostly hollows of my imagination. I was so happy I wanted to kiss Elizabeth, but I restrained myself. Instead, I pressed for more answers.

"So how did you meet Aaron?" I asked.

Her expression hardened slightly. "We were in the military together."

I nodded, feeling more confused than ever. Getting just these tiny bits and pieces almost made it worse.

"Before he went into Special Forces, we started dating," she continued.

My blood chilled. Aaron was in the Special Forces?

Elizabeth let out a sigh and shook her head. "He didn't tell you that either?"

"No," my voice barely squeaked. "Aaron and I apparently have a lot of catching up to do."

Elizabeth reached for my hand and squeezed

it. "I shouldn't have come by. I just hadn't seen him in awhile and debated about stopping by. Listen, he really loves you. He lost sight of what was important to him. You showed him that again. With everything you've been through, I'm sure he didn't want to burden you."

"It wouldn't be a burden," I whispered, looking into Elizabeth's eyes.

"You and I both know that, but that's not how it works for a certain kind of man. He sees himself as a protector. That's how he was wired."

I nodded.

"Don't hold it against him. I promise you have yourself a good man. He might need a little bit of work around the edges. I shouldn't be saying this but have you Googled him?"

My cheeks blushed and I smiled.

She laughed. "Who hasn't, right?"

"I didn't find anything though…I mean other than all the beautiful women he's dated over the years. It was all pictures from the social pages and the events he either sponsored or escorted someone too. Nothing that would give me reason—"

Elizabeth looked perplexed and then a wry smile surfaced. "You looked up Aaron Sullivan."

I nodded.

"Try Thatcher. That's what he went by in the service. He changed it briefly to Bernie's last name."

I felt absolutely gobsmacked.

"When did he change it back to Sullivan?" I asked.

"When Mr. Sullivan decided to start speaking to him again. He figured it would be better for business. Bernie might have been his biological father, but he didn't raise him. Aaron said it didn't feel right to turn his back on the man who had."

"But Mr. Sullivan turned his back on Aaron when he found out. He stopped speaking to his own son."

Elizabeth nodded. "Yeah, but he did eventually come around."

I shook my head. "It just never occurred to me."

"I only knew because I was there during all the turmoil."

"So you must know Jason?" I asked

She smiled. "Absolutely."

The click of the door opening alarmed Elizabeth, and she spun around and took off before I even had a chance to say goodbye. I glanced up the steps and saw Aaron poke his head out.

"Everything okay?" he asked.

"I have no idea," I said, walking up the steps. "But I have a feeling it will get a lot more intriguing soon."

Aaron gave me a quick peck on the cheek as he slid his hand into mine. "I was getting really lonely."

Guilt worked its way through me and I smiled, taking another flute of champagne off the tray as we entered the foyer.

"Are we okay?" Aaron whispered, his eyes

connecting with mine.

"We're always okay," I said, sipping my champagne. "But I think it's time we both start sharing a little more."

Beautiful music began funneling through the hallway, and as if on command, I watched as all of the people began trickling out of the sitting room, following the beautiful melody down the hall. I finished my champagne and placed the flute on an empty table as the music poured into all my senses. I absolutely loved waltzes. It sounded as if a small symphony had joined the evening's festivities.

Aaron slid his arm around my waist and pulled me to him.

"I'm sorry for not telling you everything. Do you forgive me?" he whispered next to my ear. My skin tingled as his lips lightly touched my ear lobe before his hand slid up my back.

I looked into his eyes, feeling dizzy with emotion, and nodded. "I'll forgive you if there are no more secrets."

"Then I have a lot of explaining to do," he whispered, as he brought my body to his.

A waltz echoed down the hall and he smiled. "I think the festivities have begun."

"I thought these were the festivities."

He smiled and backed up a few steps, giving a slight bow. I knew he was teasing, but I had to admit that being in this new city, surrounded by ghosts from another era made me fall right into his plan. I was forgetting the earlier events already. I was forgetting Elizabeth.

Arching my hand in his, we walked down the hall and turned into a room that made my jaw drop. It sounded like a symphony was playing because one was playing. The orchestra was set up in the far corner of the ballroom, and the entire space was filled with graceful couples waltzing on the gleaming marble floor. It was like a scene out of a movie. I looked up to see not one, but three crystal chandeliers hanging from the ceiling. The walls were painted peach, which somehow fit the entire décor. Ivory and gold columns and pedestals were spaced evenly down three of the walls, and the fourth wall was filled with paintings and sculptures. It was absolutely fanciful, and I was beyond grateful to Aaron for picking out my dress. Seeing the women dressed in their beautiful gowns as they glided across the floor made my heart override my mind as I looked on in awe as the entire crowd swayed from one direction to the other. This was what I wanted to remember from my first night in Paris.

The waltz drifted away and the crowd stilled, and I suddenly felt all eyes on Aaron and me as he took my hand in his and walked me to the floor.

Gregory Sennet announced to the room that Aaron Sullivan would be taking my hand in our first waltz in Paris and my entire body seized up. I suddenly felt like I was thrust into a high society gambol that I wasn't fit for. Gregory repeated what he said in French and before I had a chance to object, Aaron brought me into his arms as Shostakovich's Jazz Suite II hummed through the air. It was my favorite waltz in spite of it appearing in *Eyes Wide Shut.* I was surprised that Aaron remembered, but that was who he was. Regardless of what information I'd found out tonight, this was why I loved this man.

"You are way too slick," I laughed, feeling his arms tighten as our bodies melted into the waltz.

Our bodies swayed and flew to each beat of the waltz as the rest of the couples joined us. We were swallowed into the ballroom as the waltz serenaded through the air, and my world felt whimsically misplaced.

"I love you more than anything, but you have a lot of explaining to do," I whispered.

"Don't I always?" His eyes twinkled and between the bubbles of the champagne and the magic of the moment, I let myself drift into another world as he carried me across the floor.

CHAPTER EIGHT

I pushed down the sheets and stretched my arms as the bright light shone through the sheer curtains, introducing my first Parisian morning. I saw brioche and a glass of orange juice sitting on the small table by the window. Aaron had gotten up a couple hours earlier. I vaguely remembered him kissing me and telling me to sleep as long as I needed and that he'd be in the studio. Every so often, I'd hear a scrape of metal against the wood floors or his footsteps walking quickly across the floor upstairs, but I generally slept through most of whatever he was busily working on.

Now I was faced with nursing this slight headache from too many flutes of champagne and too little to eat. We were out late last night, and I'd crawled right into bed the moment we got back to our apartment. Between the champagne and my flight, I was completely exhausted and every welcome home move I'd thought about unleashing on Aaron was extinguished the moment my eyes closed. It also didn't help that I ran into his ex-fiancée.

Elizabeth!

I grumbled aloud and slid my feet into the slippers next to the bed as I almost wished myself back under the covers. The longer I was awake, the more our little encounter wedged itself in my mind.

I had to find out what Aaron had been hiding, but more importantly, I needed to understand why he didn't tell me. Our relationship had steadily grown into something profound and beautiful, and the thought that there were pieces of his history that I wasn't privy to made me internally cringe. No matter how foolish it sounded, it made me doubt who he was or at the very least how he came to be. I felt like it was impossible to see him as a whole person if I didn't get invited into his life fully.

I trudged over to the table and took a sip of orange juice before toothpaste wiped out the pleasure of fresh squeezed juice. I picked up the brioche and inhaled the buttery scent as I smeared more butter on top and crowned it with a tiny amount of jam. Taking a bite, my tongue met with the buttery goodness, and I took a seat on the chair next to the window. I opened the curtain and looked out onto the street below. People were walking down the sidewalks, and cars were driving by on the street with places to go. I leaned against the back of the chair and pondered this last revelation. I didn't have any place to go. I wrinkled my forehead and took another bite. I'd have to change that.

Polishing off the brioche and juice, I saw that Aaron had already connected my iPad and phone to the wireless. He had them sitting on the chair. My stomach knotted as my grogginess exchanged for trepidation. With only a few swipes I might be able to see what Aaron Thatcher was hiding from me. I took in a deep breath and reached for my iPad. I'd never been one to sit and speculate when I had answers so close to my fingertips. I swiped my fingertip along the screen and waited for the home screen to flash on. Quickly typing in Aaron Thatcher, I waited impatiently for the results but was interrupted by someone's footsteps, but I couldn't tell where they were coming from.

I set my iPad down on the bed and followed the mysterious noise down the hall and through the kitchen, only to find Aaron pushing open the hidden door in the dining room. It was going to take some getting used to all these strange noises in such an ancient building.

Aaron's snug-fitting jeans were splattered with solder, and his thermal shirt had a thick coating of metal dust entwined in the fibers. His hair was completely disheveled, and he had a few dark smudges under his left eye, and for some reason, that combination was sexy as hell. When his gaze landed on me he grinned and shook his head.

"Good afternoon, sleepyhead," he teased, closing the door behind him.

"Do you blame me with all that champagne you force-fed me." I smiled and walked over to him. He placed a quick kiss on my forehead and was about to go for my lips when I shook my head and took a step back, bumping into a dining room chair.

"I haven't brushed my teeth yet."

Aaron rolled his eyes. "Like I care."

"You would. Believe me," I teased, following him through the hall. "Thank you for the delicious breakfast."

"The least I could do. Would you like a mimosa?"

"Hardeeharhar, Mr. Sullivan." I narrowed my eyes at him. "I think I'm just fine in the booze department."

"I was only checking." His playful grin made my world spin more than it already was. He opened the fridge and grabbed a bottle of Perrier. "Would you like one?"

I shook my head. "I prefer not to burp after water."

Aaron laughed and shut the fridge door. "I think I prefer that too."

"Did you get a lot of work done?" I asked, reaching for a glass to get some tap water.

"I did. I had a lot of time to think as well."

"Did you?" I asked, filling my glass.

He nodded. "Do you know what time it is, by any chance?"

"No clue."

"It's almost four o'clock."

"In the afternoon?" I almost choked out.

He smiled and took a sip of his water. "Yep. I knew you were tired."

"That would explain why I feel so rested...slightly sore but completely rested." I stretched my arms in front of me and caught Aaron's gaze traveling along my bare skin. I was only dressed in a skimpy top and loose, cotton boxers.

"Alas, I think the only thing we can blame the soreness on is too much champagne. I hope to change that soon."

"What exactly do you have in mind?" I asked innocently, as I walked past him with a little extra wiggle.

He let out a slight growl and followed me down the hall. I reached our bedroom, and moved my suitcase to a better place to spread out. I unzipped it and searched for my toothpaste and toothbrush. Finding my baggie, I snatched it up just as I felt Aaron come up behind me. I stood up, almost crashing into him, as he glanced at the iPad I had tossed on the bed.

His gaze dropped to the floor, and he chewed his lip slightly as he contemplated what I'd so carelessly left on the screen.

Damn me for never programming it to sleep!

"So... you haven't brought up what Tracy mentioned, and I don't remember it entailing that." His eyes moved to the iPad and then back to mine.

"You mean that or who?" I arched a brow and he nodded.

I also hadn't brought up running into who she mentioned either, but I might leave that for another conversation. So far nothing was going as planned.

"I was hoping you'd bring it up," I confessed.

"Well, I guess I just did…"

"You sure did." I breathed a long sigh as I walked over to him. He picked up the iPad and tapped a link with his index finger.

There was an awkwardness resting between us that never existed before, and I desperately wanted it to stop.

"So what did you find out about me?" His gaze didn't leave the iPad as he continued to read over whatever information he came onto.

"Absolutely nothing and would you mind giving that back?"

"I'd say you found out more that nothing, judging by this story."

I was so irritated and I wasn't even sure at who. "Believe it or not, I hadn't clicked on any of the links yet."

"I'd say not. As nosey as you're, I can't imagine you not clicking."

I wanted to protest, but the truth of it was that I was nosey, which was why I loved the idea of practicing law. I'd be able to stick my nose where it didn't belong. The last thought took me by surprise. Ever since the accident, I hadn't thought much about law one way or another.

"I'd take complete offense to that if you

weren't right, but it just so happens, I heard you come down the stairs before I managed to click on anything."

My heart raced as my mind shuffled all kinds of answers that I wanted him to give me without having to look them up. The problem was that I continued to wait. He offered no answers as he threw the iPad back on the bed.

"Aren't you going to explain things to me?" I asked, trying to hide my anger.

"Explain what to you? It looks like you've got a good handle on it. I'm gonna take a shower. Get this dust off me." He walked toward the bathroom, and my pulse went through the roof.

I detected the same aloofness I'd felt when I uncovered he was flying off to China, and I began to panic. What was happening? What had I stumbled onto that would threaten what we'd built? How could things crumble so fast? Was that why Elizabeth was so helpful in planting these tiny seeds of information? She knew this was how he'd react?

"You're not going to explain to me what's going on? You're just going to take a shower?"

He glanced over his shoulder, but there was coolness resting behind his eyes. "Seriously, just read a couple of those articles, and you'll be all caught up." He winked at me and that was when I popped a cork. The dryness in his tone sent me right back to when I ran into his translator, and I wasn't going back there again. Enough sidestepping. I wanted answers now.

From his mouth, not the internet.

"Are you serious?" I demanded, following him into the bathroom.

He'd already turned on the shower, and steam was rolling out of the tiled basin.

"Deadly," he said, stripping out of his thermal. My eyes coursed down his sharply defined torso, and my heart literally fluttered despite my best efforts to control myself. He knew what he did to me, and I was having no part of it as I turned around and spoke to the blue tiled wall.

I heard him unzip his jeans and found myself pressing on the wall with the palms of my hand.

"Do you actually think that this is called for?" I asked.

"What in particular?" His voice changed, and I realized he was already under the water. I was safe to turn around.

"Keeping something like this from me?" I seethed.

"So you do know what it is."

"No. I have absolutely no idea what it is."

"Then how do you know I'm keeping anything from you?"

A guttural sound rolled out of my mouth as I fisted my hands. "Forget whatever it is you think I saw on the internet. We both were there when Tracy happened to mention your ex-fiancée, Elizabeth. Let's not forget the obvious. You never once mentioned you had a fiancée."

"I told you last night, it didn't mean anything."

"And like I mentioned last night, that's more horrifying than finding out you had one."

"And why's that?" he asked, baiting me.

"Would it have changed things between us if you knew?"

This was the Aaron I rarely saw. The cold and calculating businessman who knew how to argue deals for the win and always came out on top. But there was a reason I was the captain of the debate team in high school and college. It wasn't that I always wanted to win. It was that I never lost. I was just that good.

My cheeks were warm with anger as I marched closer to the shower.

"It has absolutely nothing to do with whether it would have changed things between us. I've told you everything about my life. You know things I haven't even told Gabby and Lily and none of those things include a long, lost fiancé."

"Well, she's never been lost. I've known right where she's been this whole time."

His hands reached out of the shower and pulled me under the droplets with him. I pounded his chest in pure frustration as his body shook with laughter. I didn't have a chance to argue my side. He wasn't playing fairly.

"Do you think this is funny?" I scowled.

"I'm laughing, aren't I?"

"Who are you and what have you done with Aaron? I want my kind, caring, compassionate man back. The one I flew across the globe to be with."

"He's here, babe. He's just trying to get you to relax and realize that he wouldn't ever do something to you to hurt you."

"Quit talking in third person," I muttered.

He chuckled and poured shampoo onto my hair.

"Seriously though..." he paused and lathered the soap through my hair as my top and boxers continued to drip with water. "It was a time in my life that I'd like to forget. I'd abandoned my little sister, the only father I'd known rejected me, and things outside of my control happened. Being with you has let me escape all that, and I never wanted to bring it up. Not because I was hiding it from you, but because it wasn't a version of myself that I was proud of."

"How many versions of you are there?" I asked.

"Too many," he murmured, his hands sliding along my bare arms. "And to be honest being over here the last three weeks alone with my thoughts, only made things more confusing."

He rinsed the shampoo out of his hair as I maneuvered around him in the small shower. The tenderness in his touch as he swept my wet hair out of my face made my body crumble into his, but I was too riled up.

"It's really difficult having this conversation with you like this," he groaned, as I pressed my back against him to rinse the shampoo out of my hair. I'd managed to strip out of my boxers and top, but I kept my body turned away from him.

"Then hopefully that's incentive to get you talking."

"You have no idea." He reached for the white towel hanging outside the shower and stepped out of the way of the stream as he dried off.

"So you haven't clicked on any of those links?" he asked.

I shook my head and let the warm water run down my back as his eyes ran over my body with heated desire.

"How did you know to look up Thatcher?" He glanced over his shoulder and waited for my response, but I didn't have one to give. I'd just given him hell for not being open with me, and I'd failed to mention that I ran into his ex-fiancée.

I turned off the water and Aaron handed me a towel to dry off with.

"Why aren't you answering my question?" Aaron asked. He wrapped the towel around his waist and walked out of the bathroom as I wrapped my hair in a towel and followed him.

"It's complicated." I reached into the suitcase and pulled out a pair of panties and a matching bra. Quickly fastening my bra, I pulled an oversized shirt over my head and pulled up my underwear.

"Shouldn't be that complicated." He buttoned his jeans and sat on the bed, waiting for my reply.

I pulled on a pair of leggings and pulled the towel off my head.

"I ran into Elizabeth last night."

Before I even had a chance to continue, Aaron bolted out of the room.

"I changed my mind. Just check out the links. It sounds like you'd rather find everything out through secondhand sources anyway."

I'd only managed to make it to the dining

room when I heard the front door click shut.

"Fine. Don't mind if I do," I whispered to myself as I walked back to the bedroom and picked up the iPad.

With a quick swipe of my finger and a couple taps, I stared down at the screen. My body slid onto the bed as I realized I'd never be able to look at Aaron the same way again.

Chapter Nine

I couldn't stop looking and clicking on link after link. Each one painted the same picture of Aaron Thatcher, and it was all I could do not to shatter into a million little pieces. Every image of Aaron tore at my heart, and it created more uncertainty with each new click. I didn't understand how a man I loved so deeply could hide something like this from me. The images flooded my mind as I scrolled through the online reports and stories about Aaron. My hands were slick as anxiety pulsed through my system, and all I wanted was to hear it from his lips.

Closing my eyes, I tossed the iPad on the bed and fell backward as the first tears of deception fell down my face. How could he not tell me these things? My thoughts were scattered as my emotions turned from one thought to another. I wondered if Gabby knew any of this, but as quickly as I thought about her, my mind went back to Aaron. Did he expect to hide this our whole lives together? My mind was racing with uncertainty and confusion, and all I wanted was to be back home.

As the tears continued to cascade down my cheeks, I half-laughed and half-sobbed as I thought about my first day in Paris. Crying on the bed wasn't what I'd planned. None of this was what I'd planned. Taking a big sniff in, I reached for my phone and texted Gabby. I was turning into a complete basket case, and I didn't know how to stop my free fall.

Did you know about your brother?

I waited impatiently for a reply as I became a mess of tears and snot. Things weren't going well. I used my shirt to wipe the tears, and I continued to stare at the ceiling. The misery of being lied to by omission was more than I could bear, and I felt completely stuck—mentally and physically. Not to mention I didn't understand why Aaron ran off. Leaving me to discover these things without him only made it worse.

Gabby responded, and I picked up the phone.

Know what about my brother? Is everything okay?

I let out a small amount of air as relief settled

over me. At least my best friend wasn't keeping secrets from me. My hands trembled as I held the phone. This was exactly why I shouldn't have fallen in love my best friend's brother. The situation was too sticky, and the thought of losing both Aaron and my best friend...

I shook off the almost paralyzing sensations and texted back.

Look up Aaron Thatcher. That will tell you everything. He took off because I learned of his "other" last name and was going to Google him.

I pressed send and walked to the bathroom. I had to get a grip. If I was going to be getting on a plane to head back to the states, I at least needed to look somewhat decent. If I washed my face with cold water and started over, maybe I wouldn't look so terrifying. Opening the cabinet door that housed the towels, I searched for a washcloth and came up empty-handed. I opened the armoire that was in the hall and only found sheets and more towels. Why was it this hard to find a washcloth?

Letting out a sigh, I trundled back into the bathroom and turned on the cold water. My phone rang in the other room, but I didn't even care. As I splashed the water on my face, all I could do was picture Aaron wandering the streets of Paris alone, and my chest tightened. What was he thinking? Why didn't he just tell me? Would this pattern ever stop?

I grabbed a towel and dried my face. Feeling

slightly better about life until I looked in the mirror, I grunted at the madness that had developed in the last twenty-four hours. Was this a sign of things to come? Brandishing these fleeting thoughts around was teetering on insanity. I had to get back to the first problem. Aaron had hid a couple of doozeys from me, and I needed answers. Simple as that.

I dabbed lotion on my face to tone the redness down, but it didn't help. My eyes and the tip of my nose were red and my chin was all blotchy. This wasn't a good look, but it would have to do. I needed to find Aaron, but I didn't want to frighten the Parisians on the way. Something about this scenario had to change. I hated inaction, and that's what my world consisted of in this very second. Everything in life was in a holding pattern. Being mopey wasn't going to solve our problems, but my body was completely useless as I trudged back into the bedroom. Whatever I was experiencing was far worse than jet lag. Every second felt like too much for me to handle. I loathed being this out of control with my emotions, and Aaron's refusal to discuss only added to the helplessness pummeling through my veins.

I groaned at the inconsistencies as my thoughts contradicted themselves. Which was it? Would I powder my cheeks and face the world or hide in the apartment until he returned?

We needed to talk. I shouldn't have gone behind his back, but he shouldn't have hid things from me. Not to mention Aaron Thatcher was a man I wanted to know. I needed to learn about him, uncover what drove his actions. After all, the actions of Aaron Thatcher created the man who was now Aaron Sullivan.

That was it. I would go find him in a city I didn't know, looking like I rolled out of the catacombs. No sense in being vain now.

I glanced at the phone and saw the text from Gabby.

Holy Shit. I had no idea. None. I'm at a complete loss for words...

You and me both. I drew in a long breath and texted back. Not wanting to mention the fact that Jason had failed to mention this to her as well.

I'm off to track him down. I don't know where he went. Day one in Paris is going really well. So glad I came. You Sullivans have some really bad habits.

She texted back.

Don't get lost. Stay close to the apartment.

Here I was about to venture onto the streets of Paris, looking for someone who didn't want to be found, and I had no idea what I even wanted to say to him. I was hurt that he didn't tell me about any of these developments, and at this point Elizabeth was a small part of the whole situation. I tossed my phone on the bed and grabbed my makeup, opening it up and quickly patting powder on my face to take away the red. Sort of.

I changed shirts and grabbed my passport and tucked it in a small purse, along with some credit cards. Even though I knew he wouldn't pick up, I dialed his phone and it went to voicemail.

I grabbed the set of keys off the dining room table and made my way through the apartment. Even with the mess going on, the space was calming, and I hoped with all my heart this wouldn't be the last day I enjoyed it.

I locked the front door and rather than take the elevator, I found the stairs and descended quickly. With my luck I'd get stuck in the elevator and no one would find me. I hadn't had the best of luck with elevators, but at least this one didn't argue with me.

Since I didn't remember the code to unlock the door to get back into the apartment building, it made me all the more determined to find Aaron. I opened the door and took a deep breath of cinnamon and sugar as I stepped outside to feel the warm air against my skin. I closed the door and began walking down the sidewalk away from La Crêperies Parfaites when a strange sensation ran through my body.

I paused and scanned the sidewalk, and rather than continue walking away from the café, I walked toward it. There were several outside diners sitting at the tables, smoking and chatting. I reached the corner and glanced down the sidewalk to see even more outdoor seating. All the umbrellas were open to shield the patrons from the blazing sun, which made it difficult to see the faces of the people sitting at the tables.

But my heart fell when my gaze managed to stumble upon one figure in particular. I knew it was Aaron. I'd recognize that body anywhere. I didn't need to see his face to know it was him, and I didn't need to see Elizabeth's either. I watched Aaron take a sip of a cappuccino as he stared at Elizabeth. She was sitting across from him, leaning over the table as her lips moved incessantly.

I wanted to spin around and run away. I finally understood the comfort that seemed to bring to Aaron and Gabby, but I had nowhere to go. I couldn't open the door to get back inside. I'd just be running through a city that didn't seem to want me.

Aaron set his cup down and continued to stare at Elizabeth. He didn't say a word. He listened, and my heart twisted in knots as I thought about the chance he was giving her to explain her side of things; yet with me, he fled.

And he fled to her.

The last thought that pumped from my mind to my heart about did me in. I so desperately wanted to be anywhere but here. I begged for the cracks on the sidewalk to open up and swallow me before I burst into tears again. I certainly couldn't do that in front of her. I wouldn't give her that satisfaction.

Or him for that matter.

With that last thought, I spun on my heels and

ran right into the server who had a tray full of cappuccinos. His quick movement wasn't quick enough as one of the mugs slid off the tray and crashed onto the concrete below. I gasped and glanced over my shoulder as Aaron stood up and Elizabeth grimaced from her seat.

"Excusez-moi, Mademoiselle." I turned my attention back to the server, who was now apologizing profusely even though the fiasco had been my fault. I shook my head and uttered a feeble apology in French and walked around the mess as another server came to help pick up the heap of espresso, foam and ceramic.

I quickly rounded the bend, when I felt Aaron's fingers grasp hold of my arm and pull me to a stop. Even his touch had the power to break me, and all I wanted was to shrink into the pavement.

"Brandy," Aaron's voice was completely calm and collected, yet I felt like the moment I opened my mouth, I'd break down. How was he able to shut things off so easily?

I kept my gaze on the sidewalk as he stepped in front of me. He tilted my chin up to meet his gaze, and all I could give him was an exasperated sigh of defeat. Resentment was beating its way into my mind as I stared at the man who I loved more than anything in this world.

"Don't you need to go back to Elizabeth?" The moment I uttered the words, I hated myself for it. I wasn't that petty person, yet he reduced me to a sniveling muddle of emotions while he stood strong without a stitch of regret.

"It's not like that," he murmured.

"Of course it's not." I glared at him, but my trembling lips gave away the true state of my emotions. "Nothing ever is, right?"

Aaron let go of my arm, and I stepped back, relieved that this section of the patio was clear of diners.

"Would you mind letting me know what the code is to the apartment? Now that I've found you, I don't know what to do with you... so I'd just like to go back upstairs and pack."

Aaron let out a sigh and ran his fingers along the stubble on his chin. "I messed up."

"Sherlock would be proud." I stared at him and saw a slight twitch of his mouth, which only infuriated me more. "The code. Do you mind?"

"I do mind. We need to talk, and I think we should find a neutral place to discuss things."

"Neutral?" I asked, narrowing my eyes at him.

"Yes. Neutral."

"This isn't really anything I want to go over in public. I'm wrapped in knots inside. There is no end to my confusion. My mind's a mess, and there's no undoing it unless you explain what I saw online. I need to know why you wouldn't tell me something so important... so life altering..." I stopped myself from saying something I would regret. "It makes me feel like you don't think I'm worth opening up to and doing this all over a cappuccino isn't my idea of getting to the heart of the matter. Maybe it works with Elizabeth, but it doesn't work with me."

His jaw tensed, and he looked over at the door

to our building. "I deserve that."

"You deserve more than that."

Ignoring my comments, he reached for my hand and cupped it in his. "Let me take you somewhere that's secluded. I'll answer any questions you have, and I'll tell you everything. I don't want us to discuss this where we plan on spending the rest of our time while in Paris. The apartment isn't big enough."

I let out a sigh and avoided his gaze. "Who's to say, I'll be staying."

"Only you, but I beg you to hear me out..." his voice trailed off and the coolness I'd detected earlier was long gone. "Look at me, Brandy. Please."

My heart and mind were racked with chaos as I slowly brought my gaze to his. Deep pain plagued his expression, and I wanted nothing more than to forgive him and move on, but I was smart enough to know if we didn't deal with these things now, they would forever haunt our future. And I wasn't prepared to donate what time I had left on earth living as a tortured soul, waiting for the next big revelation to surface.

He squeezed my hand, and I nodded slowly. "Don't you need to let Elizabeth know you're not returning?"

"Believe me. She knows." His gaze hardened, but he didn't say anymore as we began walking down the sidewalk. With every step, my heart frayed a little more knowing that our lives would never be the same.

CHAPTER TEN

I had no idea where we were in the city, but he led me through a wrought iron gate that had a matching fence encircling a meticulously maintained garden. Scarlet and purple flowers dripped from the beds, spilling onto a gravel path that led to a row of empty benches. Tall laurels provided a wall of privacy from the bustling street. It felt like we'd been sucked into a hidden world miles away from everything and everyone, but the same problems still existed.

On the way, and despite my protests, Aaron bought sliced meat and rolls. Placing the bag on the bench, he motioned for me to take a seat. If we weren't about to embark on something so serious, I would've enjoyed wandering through the garden, but all I cared about was getting answers.

He took out a bottle of water and offered it to me. I gladly accepted, twisted off the cap and began sipping it while he sat quietly next to me. There was a stubborn silence as if neither of us wanted to break the barrier that would begin the barrage of questions and answers. My mind was ready, but I wasn't sure my heart was prepared.

"So I'm guessing you looked at the links this time." His gaze fastened on mine, and my voice wouldn't come. I nodded in response and tucked a leg under my body, turning toward him. Our bodies were close but not touching. I needed it to be that way so I wouldn't dissolve into him.

He took a sip of water and looked at the gravel beneath his feet. "I don't know where to begin."

"How about we start at the beginning," I said, after a few seconds of silence. "When you took on your biological father's name. Let's start there."

He sucked on his lip and a flash of his tongue piercing glistened. I couldn't help but smile at the distractions this man always seemed to deliver. He was full of contradictions and surprises. Often one led to the other, but it was the unknowns in between that worried me. I glanced across the path at a white rose and slowly slid my hand to his knee.

Aaron let out a deep breath and scratched his chin. "Well, you already know that I was in the Marines, alongside Jason. I changed my name before joining. It was foolish, but things always happen for a reason, I suppose. I was thankful I had Sullivan to go back to."

I nodded, and my body began to relax as our eyes connected.

"Jason and I wanted more out of our time in the service. So when we returned from our first tour, we put our sights on the Special Forces unit. It was a grueling process and both of us wondered what the hell we'd signed ourselves up for once we started. Soldiers began dropping out on the very first day of training, which only made me want it more. I wanted to prove that I could do it. That I was worthy of carrying out the most sensitive missions our country had to offer. It was what I clung to in order to get through the training. Every day I thought it couldn't get worse and then it went downhill tenfold the next day. What they demanded of us was nothing less than perfection, and I needed to prove to someone somewhere that I was needed. That I had a place in the world."

My heart stung at his admission, yet I kept my gaze steady on his. I knew he wouldn't want anything misconstrued as pity. What he didn't realize was that all I had for him was admiration. The moment I read the articles online, I was in awe. I didn't understand why he wouldn't tell me. Why he wouldn't share such a huge part of his life with me.

"I became part of the 1st MSOB division…" He saw the look of bewilderment on my face and backed up. "Sorry. It stands for Marine Special Operations Battalion. It falls under another alphabet game, MSOC. Marine Special Operations Companies."

I wanted to ask if that was before or after Elizabeth, but I kept my mouth shut.

"I was really proud of my accomplishment, but I had no one to share it with. No family to tell. Unless you count Jason." He grinned, and the tension between us continued to dissipate. I was finally beginning to see the side he'd hidden for so long.

"He'd probably be offended if you didn't." I smiled, and we both knew it was true.

"A week before Jason and I were scheduled for our first tour, I met Elizabeth. We met at a bar. She was with some friends. It turned out she was headed to Afghanistan as well. I never saw her as anything more than platonic. I thought we were on the same page."

I tried to swallow discreetly, even though it felt like I was trying to push a boulder down my throat. I hadn't expected Elizabeth to factor into his story so quickly. I started to feel a little lightheaded and realized the brioche from earlier wasn't cutting it. I pointed at the bag and Aaron smiled.

"I told you I knew what I was talking about. This kind of discussion requires sustenance." He pulled out a napkin and placed a roll and a couple slices of meat on it.

I ripped into the roll and put the meat inside. For some odd reason, it provided the distraction I needed as he continued.

"When we were in Afghanistan absolutely nothing happened between us."

I cringed knowing that meant at some point

something may have.

"She was persistent, and I'm sure I gave her the wrong signals." He took a sip of water. "When we returned from Afghanistan, Jason and I needed to concentrate on MSOC. Jason liked to joke that I wanted to join purely to avoid dealing with Elizabeth."

My heart stumbled at the pattern of avoidance that never seemed to stop.

"Was it?"

He shook his head and then contradicted his gesture. "Well, maybe. Anyway, she got transferred to another base, and I assumed that would be where the friendship ended. We never had a date, let alone a relationship of any kind. When Jason and I made it through training and into MSOB, I never gave her another thought. I thought the friendship had run its course."

I slowly chewed my sandwich and braced myself for whatever might be coming next. He wasn't in the military all that long and so far, he'd relayed events that covered quite a bit of time.

"I know I sounded like a dick last night and today. I don't take being in love lightly or being engaged. I just figured I'd have time to tell you everything before it got twisted, but I was wrong. I left that part of my life behind for a reason, and I honestly never had any intention of bringing it up again. It's nothing I'm proud of."

I knew what I saw online, and his sentiments toward the entire situation made no sense.

"I don't understand." I scooted closer and

touched his hand. "Your actions saved countless lives. How can you not be proud of that?"

Scathing laughter cut through me as he shook his head. "Our military is the most powerful organization on the planet. They'll make even the most deplorable of situations seem okay."

I refused to take his simplified answer. "Are you telling me you didn't save those people I read about?"

"No. I'm not telling you that, but I'm also willing to tell you that I was responsible for twice as many deaths."

A prickle of apprehension ran across my flesh as my mind tried to comprehend what he was trying to tell me.

"But you were in war. We are in war," I offered.

He nodded. "Doesn't make it any easier."

Part of me wanted to know the details, and the other knew not to ask. My father had always told me never to ask a soldier questions I didn't want answers to. I learned that lesson the hard way when one of his vet friends, from the first Iraq war, sat in our living room at Christmas. I had asked him if he'd ever killed anyone. The question sent a shockwave through the living room, but it was nothing compared to his answer, which was that he'd happily killed more than one. Granted, I was only a child when I asked, but it was something I never should've brought up, and something I'd always regretted. It was rude on so many levels.

Now I wanted to help carry that burden for

the man I loved, but I knew it was too much for even our shoulders combined. Taking another life, no matter the reason, had to pierce one's soul.

"I'm so sorry," I whispered.

"Don't be. I knew what I signed up for. I wanted to be in the most elite killing squad the world had, and that's what I achieved. It would have been fine." He nodded. "That was my job, but to get slapped with a hero status when I came back. I could reconcile being one or the other, not both..." his voice trailed off.

And that was when I realized Aaron was a man full of contradictions because his life had been built with them. I took his hand in mine and squeezed it.

"If you hadn't done what you did, dozens of families would have been without their children, their parents. You said it yourself. What you did in Afghanistan was your job. You were fighting for our country. When you came back on our soil, you didn't have to do what you did."

"It's not that simple," he said.

I had read the countless articles explaining Aaron Thatcher's heroics. A gunman had opened fire at a church in Massachusetts. According to the articles I read online, it was pure chance that Aaron had been at the church. He was visiting a friend in the area, and that was when it clicked. That friend had been Elizabeth.

"You may not want to see yourself as a hero, but that's exactly how I see you. How I've always seen you. Fighting for our country automatically put you in that category whether you like it or not. And I have to admit that no matter how much I love Gabby, I always connected with your side of it more. I knew there was more that you weren't sharing."

He let out a deep breath.

Our legs were touching, and I felt the strength in his grip as we silently looked at each other.

"You did what you had to do," I finally whispered. "And I won't pretend like I know what that feels like."

"I wouldn't want you to," he replied. He pressed his lips together and leaned against the back of the bench.

"So you were visiting Elizabeth?" I asked.

He nodded. "She was training at Fort Devens, and I had some leave and always wanted to see that part of the country. She had continued to stay in touch, even though I really hadn't, so I took her up on her offer to be my local tour guide. Jason warned against it, but none of us knew what would transpire. I'd already been in the New England area touring around for five days before I stopped in to see Elizabeth. I got into town on Thursday and by that Sunday, my life changed forever. We went to the early morning service. I really hadn't wanted to spend my vacation at church, but I figured I had no choice. She'd been gracious enough to show me around. I picked her up late, but she refused to let that stop us from attending church. We'd gotten there about twenty minutes late, which was fine by me since we missed the singing.

Anyway, we sat in the back, and I hadn't really been paying attention to the sermon. I noticed a guy come in, and he seemed overly jumpy. He was wearing an overcoat that he never took off, and the place was really warm so he had to have been uncomfortable. The guy didn't take a seat. He stood behind the back row across from us. Within minutes of him being there, I began to feel what I'd felt in Afghanistan right before I pulled the trigger, but I wasn't the one behind the gun."

Aaron took another sip of water and then continued, "That's when I realized that sensation was rolling off the man. He was about to open fire. I didn't reach him in time. He wounded some folks before I was able to take him out with his own gun. He died before the medics got to the church. I wish I could tell you I had remorse, but I didn't. I saw the look of pure hatred resting in his eyes. He had intended to kill as many innocent people as he could. I remember hearing the screams and cries from everyone in the church as the pastor ushered everyone through a door behind his podium, which led to a small chapel. I made Elizabeth follow them all as I stood there with the man's blood pooled on the floor, dripping from the pews, and splattered against the wall. It was my worst nightmare, but I was in my own country. Everything happened so fast, and it didn't take long before the media arrived to film me coming out of the church. It was a madhouse and I couldn't run from it. It followed me everywhere I went. Elizabeth had been by my side the entire time things unfolded, and people began referring to her as my girlfriend. That was the least of my worries so I never bothered correcting anyone. I didn't realize the ramifications that would have. I didn't understand how big the story was going to get. My life became a circus, and I wanted nothing to do with any of it. The press was making a big deal out of nothing."

I stared at him in awe.

"The military really spun things to their benefit as well. I knew they needed to do that. Press about the military isn't always the best," he sighed.

"You don't say."

He grinned and licked his lips before taking a sip of water. "Honestly, it's nothing I like to talk about. The attention was undeserved and quite lopsided when I frame it up with everything else that I'd done in my life."

I shook my head in disbelief. The many sides of Aaron seemed at odds with each other, yet they were all needed in order to define the man he'd become. Learning about this put into perspective so many inconsistencies that I didn't understand. There was much more to his story than he even told Gabby. The depth to Aaron was staggering, and it seemed like I'd only scratched the surface.

"Oh, my god," I whispered.

"What?" he asked.

"I remember you. I remember the story. I can't believe I didn't put two and two together."

"Why would you? It was a long time ago…"

"But still. I remember now. It was on all the channels. I was in high school."

Aaron nodded. "My worst fear about the whole thing was that Gabby would see something about it in the news. I was a complete fraud. I abandoned my little sister because I was too cowardly to stand up to our dad, and here I was being declared a national hero. It was complete garbage and wrong on so many levels. The least of things she needed to see was her long-lost brother being hailed as a hero. I was no hero. It was just happenchance that I was there."

"I don't know how she didn't see it," I muttered, shaking my head. "You were everywhere."

Aaron let out another sigh. "Yes. I was."

"How in the world she didn't notice you if not on television, at least at the grocery store. You were on all the magazines."

He nodded and had a pained expression. "When I left Gabby, I looked a lot different than I did when everything happened. The military will make a man out of even the most scrawny individual." He attempted to grin, and I couldn't help but smile at the man who I'd so deeply misunderstood. "Not that I was ever scrawny."

"So over about the spread of six months, Elizabeth somehow became known as my fiancée, even though I never asked or gave her a ring. I didn't question how that story got spread. I didn't want to know. Anyway, I went on with my life and as quickly as I was thrust into the spotlight, I fell from it. Jason and I developed our product and then we both jumped ship the moment we could."

"The sad thing is that I think Elizabeth actually told her friends that we were engaged. I'll admit I leaned on her a lot during that whole time, but I never thought I gave her that idea. Shit. I mean, we didn't even sleep together. I mean…come on." He flashed a devilish grin, and my cheeks reddened at this revelation.

Having all of the pieces of Aaron's hidden life emerge and paint a complete picture of the man I fell in love with made my spirit rise to the occasion. I never should've second-guessed him, but I hoped that going forward, we wouldn't hide anything big or small.

"I felt bad that she got carried through all that. Some story even ran about her being dumped by me. I have my suspicions who leaked that one."

"Tracy?" I asked.

He nodded. "But whatever. When Elizabeth got out of the service, she worked a few low-paying jobs, and then she came up with the idea for her business. By the time she reached out to me, I was already working with my father again. I thought it was the least I could do to help get her on her feet. Plus, she had a really good idea. It honestly never occurred to me that the worlds would collide, so to speak."

"It's so damn hard to stay mad at you when you have such good excuses. I'm the one who should be apologizing. I should have trusted you and what you had to say last night. Instead, I've spent my first day in Paris sleeping and raising hell."

Aaron laughed and threw his hands up. "Let's not get carried away. I should have filled in the woman I want to spend the rest of my life with."

His admission sent me to the clouds and back, and I hoped one day I'd be lucky enough to fulfill that wish, but in the meantime, I needed to understand Aaron's motives and take comfort that he'd begun to share with me parts of his life that he'd tried to forget.

CHAPTER ELEVEN

"*Patience* has never been one of my virtues." I folded my arms and stood outside the door to the studio. I was perched on the top stair waiting for him to let me see what he'd been working on the last three weeks.

"That's okay. I love all your others. Now give me one more second," Aaron hollered into the hall.

"Okay. Your one second is up."

"How about two seconds," he laughed.

"Come on. I flew all the way across the world to see your work, and now you're going to hide it from me?"

Aaron appeared in the doorway, his expression solemn. "I thought you flew all the way across the world to be with me."

"Well, maybe. But your work comes in a close second." I grinned as he drew my hands into his.

"You have to shut your eyes, and you have to realize that absolutely nothing is put together yet. You're just seeing the pieces. I'll be constructing it somewhere else."

"I got it. Now let me in."

"Close your eyes."

I huffed, but I squeezed them shut and allowed him to lead me into the studio. I walked about ten steps before he had me turn to the right. My hip bumped into a sharp object and something clunked onto the floor and I let out a gasp.

"It's okay. It was just a ruler." He stopped walking, and I detected a slight change in his breathing patterns. "Ready?"

"More than."

"Open them up."

My eyes flashed open, and he stepped away allowing me to see his pieces propped against the wall and arranged on the floor. Directly in front of me, metal streamed out of an opening that twisted into itself. The shapes reminded me of something from the ocean. The beauty he managed to capture in his pieces always exceeded my expectations, and these were no exception. Whether it was brutality or sensuality, Aaron's work was full of emotion, and the simplicity and clean lines of his pieces screamed perfection. I knelt down and studied the piece closest to me on the floor, my finger tracing the outline against the wood floor.

"These are incredible. Breathtaking actually. This piece reminds of a scion, but one who was taken from her family in the sea not the land..."

"Is that so?" Aaron asked, narrowing his eyes as I spoke of the piece.

"These metal shards streaming away, look like the ties to her family she's trying to cut from her life or her way of existing."

He knelt down and his gaze darkened as I lifted my hand away from the piece.

"Anyway, that's what I see in this one." I glanced across the room to distract myself from the intensity sitting behind his expression.

"It's not even fully constructed yet. I'm amazed you can see all that from so little."

I shrugged and stood up, moving to his next sculpture. This piece was different than the other one, but it still felt like the subject was reaching for something it couldn't obtain. The sorrow that dripped from it was terrifying, and I couldn't help but see Aaron in this piece as I thought back to his confessions from the day before. The hollowness of the metal contributed to the melancholy feeling that washed over me when looking at the sculpture. It felt like two worlds collided whether it was peace and war or love and hate, but the longer I looked at the metal, the more I felt I was staring into a portion of Aaron's soul.

He walked over to me and slid his arm around my waist. I rested my head on his shoulder, and my heart felt heavy as I stared at the piece in front of us. The half completed sculpture told me so much more about Aaron than he even knew.

"What do you think?" he whispered.

"I think you might have found your calling."

He squeezed my waist and sighed. "I'm not that sure about that."

"That's just jitters. Believe me when I tell you that your work is out of this world."

"Now that you've seen what I've been working on up here, will you finally let me eat and take you around a little bit?" he asked. "I need a break."

I nodded and smiled. This was how I saw my trip to Paris unfolding, but I wouldn't take back the last forty-eight hours for anything. It brought me closer to the man I loved. Questions were still swimming around inside my mind, and I'd find a time to ask them, but now wasn't the time. I wanted to play tourist in my new city.

"So what do you have in mind? The Louvre or the Eiffel Tower or a walk along the Seine..."

"How about none of those." His brow arched.

"What?"

"The Eiffel Tower is overrated, and we can do the Louvre another day when we can get an early start."

"How in the world can you say that the Eiffel Tower is overrated?" I was halfway down the stairs and came to a screeching halt at his latest curve ball. I was here to explore the city.

"It's just a tourist trap. The lines are outrageous, and the space needle is just as awesome." There was something mischievous lurking behind his expression, and I decided not

119

to fall into his plan. I mean maybe he'd seen it a few times with all of his travels, but come on. It was the Eiffel Tower.

I dropped my shoulders and flipped my hand, dismissing the idea entirely. I'd get there one way or another. "So what have you got up your sleeve?"

"I thought you might like to picnic in Jardin du Luxembourg. We can pick up some macaroons from Ladurée and wander the gardens and see the statues, or we can find a quiet place to enjoy one another's company."

"Both options sound heavenly." I walked down the last couple of steps and pushed open the door leading back into the dining room and was pleasantly greeted by a warm breeze from the open window. "I still need to try the crepe place, but I'd like the embarrassment of the cappuccino catastrophe to blow over."

"I'm sure they've long since forgotten," Aaron assured me.

"In a day?" I laughed.

"Well, soon they won't remember..." He winked, and I just shook my head at his feeble attempt to gloss over the fiasco.

"Do I need to bring anything special?" I asked.

"I don't even think you need a sweater. It's been warm from the moment I arrived and I don't see it letting up."

I strolled to the window and poked my head out the opening, thrilled at the thought of getting to stroll through Paris. Today had been exactly as I'd imagined it. We both woke up and shared breakfast. While he went up to work, I spent the morning reading and felt absolutely no guilt for doing so once in my life. I was wearing a green, fitted dress and had no plans to change. Jeans might be more practical, but this dress made me feel amazing.

Just as I turned around from the window, Aaron picked up my phone from the dining room table and handed it to me. "It looks like you got a text earlier."

I glanced at the screen and typed my password, which revealed a text from my mom. It must have come over while I was reading, but my heart fell when I saw the subject of the message.

Did you see the news I forwarded you about Derek?

News? What news? I hadn't looked at email since I arrived. The whole purpose of being in Paris was to hide from it all. Even though I didn't want to ask, I knew it would bother me the rest of the day if I didn't get the details.

No. What's going on?

Even though it was early in Seattle, my mom texted back.

Jury selection is underway and with Derek's online presence revealed in court documents, the local news has been eating it up. It's good you're

out of town, but I want you to be aware. Love,
mom

The news chilled me to my core. My plan had been to be as far away from the spectacle as possible. Unable to focus on anything, I leaned against the wall and stared directly in front of me. The dull ache that stretched from my hip down to my leg worsened as the words settled over me. I would be connected to what this predator did for the rest of my life.

"Brandy, what's wrong?"

I shook my head and handed him the phone as the anger threatened to overtake my world. Derek didn't deserve attention. He was getting exactly what he wanted. A platform.

I just wanted everything to go away. It was bad enough that I had to be reminded of what he did everyday when I got up in the morning or bent over to grab something. It was the simple things in my life that would forever connect me to Derek.

"If any of the press try track you down..." Aaron's agitation cut through the room. "Why can't they leave well enough alone?"

The disgust in his voice spoke to the depth of emotion that swarmed and muddled my thoughts, pulling me in every direction.

"The press must be hounding my family and my mom didn't want to tell me," I whispered.

"I'm so sorry, babe. I know you hoped to avoid most of it while you were here. The media feeds off things like this. It's sick." His jaw tensed, and I realized his words meant more to me than they ever had. He'd been in my shoes. Against his wishes, Aaron had been thrust into the spotlight. It was something very few could understand, but he did. "If any of those story suckers are on the other line when I pick up the phone..."

I laughed. "A story sucker?"

"I refuse to call them journalists. Journalism is reporting the facts not sensationalizing the situation." He balled his hands into fists and shook his head loathing the story-making machine our news had become.

I nodded in agreement as the tension that I'd been feeling in my shoulders and body begin to dissipate as I watched Aaron carry the burden for me. I hadn't asked him to, but he did it without question.

"You still up for the park?" Aaron asked, taking my phone from my hands and placing it on the table. He tangled his fingers with mine and pulled me closer to him. Leaning my head against his chest, I breathed in everything about him and nodded my head.

"I think it's the perfect idea to get my mind off things."

Aaron wrapped his arms around me and held me tightly as I kept my eyes closed. Listening to the steady beat of his heart lulled me to a place of calmness that only moments before I didn't believe existed.

"I don't know what I'd do without you," I murmured.

"It goes both ways, my love."

His grip lessened and I took a step back. "I'm not going to let this bastard spoil my first official second day in Paris."

Aaron smiled and gave a quick nod. "Agreed. I'll go grab my wallet and we'll be off."

I watched him walk out of the dining room, and my mind circled back to everything he revealed to me yesterday. There had been such a flood of information all at once that I was still waiting for the pieces to settle in place. It was hard to believe the man I'd fallen in love with had been a hero-in-hiding. I knew the events that unfolded that day in the church changed him forever, but I also understood the events prior to that had changed him as well. Some good. Some bad. It was up to me to navigate between the parallel worlds and discover the man behind the façade. Puzzling away, I imagined a lovely day with Aaron as I slowly made my way to the front door and waited for him to reappear.

"You ready? I grabbed two waters. It gets pretty hot in the afternoon here."

I nodded and put both bottles in my bag and followed Aaron into the hallway. He locked all the deadbolts and we were off. Excitement pulsed through my veins at seeing Paris in the light of day and leaving my baggage behind.

CHAPTER TWELVE

I allowed myself to imagine the beautiful Parisian days looming ahead of me—filled with delightful exploration and indulging in the sinfully delicious. I saw a simpler way of existing while I tried to unravel the madness of the life I'd left behind. I wasn't going to be held prisoner in thought or action because of a choice that someone else made. Trusting the legal system would need to be enough for me. But what if it wasn't? What if the actions of another dictated how my life would be? It also didn't help that I played peek-a-boo with someone who's clearly in love with my boyfriend. I felt like if there was ever a moment when I might come undone, now might be the time. I only hoped it wasn't at Aaron's expense.

But I felt like a ticking time bomb.

"Try the yellow one," Aaron said, handing me the box of macaroons. "It's way better than the green one."

Hearing Aaron's voice brought me back to the present and the very life I'd been daydreaming about. We'd managed to sample about every single color and type of macaroon we'd purchased. It started with the first one, raspberry, and my control steadily went downhill after that first bite. I couldn't stop myself from trying every single one. We'd been lucky enough to find a large shade tree in Jardin du Luxembourg where we sat and watched the world go by. Other than the fact that the wrought iron chairs were a little uncomfortable, this moment was what I'd envisioned.

"I could get used to this." I dipped my hand into the box and snatched the only yellow one remaining. "But this is the last one I'm eating, or I won't be able to fit in that tiny elevator of ours."

Aaron gave me a wry smile and picked a chocolate macaroon out of the box, closing the lid. "I say eat the extra macaroons. Who cares if we fit in the elevator? There's also the stairs we can take to our floor."

I took a bite of the macaroon and lemon melted in my mouth. Aaron was right. This was the best flavor out of the bunch. I eyed the box of treats as he slid it into the paper bag and wondered if I should stop him to get one more...

"You've been pretty quiet," Aaron said, dropping the box the rest of the way in the bag.

I drew in a deep breath and glanced around the park packed full of couples and families wandering the grounds. The gardens were in full bloom, and the lawns so perfectly manicured there were chains to keep people off them. "I really like it over here. The people are so friendly, and it's a million miles away from reality."

"This is reality. This is our reality," Aaron said. His eyes steadied on mine, and I felt that energized current run between us.

I understood what he was saying, but I honestly felt like recently I'd been living in a fog. The only moments of clarity seemed to happen in Aaron's arms.

I shook my head. "I feel horrible about how things are turning out. I'm over here sitting in a park, eating macaroons, while the press is harassing my family. That should be my reality. I feel like a complete coward."

Aaron rested his hand on mine, but he didn't say anything for a few seconds. He didn't need to. I saw it in his eyes. He recognized something I hadn't wanted to admit. I was broken, and I wasn't sure if I could be fixed. Everything I held dear and worked for my entire life had been stripped away from me. The drive and determination I'd always cherished vanished the moment I awoke in the hospital bed. I had always been enamored with law. Rather than play house with my friends, I wanted to play courtroom. My entire life had been built around getting into law school and finishing law school.

Now I didn't care if I ever stepped into the law library again.

"You're not a coward, but I know me telling you that won't change your mind. Nothing will change your mind except your own will."

The gloom hummed between us as I thought about the empty shell of a person I'd become. I'd hid it from my friends as best I could, but Aaron knew better. He saw my frustration when my leg gave out, or when I got tired of trying to convince myself that everything I thought I wanted, no longer seemed important.

"I'm tired of pretending that everything is going to be okay." I leaned back in the chair and went silent as a couple walked behind us, waiting until they were out of earshot before I continued. "What if it's not? What if Derek's not found guilty? What if he gets off? What if what I've worked toward my entire life doesn't interest me any longer? What if I just don't care?"

"I don't believe that you don't care."

"What if I don't want to go back?" My shoulders slumped at my admission.

Aaron shook his head and leaned forward, balancing his elbows on his knees, as he chose his words carefully. "Sometimes life's choices and unknowns seem endless, don't they?"

I nodded, wishing I wasn't in this chair. The entire park was dotted with chairs. There wasn't one bench that I could spot, and all I wanted was to be curled next to Aaron. I needed the comfort he offered.

"Your mind is rattling around all kinds of

scenarios, and it's distracting you from what is important. I know. I've been there. You manage to spin every possibility into a worst-case scenario. It's exhausting. The clutter is absolutely overwhelming."

"It is wearing. It makes life draining," I hesitated.

"There's something else you're not sharing..." he prodded.

I chewed on my lip for a second before answering. How did I bring this up without sounding like a crazy, jealous girlfriend?

Aaron's gaze was sprinkled with hesitation as he continued to silently watch me. I heard the cheerful laughter echo through the air, and sounds of the carnival behind us as I tried to center myself in this moment.

"It's so easy to get lost in the emotion of everything," I sighed.

"It is." His voice was uncertain of the direction I was heading, and that only made me more nervous about bringing up my concerns. Aaron was several years older than me, and I never wanted to seem petty, but I'd been unsettled ever since seeing Aaron with Elizabeth.

"Why did you meet with Elizabeth?" I held in my breath as I waited for his answer.

"I wasn't happy finding out she'd snuck behind my back and talked to my girlfriend."

I let out the air I'd been holding in, but I didn't feel any better after hearing his answer.

"Couldn't you have called her on the phone?"

"I did, but she wanted to meet in person, and I

didn't feel like going back to the apartment." His gaze stayed fixed on mine as I debated whether or not to press for more information surrounding their relationship.

I found myself nervously sucking my lip, but I didn't proceed. I simply sat there stewing.

"What else is bothering you? I can tell there's more." His brow arched slightly, and he folded his arms on his chest.

"Is there a reason other than business that you talk with her almost daily?" I questioned, watching his jaw tense slightly. "I mean that seems kind of excessive. What is it that she needs that much help with, and why have I never stumbled in on you speaking with her?"

Aaron sat silent and stone-faced as the words tumbled out of my mouth. Between the trial and this development, it was hard to even figure out what was actually bothering me in a typical day. An hour ago, I was plagued by the looming trial, but at this particular second, I'd say the Elizabeth matter was most unnerving, particularly because she was here in Paris.

"The whole secrecy thing isn't sitting well with me. I thought I was fine with your explanations, but sometimes I'm slower on the uptake than I realize. Sometimes I need a day or two for things to soak in before I tackle them, but I'll get there."

Aaron sniffed in and scratched his face without saying a word.

"Something seems off. And she's in Paris of all places?" I studied his expression as I waited for his reply. He looked disappointed in something. I wasn't sure if it was my assessment or how the afternoon was turning out. So far I'd been striking out in Paris.

"I don't know what you want me to say. I feel like it's a trap. Anything I say will be wrong." He shifted in the seat and crossed his leg.

"I'm insulted at the implication. I've never been someone who's paranoid or sets traps for you to fall in. I have a legitimate concern. I don't think you'd be thrilled if all of a sudden you ran into an ex-boyfriend of mine who you found out I spoke with on a daily basis. It wouldn't matter if I called him a study partner or a business partner, I'm sure it wouldn't fly."

"I wouldn't have a problem with it."

"That is complete baloney."

A flicker of amusement pulsed through his expression and I didn't let it get to me. This was a serious discussion, and I wasn't going to be swayed with his ridiculously charming ability to distract me. After all, I was the one who ran into Elizabeth ogling at Aaron through the window. That was just another memory I tried to sidestep.

"Baloney?" he asked.

I shrugged. "Don't try to change the subject. You wouldn't be fine with it, but this discussion isn't about me, it's about you. What's with the daily phone calls?"

The knowledge that Aaron was chatting away daily with another woman was a painful revelation. One I hoped he would clear up, but his silence only added to the heaviness in my heart as he looked on. Seeing that we were getting nowhere, I tried again.

"Do you two only discuss business?" I hated that I was doing this, but there was an unease driving me forward.

"No, of course not. I'm sure personal facts enter into our discussions as well."

I steadied my breathing and tried not to explode. I didn't like the clipped responses I was receiving from Aaron. This wasn't like him. No, that wasn't true. This was like the old Aaron. I thought we'd moved past this.

"What is her business? What is it in life that makes her so unsure that she needs to have her hand held?"

"It's not like that."

Wrong answer.

"Then why don't you tell me what it is like?" My brows furrowed and the macaroons churned in my stomach. How did I manage to get an absolutely lovely afternoon so twisted into something like this? Was it nerves? Was I overreacting because of all the stress?

"She has low self-esteem. She made some bad choices in the beginning that cost us both quite a bit of money, and since then, she likes to run things by me."

Not good enough.

"I hate to be the bearer of bad news, but maybe she's not cut out to run a business. Shit happens. There's always risk and if her personality is too sensitive to bounce back then maybe it's too much."

Aaron grinned and shook his head. "Is that so?"

"It is so."

"Well, not everyone has been as fortunate as you to know what they've wanted to do since they were in kindergarten." He was still grinning, and I got the distinct feeling that he enjoyed this discussion a little too much.

"You'll be happy to know that I have no idea what I want to do with my life."

"That doesn't make me happy at all," he countered.

"All I'm saying is that my intuition tells me that there's more to Elizabeth's calls than you realize."

"I doubt that very much."

I snickered and threw my head back. He was being so dense. He was one of the most attractive men I'd ever laid eyes on, and somehow he seemed to think that women wouldn't think up reasons to stay in his periphery? I needed to try a new technique.

I leaned forward and began my assault.

"Did she know about me before my accident?"

"Absolutely."

"Did you talk to her while I was in the hospital?"

"I did."

"Did she know I moved in with you during my recovery?"

"Of course."

"Did she know you were leaving for China?"

"Yes."

"Did she know you'd be leaving me behind?"

"She did."

"Did she try to talk you out of it?"

"No."

"Did she try to talk you into it?"

"I don't know. I never really thought about it."

"I think it would be a mighty good idea if you thought about it now."

I sat back in the chair and smiled as the realization slowly came to him, but I also saw the stubborn side of Aaron emerge.

"That doesn't necessarily mean what you think it does," he replied.

"I won't argue that." I smiled and looked across the lawn before turning my attention back to him. "But we both know I'm right. So what's her business?"

He let out a deep sigh, and I knew this was about to get good.

"She has a patent on an eyelash curler."

"And has it taken the beauty industry by storm?" I quirked a brow.

"It's done quite well."

"And you're the expert on curling eyelashes because…"

"Business is business."

"I'll give you that, but going with that principle, I'd say that business is not for her if you're holding her hand every step of the way. There'll come a point when having a good product won't be enough. Competitors who know how they want to run their business will run her over."

"I don't disagree."

"You don't?"

"I don't. I've tried to explain that to her many times. My belief is that she should sell the company while it's profitable."

"That makes two of us. So what on earth would make her want to keep a business she isn't capable of running on her own?" I put my finger to my mouth and looked toward the sky.

"I hear your message loud and clear, Brandy." He couldn't help but smile as I brought my gaze back to his. "But it's not that simple."

"I'm going to be straight with you. What is simple is that I don't feel comfortable with the fact that you speak to a woman on an almost daily basis who has known things before even I did, like your move to China, and shares a pretty intense history with you."

He stretched out his legs and linked his hands behind his head. "I see where you're coming from."

"I wish you saw it before I had to explain it to you."

He nodded and furrowed his brow. "I'm still trying to get this relationship thing down. I wouldn't do something to intentionally hurt you. That's the last thing I'd ever want to do."

"I'm not saying these things because I don't trust you. I trust you with my life."

"I know."

"But I've got to ask. What on earth is she doing in Paris?"

He shook his head and groaned. "She's launching the product in several boutiques throughout the region."

"How fitting. I'm just glad the irony isn't lost on you." I smiled.

"You said something that bothered me."

"Only one thing?"

Aaron laughed and nodded. "Yes. Only one thing, but it's a pretty big thing."

"What's that?"

"Your uncertainty for going after the things you used to want..."

I craned my neck and remained quiet.

Aaron stood up and helped me to my feet. "So how about we walk along the promenade, and we work through each of those thoughts that are shaking you up. We can get to the bottom of things."

I snatched the bag of macaroons from the ground and slipped my arm around his waist. Aaron kissed the top of my head, and we began walking along the statue-lined promenade.

"I think that sounds like a lovely idea."

"So the way I see it, there aren't that many possibilities for your life choices to go up in smoke. The odds are in your favor, really. They always are." Aaron smiled as we stopped to look at the beautiful statue of Bathild. The dress wrapped gracefully around the woman's figure as she stared straight ahead, daring the future to unveil itself, and I wondered if I'd ever get that look of determination back again.

"You're probably right," I confessed.

"I know I am. Let's break it down. What concerns you about your future?"

"You're using my tricks against me?"

His laughter echoed through the air, and I couldn't help but love Aaron even more for caring. "So let's have it."

"Not knowing what I want out of life...Always being scared...Fearful of what the future holds or doesn't hold."

"Fair enough. Let's strip away some of the things you have no control over."

"Like what in particular?" I asked, turning to face Aaron.

"The trial. It's out of your hands. The press. You have no control over their spin on the story. So let's imagine your life before the accident. Before all of these things that were out of your control began to warp your view of reality."

I twisted my lips and stared into his dark eyes, but I wasn't able to imagine what he was asking of me.

"Okay. This isn't working. Will you do me a favor?" he asked.

I nodded and smiled as he moved me forward. His hands didn't leave my arms as he gave me the first of many instructions. "Okay. Close your eyes and take a deep breath in."

The warm air filled my lungs as I listened to Aaron. Just the tenor of his voice made me want to melt in his arms, but I remained focused on what he was telling me.

"Do you remember that very first time we were alone?" His voice lowered, and my body reacted unexpectedly to his tone. I didn't know how this was relevant, but I also didn't care as my mind took me to another time, one that was charged with the unknown and filled with excitement for the unfamiliar.

"The elevator?" I asked, my voice hoarse. "Back at the office."

He moved closer, and I felt the heat from his body, but the space between us allowed for something more to develop.

"Yes. It was the morning after I met you at Carla's gala. I stepped into the elevator and the woman who I'd been dreaming about all night was right in front of me. All I wanted to do was slam you up against the wall, and well, I guess you can imagine the rest. But then you opened your mouth."

I chuckled at his admission.

"And pretended not to remember my name," he continued. "Do you know what that does to a guy like me?"

"Who said I was pretending?" The feelings of pure electricity ravaged my body as I thought back to that first time Aaron and I ran into each other. "And can I open my eyes?"

Bringing his lips close to my ear, he whispered, "Keep them shut."

My body trembled as his breath rolled off my skin and he continued. "Do you remember our coffee together that morning?"

"How could I forget? You were arrogant and assumed I'd fall at your feet." My mind flashed back to that morning and the intensity in his eyes, knowing full well what he did to me.

What he still does to me.

"And was I right?"

I couldn't help but laugh.

"Do you remember how determined you were to fight the feelings that we had for each other?"

I nodded.

"But we couldn't control what we felt for each other, could we?"

Unable to speak, I shook my head and waited for him to continue.

"The highest high I'd ever had was holding you in my arms, and the lowest low I'd felt was when I let you slip away. But those emotions were unlike any other I'd ever felt because I knew I had to have you. I knew I was making the wrong choice, yet I still made it. I left for China. But at least I allowed myself to feel. I allowed myself to be guided by emotion. Remember being at your brothers' lake house?"

I smiled as warmth spread through my body. "How could I forget?"

"When you held me while we were on the Jet Ski, I almost lost my mind. No woman had ever sent me over the edge like you did."

"Is that so?"

"Very much so."

"It was so exhilarating. I can still feel that rush. Being with you is like being on the Jet Ski," I confessed.

Aaron laughed and his fingers slid into my hair. Before I had a chance to open my eyes, his lips touched down to mine, and my mind began to spin as all the emotions that had carried me forward were working their way back into my life. Aaron's kisses deepened as our memories moved me in the right direction, allowing me to remember what it was like before the accident. Before uncertainty became my best friend.

Aaron's lips slowly drew away from mine, but his hand continued to cup my chin as I opened my eyes.

"One thing I know about you is that you'll never do something you don't want to do. You've always managed to make the right decisions, but now that there are so many unknowns in your life, you're frozen. You're scared to make the wrong decision so you make no decision. I know I'm the king of avoidance, but it's not your style. You're trying to adopt a way of existing that really isn't you."

"How do you know?"

"I remember the fight you had when you woke up in the hospital. You wanted to get right back into law school. You didn't want life's circumstances to dictate your outcome in life. You were so angry that you couldn't get back in."

"Somehow that has changed."

Aaron nodded. "Somehow it has. You were the first person I'd ever met who was filled to the brim with enthusiasm for school. Not just any school, but law school. I don't think that's normal."

"I've heard that a time or two." I smiled, as Aaron's fingers fell from my chin. "I was tired of feeling angry so I stopped feeling."

"I know how that happens. I recognize it and it kills me that I can't fix everything for you. I mean if I could personally escort Derek to—"

I held up my hand to stop him. He didn't need to say it. I already knew and loved him for it.

Aaron took my hand and guided me to the next statue and the next and the next. All were women of great strength and beauty, and I was surprised at the small bio that Aaron managed to give me as we stood in front of each one.

Standing in front of Clemence Isaure, I looked up in awe at the mythical figure. She looked carefree and above it all. Her legend was built on grace and poetry, and I had a fondness for what she represented. Not to mention she was the only female figure in the garden that was based on myth, at least to my knowledge.

"We can make this a tragedy or we can make this a victory. I know the woman I fell in love with was all about winning. Sometimes at any cost, but that's for another discussion." Aaron's statement took me aback.

I hadn't thought about how my story, my life, would be defined in the end, and there would be an end. There was nowhere more fitting to realize that there was an end than when standing in a garden full of statues commemorating the dead's legacies. I'd been so involved in the clutter of the moment that I didn't step back and imagine how I wanted my life to unfold. I'd lost sight of who I wanted to be and it took Aaron to point that out. He'd had this planned the whole time, and I fell right into his plan.

"I think it's time I stopped watching my life go by." I spun around and looked into Aaron's eyes. "I think I've let Derek poison my life enough."

"So what do you propose we do about it?" Aaron asked bemused.

"I'm going to stop running, and I'm going to make sure the world knows my side of the story. If I don't want Derek to have a platform, I certainly can't hand him one on a platter."

"I can't tell you how long I've been hoping to hear that come from your lips." Aaron smiled and pulled me into him.

CHAPTER THIRTEEN

*T*here was nothing like living in old-world charm yet having the conveniences of today pumping my music through the apartment. I had my iPod repeating my favorite playlist that mixed indie and alternative music. I was feeling completely reenergized after spending time with Aaron in the gardens yesterday, and I'd spent most of my morning researching Derek.

Everything was going wonderfully until our doorbell buzzed incessantly. It was like my sixth sense kicked in and told me to ignore the peculiar sound. At first I thought there was something wrong with the iPod speakers, but when it continued to sound like a crow was being electrocuted, I realized it had to be the door.

I shuffled to the foyer and pressed on what I assumed was the speaker button to downstairs.

"Hello. May I help you?" I yelled into the speaker.

The crow kept squawking so I let go of the dull red button and then pressed it again.

"Is there something I can help you with?"

Two more cackles echoed into the foyer, and I'd about had it. What the heck was I doing wrong? I pushed on the button once more and leaned against the door as I spoke to the anonymous person downstairs. As I vented into oblivion, I looked over and spotted another contraption that looked very similar to the one I was using, except it looked newer. Like maybe from this decade. I released the button and glanced over my shoulder, thankful no one was around to see my brilliance shine through.

I pressed the shiny red button and spoke into the speaker box.

"Can I help you?"

"I hope I'm not interrupting. This is Tracy Sennet. I'm here to see Aaron."

Well, that's just wonderful.

"Oh, sorry. He didn't mention he was expecting anyone. He's been working in the studio all morning. I'll buzz you up."

"Thank you."

I released the red button and tilted my head as I looked at the row of black buttons. I wondered which one it was. Only one way to tell. I started at the top and worked my way down until I heard a beep. Huh. Wonder why it wouldn't just be the top one.

I glanced in the mirror and congratulated myself on my choice of wardrobe. Since I hadn't planned on going out today, I was in a pair of ripped jean shorts and one of Aaron's button-down shirts. My hair was a bit of a frizzy mess, but at least it was all collected on top of my head in a bun. Who was I trying to impress anyway?

Yeah right, the best friend of the woman who was in love with my boyfriend.

The knock on our door boomed through the air like a judge's gavel and completely disoriented me. I smoothed my shirt down with my palms and took a deep breath. At least it wasn't Elizabeth on the other side.

Flinging open the door, I greeted Tracy with open arms and air-kissed my way to hell and back as I invited her in. Unfortunately, she walked in and knew right where to put down her purse as she slithered—err walked—into the living room.

So she'd been here before. Being the daughter of the gallery owner that would make sense. No need to overreact.

"Again, I'm so sorry. Aaron didn't mention he was expecting you or I would've had been more prepared."

"Oh, you're such a dear. You look fine." Her smile was saccharin as I let the knives slowly work their way into my back.

"I meant I don't have any tea or coffee to offer."

"My apologies." She continued into the dining

room with me on her tail.

"No need for apologies," I laughed as I bit my tongue to stop it from lashing out. "I'll go get Aaron."

"You've done enough. I'll go check on him."

And before I had a chance to say or do anything, she'd opened the not-so-secret door and shut it behind her. I stood in the dining room for a few seconds reenacting what just went down. Obviously I didn't want to do anything that would jeopardize Aaron's show but what the hell just happened?

I shook my head and trudged into the kitchen and grabbed my phone from where it was charging. I unplugged it and texted Lily.

You know that moment you just want to smack a...

It was midnight in Seattle, and my hope was that Lily was still up. She was a night owl like me so the odds were in my favor. When I saw the little bubbles on my screen indicating that she was responding, my insides lit up with hope. I missed my girls. I wished I lived in a world where we didn't need backup, but apparently that was only in the land of fairytales.

Lay it on me. Who do I need to visit when I get there-lol

She brought a smile to my lips, and I let out a nice big sigh. If only it were that easy.

The daughter of the gallery owner just waltzed in and up to see Aaron. She also appears to be the best friend of the woman who is still in love with Aaron. Yes. That's right. I've failed to mention a few things since I landed in Paris. I was hoping my predicament could wait until you arrived in two weeks but...Grrrr. I hear her laughing upstairs.

Lily was typing so frantically, her texts were coming over in pieces and I had to laugh.

What...

are you...

doing still...

downstairs if she's upstairs?

What...

the heck is going...

on over there?

I wondered the same thing and scratched my chin before beginning a new text.

You're right. I'll go check on what she wants. I just didn't want to

I didn't even have a chance to finish before Lily's words landed on my screen.

Get your butt up the stairs...

like now

I shoved my phone in my pocket and grabbed bottled water out of the fridge for Aaron just as laughter hit the airwaves again. I squeezed the bottle and marched back into the dining room and opened the door just as Tracy appeared at the bottom of the steps.

"Oh, sorry. I was bringing Aaron a water."

Her look said sure you were, doll, and all I wanted to do was bop her on the head, but instead I took a step back and placed the water on the table so I could gladly lead her out of our apartment.

Tracy's gaze fell onto some of the papers I'd printed out regarding the case and I froze in place.

"You've got your hands full," Tracy said. I caught a trace of a smirk, and I was unsure what she was referring to in particular. She brought her eyes to mine and I smiled.

"Was he able to help you with everything you needed?"

"More than you know."

"Well, that's good." I began walking to the door, but she stayed anchored in place so I spun around to see what else she had in store for me. Aaron already gave up a lucrative position in China for me. I didn't need to jeopardize his next opportunity, and I felt like one wrong move on my end and that would be precisely what would happen.

"I don't know what Aaron has told you about Elizabeth, but as her best friend, I can assure you that their bond is unbreakable."

I pushed down the lump in my throat and continued to stare at Tracy. Amazed at how only minutes before I felt alive and ready to take on the world, and now my existence felt very fragile. One wrong move and I was certain I'd shatter the world Aaron was trying so hard to create.

"I've not questioned their bond and pardon my bluntness, I'm not sure how any of this is your business."

Tracy's smile widened. "Did I touch a nerve?"

I looked around the room positive I'd somehow managed to sink into the Twilight Zone. In fact, since I set foot in Paris things had felt slightly off, like the earth was skewed and reality distorted. Bringing my gaze back to Tracy, I shook my head and folded my hands in front of me. "Not at all. I'm very secure in the relationship I have with Aaron, not that it's anyone's business."

"So is Elizabeth."

I shifted my weight and unclasped my hands. "I'm not sure what you're getting at. I apologize if I've given you the wrong impression. I'm not in competition for Aaron's affections."

"It's got to feel awful to feel like you need to be taken care of all the time." She crossed her arms and waited for a reaction that I refused to give.

"It probably would if I felt that way, but I don't."

"At least you didn't hold him back from coming to Paris like you did China."

I could feel the tension building in my shoulders, and for the first time ever I wanted to hit someone. I—an aspiring attorney—wanted to feel what it would be like for my fist to connect with her chin. My brothers had obviously worn off on me, but I resisted the temptation and just stood tall, infuriated by her outburst but completely at her mercy.

"I'm sorry you and Elizabeth feel that way, but I don't care to go into things that are as personal as the choices Aaron and I make together as a couple."

"Don't you find it odd I know all of this? That Aaron would be willing to reveal so much to Elizabeth? It's always been this way, you know."

Yes. I do, but you'll never hear it from my lips.

"Well, that's what life is about. You learn something new every day. I don't mean to be rude, but I have a lot of work to get back to." I motioned toward the door, but Tracy stayed put.

"Do you think Aaron's pieces would be in my father's gallery if it weren't for Elizabeth? An artist without any branding or history behind him?"

My heart shattered at this wicked woman's revelation, and I prayed to God he didn't hear this witch's accusations. His work was phenomenal, and if she didn't recognize that someone else would.

My veins burned with fury as I stared at Tracy and waited for her to leave. It took everything I had not to say something that would completely ruin Aaron's chances. My fists were balled so tightly, my nails etched into my palms.

"His work has appeared in several galleries to critical acclaim."

"I think you know what I'm talking about. Well, I enjoyed our visit. I'll show myself out. But please remember as quickly as we put Aaron in the gallery, we can take him out."

"Thank you for coming over, Tracy, and please give Elizabeth my best."

Tracy grabbed her bag and walked out of our apartment, quietly closing the door behind her.

My hands trembled as the anger finally spilled out of me. I didn't understand in the slightest what had happened. I had two best friends who would do anything for me, but never in a million years would they stoop to something so grotesque. I took a step back and slowly slid down the wall as I tried to comprehend what kind of evil person just swept through the space. Between the accusations and very real threats, I didn't even know what she actually wanted from me.

What angered me most of all was the only thing I knew to be definitive was that she was not a very nice person. I couldn't argue the fact that Aaron had obviously told Elizabeth more than I imagined, and what I wanted to do with that information I didn't know, but I needed time to regroup.

I sat on the floor for well over an hour as I went through all of the things I wished I could say or do. It was a frivolous rehashing of another reality, but somehow it became quite empowering. And I realized I might not be able to make any headway with that kind of crazy, but maybe I could make a difference in my world—a world that I created. I didn't want to interrupt Aaron with this nonsense because that really was how I felt about it. It was like a flashback to high school except one of us had already graduated.

Miraculously, the anger I bottled up about Tracy manifested itself in the best possible way. I began combing through the articles at a feverish pace. I was able to zero in on how Derek wanted to be painted. He was the poor misunderstood victim in all of this. After all, he was the one without his mother. The press had fallen for it and that was going to change.

My stomach knotted at the thought of my poor mother and everything she'd worked toward. She was being picked apart because Derek painted her as an incompetent attorney when it came to defending his mother. My mom only wanted to help people, and this criminal somehow threatened to undo all of her wonderful work with a handful of lies. My mom's philosophy had been not to dignify his statements with a comment, but I couldn't help but feel this was my fault and I wanted to fix it. My cheeks warmed as the anger continued to boil over.

The final straw was seeing a description of myself in a headline. They referred to me as a Law School Dropout. That was all it took. I was tired of having someone else give a voice to my story. I left school because I was hospitalized and in physical therapy so I could walk again. This was absolutely absurd. My pulse was on a wild adrenaline ride as I continued to sort through my research.

I quickly blasted off an email to the prosecuting attorney's office to ensure that I wasn't overstepping my bounds. I wanted to know exactly what I could and couldn't say to the press. I didn't want to do anything to jeopardize the case against Derek, but I could no longer sit idly by as something as important as this churned on.

I found the names of the reporters who had more than willingly written stories about Derek, and I sent emails requesting to speak with them. While Aaron worked away upstairs, I managed to compile all the online discussion boards and threads that Derek contributed to while he was trying to garner more support and create his following over the last couple years. The more I uncovered, the more disgusted I was by the events that unfolded, and I also understood how lucky I was to be alive.

Aaron treaded softly down the stairs, and I looked up from the dining room table to see him open the door. My heart warmed at the sight of him. Somehow our walk down memory lane was exactly what I needed to put my life in perspective, and Tracy was exactly the fuel I needed to stop the destruction of my life before it began.

"You doing okay?" he asked, closing the door behind him.

"It feels like a new day. I have you and Tracy to thank for that," I chuckled and stood up from the table. I glanced outside. The sun had set and even though we'd only been at the park the day before, it felt like a lifetime ago. Just this morning I was wallowing in my own self-pity, and now I was riding a high with a purpose and more determination than I knew what to do with.

"Tracy?" he asked bewildered.

I waved my hands. "Long story for another day."

He tilted his head, but I continued on to tell him about what I'd been working on. I didn't want to give any weight to her existence.

"I've managed to contact all the local magazines and newspapers that seem to think Derek is an intriguing individual. I plan on setting them straight."

"Do you now?"

"I do. I'm waiting for the phone to start ringing."

He looked at his phone. "It's what? About three in the afternoon back home?"

I nodded. "Oh, my gosh. Is it really that late here?"

He nodded.

"You don't let grass grow under your feet."

"I can't afford to. I have a lot of time to make

up for since I was feeling sorry for myself."

Aaron laughed. "You don't need to go to the other extreme now."

"It's how I roll. One extreme or the other."

"Well, can I tempt you with a crepe? Neither of us have had dinner yet."

"Dinner at midnight?" My brow arched.

"Time is irrelevant when it comes to crepes."

"Downstairs?"

"It's highly unlikely that the same staff is on at this hour... if that's what's stopping you."

I looked down at my shorts and shirt and took my hair out of the pseudo bun. Shaking my hair out with my fingers, I let out a breath and stared at him, wondering what in the world he saw in me.

"You look beautiful," Aaron said.

"You'd say anything to get your crepe. Do they really serve crepes at this hour?"

"They do. You'll see."

The familiar twinkle in Aaron's eyes made my heart skip a beat as I nodded my head in agreement.

"Well, I think a crepe sounds like the perfect midnight snack."

"Then it's a date. Let me go change." Aaron took off for the bedroom just as the first email from Vanessa Torlin came over.

Vanessa was the first reporter I'd sent an email to. I clicked on the message and as I suspected, she wanted to talk with me immediately. She mentioned that she'd been trying to get a hold of me, but my family hadn't made that easy. My heart raced at the thought of getting to speak with her, but I also didn't want to jeopardize the case against Derek. I wouldn't respond to Vanessa until I heard back from the prosecutor's office.

Aaron appeared in the dining room, and his eyes connected with mine as he walked over and held out his hands.

"Ready for our night out?" he asked.

"We really know how to whoop it up," I teased.

"Just wait until later," he whispered, as we walked out the door.

I was determined to enjoy my midnight stroll with Aaron and not let Tracy contaminate my mind anymore than she already had.

Chapter Fourteen

*O*ur hands intertwined, and he led me out of the apartment and down the stairs. I expected the streets to be empty, but they were packed. Every café was bustling and the outdoor seating was filled to capacity even though it was past midnight.

"Is it always like this?"

"From Wednesday to Saturday."

"I could definitely get used to this."

We wandered toward La Crêperies Parfaites and found a seat for two outside. The server appeared immediately, handing us the menus, as Aaron ordered us both a cappuccino. I sat in amazement at how active the city was at this time of night, and it wasn't only couples and friends. The patio held as many families with small children. For someone like me who was a night owl, I felt right at home.

Opening the menu, I scanned over the few French words I recognized, but I didn't see the banana crepe that Aaron had mentioned. I glanced up at him, noticing that he was watching me intently.

"Did you decide on something?" he asked.

"I would if I could read the menu."

He laughed and closed his. "Did you want the banana one?"

I nodded and sat back in the chair as the warm breeze picked up slightly.

"Did you know I was known as the law school dropout?" I asked.

"In what context?" he asked, propping his elbows on the table.

"It was in one of the articles I saw."

Aaron's jaw tensed, and he took a sip of water. "It's a hard thing to deal with. Your story isn't your own unless you claim it as such and even then they'll spin it however they want."

"Did you ever claim it?" I asked. "Your own story I mean."

He let out a deep breath and shook his head. "No. I never did."

"Do you regret it?"

"No. I don't think I do. I try not to live in regret."

"But regret is part of life."

"It doesn't have to be," he countered, as the server came back with our cappuccinos. The server slid the drinks in front of us and Aaron placed our orders.

"Are you content with your decisions?" I asked.

"Isn't that the same as asking if I have any regrets?" His eyes fastened on mine, and it felt like he was searching me for something.

"I suppose it is."

"What are you not asking me, Brandy?"

"I don't even know."

"Not sure if I believe that."

"Well, it will have to do. So what are your plans for the rest of the week?"

Aaron laughed and shook his head. "I think some of my bad habits have rubbed off on you."

"What do you mean?"

"Avoidance." He smiled and wiped his mouth with a napkin.

I let out a sigh and shook my head. "Maybe so."

"But to answer your question, I only have a few more days or so of work, and then I think we'll move the pieces to a workshop just outside of the city. It's safer to construct everything out there."

"Would we be driving back and forth or…"

"I thought we could stay there while I put the pieces together. It'll probably take me about a week." He let out a deep sigh, and I saw his posture tense.

"What's going on? What was that all about?"

Aaron glided his fingers along his jaw and stared at the table. "I'm having doubts."

"Doubts about what in particular?"

"I only have five pieces and I'm not sure they're my best work."

I almost choked on my cappuccino at his admission.

"Your work is raw and emotional. It speaks volumes to me. I know everyone will love it."

"But I don't."

"I don't know what to say."

"There's nothing you can say. It's something I have to deal with. I need to get this show over with and—"

"What do you mean over with?" I interrupted.

"I mean exactly that. I'll be happy to have everything behind me."

"I'm sure what you're feeling is normal. Everything is so personal. You're putting pieces of your self on display. That can't be easy."

The server delivered our crepes, but I could barely concentrate on the food in front of me as I saw Aaron's pained expression.

"Can you back out?" I asked, realizing the seriousness of the situation.

"Absolutely not."

"Are you afraid people—"

"I'm not afraid," he cut me off and dug into his crepe. "I was wrong about many things. I'll have to see my commitment through and reevaluate."

I stared down at the crepe on my plate covered in bananas, caramel, and ice cream that was quickly melting. I had no idea how to respond to Aaron so I took a bite full of caramel goodness.

"Crazy good, isn't it?" Aaron laughed, changing

the subject.

"I can see how these have become a problem for you while I was away."

"I wouldn't call it a problem..."

"Addicts never do." I grinned and shoved another forkful in my mouth, allowing the buttery crepe to dissolve in my mouth. Ordering two of these would definitely be out of the question.

"What are you grinning about?" Aaron asked.

"Honestly?"

He nodded.

"Whether or not ordering two of these back to back would be bad."

"I've done it." He set down his fork. "It's fine until you have to face yourself in the morning."

"Well, I guess I'll enjoy what's left in front of me."

"So have you thought about what you want to tell the reporters?" he asked.

"I planned on telling them the truth."

Aaron was quiet for a few moments. "I hate that I'm even having to say this, but you need to come up with a way to have your side outshine Derek's. I'd like to say that the truth will automatically do that but that's not how it works."

"What do you mean?"

"Once you open the floodgates, the journalists will dig up all kinds of things, no matter how irrelevant. Your job will be to steer them in the right direction. I'd spend tomorrow coming up with how you want to be seen in the public eye."

"Is that something you did?"

"Not at all. I should have, but I had no idea what I was in for, and by the time I figured it out, it was too late. Or maybe I didn't care at that point."

"I'm guessing the book I saw online wasn't your doing?" I asked.

"Completely unauthorized," he sighed, scooting his empty plate away from him.

"That's what I figured."

"I'm surprised that still comes up."

The server dropped off the check and Aaron placed a few bills and coins in the tray.

"The satisfying thing about that was that it tanked," he half joked.

"Always a silver lining."

"True."

"Do you think about the things you went through often?" I asked.

"It's gotten less over time, but some days it's worse than others."

"It's not like I ever needed to find myself...I've never been lost. I've always known what I wanted and what I imagined for a life for myself. At least until the accident."

"It's okay to change your mind."

"Yeah. I know it is, but after today, things kind of became clear."

He gave me a puzzled look and I smiled.

"How so?" Aaron studied my expression and the concern he paid made my body keenly aware of the attention.

Now wasn't the time to bring up Tracy or

anything else that fed my obsession. Tonight I wanted to focus solely on Aaron and me. Somehow I knew today's confrontation wouldn't be the end of it, and I wanted to spend a blissful evening with my boyfriend in Paris.

"I always assumed I'd be working side by side with my mom at her non-profit. She had control of hours worked, and granted she didn't make a ton of money, but she got by. That was the life I imagined for myself. But the adrenaline rush I get merely thinking about putting Derek away...and I'm not even on the case."

"You're thinking of switching concentrations?"

I nodded.

"Wow. So that also means you're thinking about going back in the fall..." his voice trailed off. "That's awesome news, Brandy. I hoped you would."

"Really? Why didn't you ever say anything?"

"I didn't want to push you in the wrong direction, but my gut said law school was where you belonged."

"I have to be back before the semester starts."

"Yes, you do."

"And it might be before we originally planned on leaving."

"That's fine with me. Whatever we need to do, we'll make it happen. Have you told your parents yet?"

A flash of guilt ran through me as I thought back to what Tracy said, and everything Aaron had already given up for me. I was angry I even allowed her in my subconscious, but there she was grinning and waving frantically for attention.

I shook my head. "Not yet. I wanted to surprise them."

"And this all transpired within the last eight hours?" He grinned widely and sat back in the chair.

"What can I say? I have an impulsive streak."

Aaron rolled his eyes, but I caught a glimpse of heated satisfaction. "Should we head back upstairs?"

"It is getting late," I feigned a yawn and grinned, but he stood up quickly and helped me out of my chair. "What's the hurry?"

"You tell me," he whispered, as he led me out onto the sidewalk.

By the time we made it up the stairs, I was breathless. I needed Aaron in every way imaginable. The way he looked at me made me feel like I was the most beautiful woman in the world. His smile deepened as he grabbed my hand.

"I've been dreaming about making love to you all day," he murmured.

My heart soared with his proclamation, and there was nothing that could take away the love I had for Aaron Sullivan. He made me feel like the most desirable woman in the world.

Aaron pulled me against him before we even attempted to unlock the door. Pushing me against the wall, I felt his hard body press against mine. He cradled my chin in his fingers as his mouth slid hungrily across my neck. He lifted my hair away from the nape of my neck, peppering my skin with soft kisses, and I knew my world belonged to him. Silent pleas ran through my mind as his mouth worked so purposefully to satisfy my cravings.

My body trembled from his slightest touch, and my breath caught as I felt his tongue glide along my skin. Running my hands through his hair, I brought his mouth up to mine. His kisses intensified as my breathing changed. I needed more of him and being stuck in the hallway wasn't helping. Our kisses only created more longing as several deadbolts threatened our sanity.

"The keys," I whispered between kisses.

"The damn keys," he mumbled without his mouth parting from mine, but I felt his body move slightly and heard the keys jangle.

I let out a delighted hum as he fumbled with each key. When the last deadbolt unlocked, we pushed the door open, barely able to contain ourselves. He shed his shirt, dropping it onto the floor, as he brought me into him. Only the pale light from the moon cascaded into the living room, showing off the beautiful contours of his body. My hands skirted up his hard body, tracing the peaks and valleys of his abdomen. My head tilted back as he placed kisses along my throat. Resting his lips on the crook of my neck, another wave of pleasure pulsed through my veins, and I could feel him smile.

"I love you more and more each day," I whispered.

"I am one lucky man." His fingers quickly unbuttoned my shirt and it fell to the ground. His thumbs gently caressed my back as he unclasped my bra and it slid to the floor. I took a step back as his gaze intensified with an urgency I understood. Without waiting a second more, he scooped me in his arms and carried me to our bedroom.

Seeing the desire in his eyes as he placed me on the bed turned my world upside down.

"You're the most beautiful woman in the world and you're mine," he murmured, as he leaned over my body.

Hearing the possessiveness in his voice created a feverish longing. I wasn't sure how much longer I could wait. Tracing his thumb along my collarbone, his lips fell right behind, placing kisses along my skin.

I needed him more than anything, more than my next breath, but all I could do was wait as he teased my desires slowly and with certainty.

"I love you, Brandy Rhodes," he whispered.

Aaron crushed me into his arms as our kisses deepened, sending shivers through my body. He was the only man who ever changed my world with just one touch, just one look. He was the one man who knew my darkest secrets and my greatest joys.

I slid my hands along his back, and he slowly raised himself off me as my breath caught with longing. He slid my shorts and panties off, tossing them onto the floor as his fingers slid along my exposed flesh. There was nothing hesitant about his fingers as they skated across my belly, searching for something we both desperately craved.

Aaron's heated gaze slid down my body as warmth pumped through my veins. I felt my body succumb to his wishes as he slowly bowed his head, allowing his mouth to trace down my belly. My body quivered as his mouth went lower and it became impossible to concentrate.

"We've waited far too long for this Paris experience," he whispered.

My veins tingled with anticipation as he teased me endlessly with his lips.

Even though today had been one from the Twilight Zone, there was nothing distorted about being held in Aaron's arms. We belonged to each other and there was nothing chance about it.

He slowly worked his way back up my body as my hands trailed along his cool skin. There was nothing more like heaven than being in his arms. My nails dug into his back as I felt his body lean into mine sending my world spinning. The more he held and kissed me, the more my body ached for him. I wrapped my legs around his waist and moved my hips into his as I took what was mine. As my mind and body released in ecstasy with his, I knew beyond a shadow of doubt that Aaron Sullivan belonged to me.

CHAPTER FIFTEEN

It was early evening, and I had just finished giving my last interview to Seattle's largest newspaper. Hanging up the phone with the journalist made me feel revitalized as I gave my story a voice. If there was one message coming across loud and clear, it was that I wasn't hiding any longer, and I wanted to see justice served. I also made sure that everyone understood I hadn't dropped out of law school, I postponed attending so that I could focus on my recovery. The press didn't need to know that Derek almost ripped my life-long dreams away from me. That could be saved for another day, and I felt that might detract from what I wanted people to understand, which was that Derek was a criminal.

The more I defined my story, the more confident I became in my life. The last several days spent researching and giving interviews gave me a sense of purpose, something I'd lost along the way this past year. I found what I'd been looking for—and I didn't even know it had been missing—but that something was finding who I was again. I loved law and didn't realize that I was letting my fears define me. I believed in the possibilities of our justice system to make things right, but I couldn't sit on the sidelines and watch events unfold.

"You have any other interviews tonight?" Aaron asked, walking into the kitchen.

I shook my head. "All done. At least for now. I think I've said enough. People will be tired of hearing about me back in Washington."

"No one could ever get tired of hearing about you." He kissed my cheek and grabbed a piece of chocolate.

"Are you ready to move the pieces tomorrow?" I asked.

"I am. I'm actually tired of looking at them all scattered upstairs. I need to start assembling, or I'll never stop messing with them."

"I can't wait to see them in all their glory." I smiled and broke a piece of chocolate off and nibbled it. "I also can't wait to get a little taste of the country."

For more reasons than one, I thought. Unfortunately, Tracy had come by the apartment once more, but I'd made myself scarce. Aaron dealt with her in the living room, and it had sounded like all business. I hadn't mentioned our encounter to Aaron and planned on keeping it to myself. He didn't need to be bothered with the wicked witch of Paris's threats while he was working hard on his sculptures. I was a big girl and could handle myself.

He pulled me into him and nuzzled my neck. "You and me both."

"You have a one-track mind," I teased.

"And has that ever been a problem before?" His eyes stayed on mine, and I felt my cheeks warm just from his gaze.

"No, and it never will be."

He placed a kiss on my lips and groaned. "The chocolate tastes even better on you."

"You're certainly smooth." I playfully pushed him away and narrowed my eyes at him as I grinned.

"I can't help it. I'm trapped upstairs for hours on end. I have nothing else to do but think these things up."

I laughed and rolled my eyes. "Somehow I doubt that."

"You ready for a night on the town to celebrate?" he asked.

"Celebrate what in particular?" I'd planned on snacking on whatever we had in the cupboards topped with cheese so his plan sounded like a much better option.

"You making up your mind about law school. That's huge, Brandy, and all it took was a week in Paris."

Ha! A week in Paris and a visit from Tracy to

remind me what it's like not to have a voice.

"I think sometimes it takes being taken out of my comfort zone to put things in perspective," I replied.

"I know how that goes." He smiled and took in a deep breath before glancing at his phone. "There's a restaurant a few blocks away that I think you're going to love."

My stomach tensed as I watched him text someone back and shove his phone in his pocket. I hated the feelings that erupted every time he picked up the phone. We hadn't really discussed Elizabeth since I told him what I thought about the situation, and I certainly hadn't mentioned Tracy because anything that might come out of my mouth wouldn't be pleasant. Either way, I was always on edge when his phone buzzed. I couldn't help but wonder if he was still communicating with Elizabeth every day.

"So what kind of French food is it?" I asked, trying to distract myself.

"It's authentic, and I'd say the best Chinese food I've ever had."

"Wait. Are you serious?" My brows pulled together.

"Totally. The chef makes the noodles right at the front of the restaurant. People can watch him make them as they're walking by. That's what snagged my interest. Anyway, the chow mein and almond chicken is incredible."

My smile widened at the thought of some delicious Chinese food, and I couldn't think of a better way to celebrate. Well, maybe one other way...

"What's that goofy look on your face?" He shoved his wallet into his front pocket.

"Nothing at all." I felt my cheeks redden and he laughed.

"I hope to explore nothing at all later," he teased, and my pulse quickened as his gaze stayed on mine a beat longer than anticipated. He really knew how to throw me over the edge, and I loved every second of it.

"Let me go change, and I'll be ready for some rockin' chow mein." I gave him a quick kiss and the stubble on his cheek tickled my lips in a wonderful way.

"It's not a fancy place," he called after me.

"I think the least I can do is upgrade from shorts to a skirt."

I walked into the bedroom and immediately felt at ease. I'd really grown fond of this room. It always felt refreshing and peaceful, and I vowed to recreate it when I got back to Washington. With law school, I would need a consistent sanctuary.

Pulling open the armoire, I scanned the dresses and skirts in front of me and decided on a grey knit skirt. It was completely casual and would allow for an extra helping of almond chicken. I kicked off my shorts and flip-flops and slid on the skirt. I found a pair of sandals and buckled them around my ankles. I decided to trade out my oversized shirt for a lightweight, gauzy blouse. Glancing in the mirror, I gave myself the once over and was satisfied, considering how exhausted I felt. Between all the research and interviews, it felt like I was about at my tipping point, but I didn't want to miss out on tonight's celebration. Paris and I were starting to get used to each other, and I didn't want to lose the momentum.

"Well, you look stunning," Aaron said, standing in the doorway.

I spun around and kicked my heel up as I laughed. "Remind me to put a skirt on more often."

"It's not the clothes," he said, shaking his head. "You have your sparkle back."

"I do like to sparkle. My hope is that will confuse them in the courtroom." I grinned and tried to squeeze by him in the doorway, and he seized the opportunity to place a soft kiss on my forehead as we stood in one another's arms.

I felt his body respond to mine, and I wondered if we'd even make it to the restaurant, but then my stomach growled so loudly I couldn't help but burst into laughter.

"Can't get any sexier than that," I muttered.

"No. It really can't. After you." He motioned through the door, and I slid through the doorway with Aaron following close behind.

We decided on the elevator and bumped into a couple returning from a day out. We said our awkward greetings in English as they returned theirs in German.

The street was noticeably quiet compared to the activity I'd grown accustomed to on the streets of Paris. Very few tables were filled as we walked hand in hand down the sidewalk. Apparently Tuesday the locals stayed in. It was about the only day of the week that seemed to happen.

We walked slowly down the street, stopping every so often so I could peer into the windows of the shops and bakeries. Things felt different and new and I wished I could bundle the feeling for when things might suddenly change.

I stopped in front of a boutique that had the prettiest purse dangling from a silver hook. The rest of the store was almost empty, except for three more purses on the back wall. If they could somehow afford the rent off of only three purses, I couldn't even imagine the price per bag.

"Do you like that?" Aaron asked, draping his arm across my shoulders as he peered into the window.

"It's gorgeous, but my guess is that it would cost the same as my tuition."

Aaron laughed and shook his head. "I doubt that."

"I don't."

We started walking down the sidewalk again and turned at the crosswalk. The buildings were just as regal as the ones from the prior block, but the vibe changed drastically. It wasn't until about twenty feet down the road, when I started seeing boutiques exchanged for flashing signs and darkened windows.

"Uh. Where the heck are we going?" I asked, as I saw several women congregating at the entrances to the mysterious storefronts. They were dressed in skimpy outfits, giggling and whispering as we passed.

"I think I made a wrong turn," he laughed.

"You don't say."

He slipped his hand into mine as we continued to walk down the block taking in the blinking signs and graffiti splattered limestone buildings. It was such a juxtaposition of worlds as neon winked its invite to a seedy underside of the city.

I heard a few whistles and was pretty sure they weren't directed at me, but it made me hold Aaron's hand even tighter. We were in it this far and there was no point in turning around. If we kept walking, eventually we'd get to the end of the street and could figure out where we wanted to go.

"This is certainly fun," I laughed, as I saw the shadow of a woman dancing on the second floor.

"Glad I could entertain you."

"I had no idea there was a red-light district in Paris."

"Me either. Learn something new every day."

"It certainly looks more classy than the Mustang Ranch in Vegas." I wriggled my brows and his jaw dropped. "What? I had cable growing up."

Aaron's laughter roared down the street, and I loved the fact that I could still surprise him after a year of dating.

We came to the end of the block at a busy intersection. "I think we should be one street over. We turned right too soon," he said, his eyes narrowing as he tried to examine where we needed to go on his phone.

"Sure we did." I grinned.

Smiling, he shook his head and led me in the direction of the mysterious restaurant.

"It's amazing how on one street, there's a high-end store selling a bag for thousands and the next street over there's, well…"

"Yeah. It's pretty crazy."

Aaron came to a stop and I crashed into him. I hadn't been paying attention to where we were going. I was having too much fun studying all of the architecture.

"Found it."

I looked up and saw the restaurant. Just as Aaron had explained, a chef was kneading dough, preparing to string noodles.

"It smells delicious. How did you find the place?"

We walked inside and the hostess led us to a table in the back. She handed us the menus and began speaking to us in French. I had to admit that I was kind of excited that she thought I might actually speak French fluently. It wasn't until I attempted to order a beverage that she smiled and quickly switched to English. She left and I opened the menu to see pictures of the food and knew I'd found my new favorite place.

"So how'd you find this restaurant?" I asked again.

"Elizabeth recommended it. She thought you might like it."

Of course she did.

"Oh, well, let's hope she's right." I smiled and took a sip of water, attempting to cool off. For some reason it felt like my entire body was on fire, and I had to use the menu to fan myself off.

Aaron let out a deep breath and shook his head. "I guess I shouldn't have told you that."

"No. Don't be silly. That would be weird not to."

"Let's not make it a thing."

"Sounds good to me." His gaze sharpened as he glanced around the restaurant. I wanted to know what was running through his mind with an expression like that, but there was a part of me that was afraid to ask.

"I bet this would be a fun surprise for Lily and everyone when they visit. We can take them here the first night. Gabby's been talking nonstop about eating all the French food she can. It might be kind of fun to mess with her."

"And crush her dreams of nightly coq au vin?" Aaron teased.

"Someone's got to." I smiled, pushing away the unease that was creeping up. "I'm really looking forward to the opening."

Aaron shrugged and his gaze dropped to the menu.

"What's up with that?" I asked. "You're not excited?"

"Not particularly. No."

"You've always been thrilled when your pieces have been on exhibit... What's changed?"

"I'm not sure." He brought his gaze up to meet mine just when his phone buzzed in his pocket.

He maneuvered his cell out of his pocket and glanced at the voicemail alert, and my heart thumped in my chest. Was it Elizabeth?

"Everything okay?" I asked.

"Yeah. I've got to go return this call. If she comes back, make sure to get two orders of the chow mein. The only downside with this place is the serving size."

"Okay," I said, my voice hoarse as he walked away, leaving me alone in the restaurant. Just when I was going to follow him outside to see who he was on the phone with, the server came over to check on us.

I muddled through ordering and wasn't actually sure what all we'd be getting, but at least it distracted me from creating a problem where one might not exist. Or where one might exist. I let out a sigh and watched him wander through the restaurant. I noticed several women smiled and cast glances his way.

Over the year, I'd managed to ignore the attention he often received from the opposite sex, but today it bothered me. It was like a constant reminder of what I'd probably be dealing with the rest of our lives together. He would always receive attention from women, whether he meant to or not.

Aaron slid into the seat and gave me a huge smile, looking completely relaxed and at ease with life, which only irritated me.

"So everything sorted out?" I asked.

He nodded and placed the napkin in his lap. "It is."

"Was it about the show?" I asked, trying to sidestep the obvious question.

He shook his head and took a sip of green tea.

I found myself squirming in the chair and couldn't take it anymore.

"Was it Elizabeth?" I blurted.

His head snapped up as his brows furrowed. "Elizabeth? No. I haven't spoken to her since you and I had our talk. You made things pretty clear."

Feeling completely sheepish, I fiddled with the napkin in my lap and stared at the painting on the wall next to me.

"I thought we'd settled everything," Aaron said, reaching his hand across the table.

We'd barely scratched the surface.

I shook my head. "Nothing was settled. I simply told you how I felt."

Aaron bit his lip and remained quiet for a few moments.

"The only way I understand to deal with a problem is to solve it, fix it. That's what I do. You told me you didn't like me talking to her, so I stopped. I don't know what else you want me to do."

"That's plenty. I'm sorry. I'm just out of sorts. I'd never been one to be insecure and it's like ever since the accident, I've been playing catch up with my self-esteem. You shouldn't have to deal with it."

"Baby, don't apologize. You've had to overcome a lot and put off lifelong dreams. None of us can predict how we'll handle things that pop up in life, and yours have been a little more serious than most." His expression softened. "Things aren't always easy or as obvious as they seem. I never would have guessed we'd be in Paris working on an opening, and I certainly wouldn't have thought that—"

Our order came and covered the entire table.

"You wouldn't have thought what?" I questioned after our server left.

It looked like he wanted to say something more, but he didn't. Instead he dug into the chow mein and placed a pile of noodles on my plate. Studying his expression, I realized there'd been something bothering him that I hadn't stopped to notice. I'd been so wrapped up in my problems that I couldn't see that he'd been wrestling with his own issues. My heart sank as I thought about the timing. Since he stopped his daily chats with Elizabeth had whatever issues he'd been struggling with gotten worse?

"You look like something's bothering you..."

"I'm just stressed with the showing. No big deal."

I took a bite of the chow mein and had to admit it was the best I'd ever tasted, but I had other concerns to worry about.

Aaron's phone buzzed again, and I watched him glance at the text quickly and reply without saying a word.

CHAPTER SIXTEEN

*D*uring our long drive to our new home for the week, it slowly dawned on me that he didn't need to rent somewhere in the country just to assemble his work. I wasn't sure what he had up his sleeve, but the farther away we got from Paris the more relaxed he became, which rubbed off on me. Aaron turned our car down another rural road. I hadn't seen a home in miles when I finally couldn't take the suspense any longer.

"Are we getting close?" I asked, staring out the window. The lush rolling hills and graceful trees were beautiful, but I was getting anxious to see our final destination.

"Just over the knoll." He smiled and glanced at me out of the corner of his eye.

"Do you think all your pieces have arrived?"

This morning movers had packed and hauled everything out of the studio. They actually had to use a pulley system and move everything out through the window. It seemed like a big ordeal, but they acted like they did it all the time. With all the tiny hallways, elevators and stairs in Paris, I imagined the team it would take just to move a couch so maybe this was the norm.

"They should have, and Tracy was going to be at the house to meet them and get everything moved into the workshop. She said she wanted one last look before I started to assemble."

My blood froze at her mention.

"What's wrong?" Aaron asked.

"Nothing."

"I mentioned Tracy's name and your body stiffened. Something is definitely up."

"Nothing worth mentioning." I smiled as the beautiful home came into view. Actually I wasn't sure it would be called a home, maybe a chateau or a villa?

Blue shutters adorned the windows and matching wooden planters overflowing with blooms hung from the base of the windows. It was right off a magazine cover, and I couldn't believe we'd be staying here. Tiny gardens speckled the entire property, and I imagined each of them had a purpose of some sort.

"Is it a hotel? Are we renting a room?" I asked.

Aaron laughed and shook his head. "Nope. The whole place is ours for the week."

"You've got to be kidding."

"I thought you would enjoy being away from

the city with everything starting..."

"This is spectacular," I whispered, my gaze fastened on to the tiny turrets at the far end of the structure. "Absolutely amazing."

"There are horses and riding pastures are behind."

I spotted a car on the side of the home where Aaron turned the car, and my chest tightened when I saw Tracy step out of her vehicle and wave. She looked so happy and perky, and I probably looked like a grump who wanted to eat her for lunch. But the best way to win in a situation like this was to match her in spirit and action so that was what I planned to do.

Aaron parked our rented Mercedes, and I took a deep breath in before opening the door. Gravel crunched under my feet as I stood up and stretched to buy time. Aaron shut his door and greeted Tracy, who was overly exuberant. She had this act down.

I walked around the car and waved, flashing a huge grin at Tracy. I leaned in and gave her two quick air kisses. I caught her completely off guard and congratulated myself on this tiny victory.

"Good to see you again," I said, still smiling.

"Likewise." She turned to Aaron and pointed toward the workshop. "The guys moved everything in. I counted the pieces and they match with what you emailed to me. Did you want to check?"

"No. I trust you."

"I wouldn't," she laughed, handing him the

keys. "If either of you need anything, my father has a home not far from here, and his staff can help you."

"Thank you. That's very kind of you," I said, glancing at Aaron.

"Very kind," Aaron agreed. "But not necessary."

Tracy shook her head and smiled. "Well, I tell you... More than a day or two in the country and I go nuts. Good luck to you both."

"It's right up our alley," Aaron assured her as she climbed into her vehicle.

"I've got a dinner to get ready for so I better get back to the city." She glanced at me and then at Aaron. "Elizabeth has been trying to get a hold of you and hasn't had much luck. I promised her you were just busy finishing things up. I'd imagine that's all it is."

"I appreciate that, Tracy. I'll be sure to give her a call."

"Avoir un grand temps." She shut her door and turned on her engine. She backed out slowly and turned around, waving her hand out the window before driving off.

"I know she's the boss's daughter, but she's an odd one," Aaron quipped, as he slid his arm around my waist.

I couldn't help but chuckle as I rested my head against his arm and looked at the beautiful place we'd be calling home for the next week. The property was so different from Paris. It was hard to believe we were even in the same country.

"Should we get our things and go inside?"

Aaron asked, pressing his lips to the top of my head.

I nodded, and he released me from his hold as I mulled over his remark about Tracy. I wondered exactly how odd he thought she was, probably not as odd as I thought she was.

Aaron opened the trunk and hauled out both suitcases, and I grabbed my bag and slung it across my shoulder. I followed him to the front door and continued to gawk at the beautiful surroundings. Flowers were in full bloom every direction I looked. This would be an excellent break from the whirlwind back home. The trial would be getting underway again just about the time Aaron and I would be having dinner tonight, and I was doing everything in my control not to think about it, but it was never very far from my thoughts.

Aaron slid the key into the lock and opened the door, pushing it in.

"Nice to only have one lock," I laughed.

"Isn't it?" He stepped inside and I followed right behind.

If I'd been impressed with the exterior, language couldn't even begin to convey the beauty of the inside. The only word that came to mind was spellbinding. It was as if we'd been transported to another century. Everything was regally appointed and enchanting. I felt like I'd been dropped right into a French fairytale, and I never wanted to leave and face the world again.

The white and blue mosaic floors spread as far as the eye could see. A large bouquet with flowers from the garden sat on a French provincial table centered in the foyer, and matching gold-framed mirrors hung on the walls. A chandelier dripping crystal and gold dangled above us, and all I could do was stare at the beauty of everything. My senses were on overload. A marble statue in the far corner of the room was as tall as I was, and I realized there was absolutely no way to reconcile the royalty this house exuded with reality. It was purely decadent and not of this world.

Aaron placed the suitcases on the floor and looked over at me, no doubt gauging my reaction to the surroundings.

"How did you find this place?" I asked.

"A friend of a friend."

"Please tell me it's not—"

He laughed and placed his hands up. "An old business acquaintance from my previous life. This is his third or tenth home... I can't really keep it straight."

I eyed one of the paintings in the hallway and walked over to it. The bold colors made the garden scene come to life.

"That's lovely," I whispered, as Aaron came up behind me.

"Down this hall, and we'll find the sitting room and kitchen," Aaron said, placing his hand on my shoulder.

"You've been here before? Did you drive out before I got to Paris?"

Aaron shook his head and grinned. "I've stayed here when I was on business. Actually in between business during one of the few breaks I took."

My brow arched, and I couldn't help but wonder if he'd had another woman with him. Not that it mattered. Okay, maybe it did a little.

"Well, show me the grounds," I teased.

He left the suitcases in the foyer and took my hand. Leading me down the hallway to the sitting room, I was in awe over the amount of artwork that adorned the walls. "The owner just leaves everything here?"

"There's a groundskeeper who lives in a cottage and looks after everything."

"I see."

The sitting room was luxurious, but it somehow managed to be inviting. I could imagine myself reading a book on the chaise and not feeling like I would break something. Built-in cabinetry filled with books garlanded the fireplace. My hope was that the books weren't all in French.

A handwoven blue and ivory rug centered the room, and another vase of flowers had been placed on a cherrywood desk that was sitting in front of the picture window. Aaron opened a set of double doors and waved me through to another large room, which had a wide dining table in the center of the space and several upholstered chairs pushed against the wall. The room opened into a spacious kitchen complete with updated appliances and a farmhouse sink. A large bowl of fruit sat on the island, and I suddenly realized I had no plans to ever leave.

"The stairs lead up to three bedrooms and three bathrooms. No bathrooms on the main floor."

I rolled my eyes and grinned. "I guess that will have to do."

Aaron laughed and led me up the steps to the second floor.

"This is our room." He opened the door and the room took my breath away. A fireplace was tucked in the far corner, and a four-poster bed was in the center of the room under a window. Sheer curtains draped the four posters of the bed, completing the dreamy sensation that had already begun downstairs. The goose down comforter had a handmade quilt placed on top, along with several matching pillows. Everything was either white or glacial blue in the room. I glanced at Aaron and smiled.

"Would it be bad if I never left this room?" I asked, sliding my bag off my shoulder.

He growled a little and brought me into his arms.

"I think that would be a dream come true," he laughed. "The chef should be here any minute to begin dinner or you'd be mine right now."

"Is that so?" I giggled, feeling his whiskers tickle my neck as he nuzzled me.

"It is so." He stepped back and let out a deep breath. "I can never get enough of you."

I smiled and reveled in this moment that seemed so unlike anything I'd ever experienced or even dared to dream about. Looking around the room, seeing the plaster walls and exposed timbers above, I truly felt like I'd been dropped into a fantasy world. Any instant, I thought I should run to the window and Rapunzel myself to the world.

"You always know what I need," I whispered, shaking my head. "This is incredible and so thoughtful. I can see how easy it will be to forget about the trial."

"I'll confess that I've been a little nervous with everything working out as far as timing. I thought it would be nice if we were disconnected a little during the trial because it's truly out of our hands."

I nodded as relief spread through me. He was absolutely right. Everything was out of my control. There was no sense in spending time worrying.

"So you want to tell me what that was about in the car earlier? You don't usually have a physical reaction to someone's name."

"I had no idea I did until you mentioned it." I smiled and walked over to the bed.

I scooted onto the mattress and patted the comforter.

Aaron's expression lit up, and he shook his head, his lip curling up. "Boy, we really are wearing off on each other. No matter how much I want to, I'm not falling for your traps, Ms. Rhodes. Answer the question, and we'll see where that leads us."

"You know..." I pressed my lips together and chose my words carefully. "It takes all kinds of people to make the world go around."

"That it does." Aaron pulled a chair away from the wall and sat down. He flashed a dubious grin and waited for me to continue.

"I've got thick skin, and I honestly don't want to give her or the situation the time of day. I'm in a wonderful chateau in the middle of France with the man I love. My best friends are coming to Paris next week and that's really all that matters. Life is good and I don't want to waste a second longer on something or someone who's just not for me."

Aaron leaned back in the chair and stretched his legs out in front of him, making the chair look even tinier compared to his long, lean body. I couldn't help but imagine the things I wanted to do to that body, but the doorbell rang.

"Must be the chef. I'll grab the door and get him settled before I bring our bags up. But seriously, I want to know what made your skin crawl. I feel like you're not telling me something quite important."

"Who me?" I grinned. "Everything's totally fine."

"Sure it is." He walked out of the room and my body fell into the comforter as I thought about what to tell Aaron. I didn't want to bring up anything that happened with Tracy, and I was totally disappointed in myself for having an involuntary reaction to her name. I'd have to work on that, especially before Aaron's show opened.

I got back up and dug in my purse for my phone. I saw a couple texts from Gabby and my mom. The messages must have come over while we were parking downstairs. It didn't look like I'd be able to answer them because we had no cell service. My mother had decided—against my father's wishes—to attend the trial. She gave me a rundown of the initial arguments for both sides and her thoughts on how long the trial was going to run. Her guess was five or six days. Though surprised by the interviews I gave, she thought they showed sincerity versus the pure sensationalist garbage that Derek had been striving for. Whenever it was that my mom wrote the text, they were on a recess. I really wanted to text my mom back to thank her for the heads up, but I'd have to wait for Aaron for that. I was glad we were somewhat disconnected, but I hoped we had wireless.

I heard the chef in the kitchen banging pots and pans around as the sounds of Aaron's footsteps bounced off the wooden steps.

"So have you given more thought about telling me what's making you so uncomfortable with Tracy?" Aaron asked, as he walked back into the bedroom.

I hadn't actually, but I did see this as a perfect opportunity to bring up last night's phone call and text.

"How about if you tell me whose call you had to take last night at dinner, I'll tell you a little bit about my thoughts on Tracy."

Aaron grunted and sat back down on the chair. "You play dirty."

"I'm not playing dirty, but I certainly could.

Come on give it to me."

His mouth pulled up slightly on the corner and he shook his head. "It was a call from my father."

"Your dad?"

He nodded and let out a sigh, knowing what was coming next.

"What made you rush out of the restaurant?"

Aaron began tapping his fingertips on his knee and narrowed his eyes, studying me closely. "Brandy, I love you more than life itself. You make me want to be the best I can be for us and for our future..." his voice trailed off.

"But?" I prompted.

"But I'm not happy. I haven't been for quite a long time."

CHAPTER SEVENTEEN

It felt like I'd had a knife right to my heart. What did he mean he wasn't happy? From the moment I touched down in France, my life had felt completely out of step. As I looked at Aaron, I saw the same look I noticed the night before. It was the same expression I'd brushed off over the last couple months, thinking he was just nervous about his exhibition. If only I'd stopped obsessing about my issues and paused to hear about his, maybe we wouldn't be in this situation where the world was coming down around us.

My shoulders slumped as our eyes connected. All the oxygen in the room vanished as I attempted my next breath. Nothing was right about this moment. We were supposed to be happy. I was happy. I thought he was happy. And then a question tumbled out of my mouth before I even had a chance to stop it, but my heart ached too much to keep it in.

"Did Elizabeth know you were unhappy?" I whispered.

Aaron's expression fell. "She knew I was feeling unsettled, but I didn't talk to her about anything in great detail, if that's what you're wondering."

I felt gutted as I sat on the bed. Details or not, she knew more than I did, and that wasn't how things were supposed to work. That wasn't how we were supposed to work.

"I don't know what I'm wondering. I'm torn. I'm hurt. I want to make things better. I want you to be happy. I thought I made you happy," I said, not wavering on one syllable.

Heightened sensitivity hovered in the air between us, and I dropped my gaze to the hardwood floors. One false move on his part and I'd break down. One wrong word from me and he'd probably wish he'd never said a word. Speaking with Elizabeth rather than me was unsettling, but what concerned me more was why he wasn't happy. At least Elizabeth and I had something in common. We both thought his behavior was because of nerves. As I took deep, steady breaths, I prayed I'd find the right words because only the wrong ones were flooding my mind. I needed to stay in control of my emotions.

"You do make me happy," he said, his voice low and full of trepidation.

I steadied my gaze on his and felt the tears

begin to prick my eyelids as he stood up quickly from the chair and bolted toward me. Bending on one knee, he slipped his arms around my waist and drew me next to his body, but it was too late. The tears were already streaming down my face. How had I been so blind?

Aaron's hands cradled the back of my head as the tears continued to fall. The wetness soaked his shirt, but I couldn't move. I stayed in his arms, hoping this nightmare would be over.

"I don't understand. I thought we were happy. I thought being here was what you wanted," I sniffed.

"So did I."

I slowly raised my head, and he used his thumbs to wipe away the dampness on my cheeks as I tried to comprehend what was going so desperately wrong in my world.

"So where do we go from here?" I asked. It felt as if my voice was disconnected from my mind and heart.

He continued kneeling in front of me and took both of my hands as I tried to imagine my life without Aaron in it. Did he need time to explore and find happiness or was it more complicated?

He let out a deep breath and held my hands tightly. "I think for now we should take it one step at a time."

I shook my head. "I can't take something like this one step at a time. I need to know what to expect. The thought of you not in my life is more—"

"Wait. What?" Aaron asked, his voice filled

with urgency. He stood up quickly and scooted me over on the bed. "I'm not going anywhere. That's not what I meant."

"But if you're not happy, I don't want to hold you back."

Aaron let out a groan and slid his hands over his face as he blew air out of his mouth. "This was not how I imagined tonight going," he said, dropping his hands to his side.

"I've felt that way pretty much from the moment I arrived in France."

Aaron nodded as his eyes fastened on mine. "Brandy, if you weren't in my life, I'd be miserable. I'm in love with you, all of you, everything about you...Every single thing I do in my life is for you and because of you. Waking up without you these last few weeks was horrid. I'd turn over and the sheets were cold and there wasn't your beautiful face waiting there, giving me that gorgeous morning smile like you do. I wouldn't want to imagine my life without you in it. I think it would be a wretched, lonely life."

I shook my head as his hands locked with mine. "I don't understand."

"I'm a pretty simple guy. I know precisely what's making me unhappy. But I didn't want to let you down. I've realized if I don't tell you the worse it will get. I had planned on waiting until after the show to explain things, but as usual, things have a habit of spiraling out of control in our lives."

"Don't they," I said.

He nodded. "I've been in contact with my

father because I miss my old job. I miss the challenge and solving problems every day. I miss being in the business world."

"What about your sculptures?" I asked.

"It used to be a way for me to cope with life. I'd take out my pain and anger on the metal. When the weight of my history was crushing, I'd channel the frustration into my metalworking. It was therapeutic. What I realized recently was that it was a hobby. Once it changed to something more, it lost the appeal for me. You're the person I go to when I'm feeling down. You're the one there for me to pick me up when I'm frustrated or sad. I don't have that same connection to my art. I don't need my art like I need you."

"Why didn't you tell me?"

"I didn't want to hurt your feelings. You were so proud of my work and all the acclaim I started receiving, I didn't want to disappoint you. Brandy, I mean it when I say you're my everything. I want to make you happy, but I realized that in order to do so, I need to make sure I'm content with where my life is at."

"I can't believe it," I whispered, shaking my head.

"Are you disappointed?" he asked.

"Not in the slightest. I can't believe you didn't tell me."

"I didn't really realize it until recently. It seemed like a great idea. I wasn't doing it for money, and I hadn't planned on things taking off the way they did."

"Your work is gorgeous. You're talented. There's no question about it, but if it isn't satisfying any longer, I completely understand."

"You'll get over not dating an artist?" he teased.

"I might make you put on the welders' mask every once in a while, but I'll get over it."

His laughter boomed through the air and I smiled. I wasn't kidding, but that was for him to find out at another time.

Feeling like the weight of the world had been lifted, I sat back on my hands and stretched my body. In the last hour, my world went from one extreme to the other and now all I wanted was to spend the rest of our time in Paris without drama. Something about this trip had to change.

"So what have you and your father been talking about?" I asked. "Are we going to China?"

Aaron grinned. "Not with law school starting. Thankfully, my father noticed how good I am at what I do, and he is willing to work with me anyway I need just to get me back to the company."

"Seriously?" I asked.

He nodded.

"It's about time."

"You be sure and tell him that," Aaron joked.

"I will."

"I don't doubt it."

"I can't believe we're sitting in France with you getting ready for a show that most artists would kill for and you're hanging up your welder's hat the moment it ends." I grinned, and he tackled me onto the bed, pinning me down. "I knew things felt off about this trip."

He leaned over and me and kissed my lips softly. "I'm sorry I didn't tell you sooner."

"Thank you. That means a lot to hear."

"I've learned my lesson," he murmured, rolling off me.

"You promise?" I asked, turning on my side to face him.

"Absolutely. No more secretly commiserating with myself. You get to share in all that misery too." He grinned, and I felt like I was riding a high.

"So you haven't spoken with Elizabeth since you and I talked about it?" I asked.

"No. I should probably meet with her and explain things."

I nodded. "It kills me to say it, but it's the right thing to do."

"I'd like you to come with me when I meet with her."

"Are you sure?" I asked.

"It's the only way. I've been thinking a lot about what you said in the park, and I never meant to lead her on, but that must be what I've been doing all this time. I didn't pick up on it because I didn't see her like that. I never intended to hurt you, and it never occurred to me that sometimes what I would say to her, I should've been telling you."

I nodded and slid my hand to his. "To hear you say that makes my world seem right again. It's been eating me up and having Tracy regurgitate what you must have told Elizabeth killed me."

Aaron's eyes darkened and his face paled. "What did you say?"

"What do you mean?" I asked, realizing I didn't even know what slipped out.

"About Tracy. What aren't you telling me?" There was no hiding the anger in Aaron's voice as his stare intensified.

I drew in a deep breath and fell against the bed, covering my eyes with my arm. "It's no big deal."

"It sounds like a very big deal, Brandy, and I don't understand why you're not telling me."

"Because I don't want you to do something you might regret."

"Why don't you let me worry about that? Now tell me what's been going on."

I turned on my side again and steadied my gaze on Aaron's.

"Tracy told me that the bond between you and Elizabeth is unbreakable." The first admission felt like the biggest weight had been lifted as I removed my arm and watched him carefully.

"She did, did she?" His brow arched.

I nodded. "I told her I wasn't concerned, and she implied I really ought to be. I tried to be as polite as possible, but I told her I didn't think it was her business, and I wasn't worried about you and Elizabeth."

The anger was building behind Aaron's gaze as he shook his head.

"She brought up you giving up China and how I held you back from what you wanted to do, and at least I didn't do that with Paris."

"You know that's not true, don't you?" Aaron's voice was urgent.

"I think so, but I have to confess it placed doubt, and that's why I've probably been so sensitive about you and Elizabeth. This last week hasn't been the greatest. I've been more in shock that you talked to Elizabeth about those things in the first place, but I didn't want to bring it up."

Aaron looked absolutely horrified as I proceeded to fill him in on the other pleasantries Tracy managed to sling my way.

"Why didn't you tell me?" he questioned.

"I didn't and still don't want to ruin what you've got going at the gallery. I can handle a woman like that. I didn't really think they existed, but I'm confident in what we have. I'm not going to let some strange woman break us apart. I had put on my big girl panties and was going to wait it out. It's only two more weeks before the show."

Aaron groaned and pulled me into him. "Don't ever keep things in like that again. I'm sick about it. Disgusted. I can't believe Elizabeth would have a friend like that, but it makes me question her judgment of character and many other things."

"The whole thing felt like a scene out of the Twilight Zone," I confessed.

"I can imagine. When did this even happen?" he asked.

"When she came to visit you, not last time but the time before. Anyway, I think it's safe to say that she doesn't care for me."

Aaron started laughing, and I buried my head against his chest.

"Anyone who doesn't like you is suspect in my book, and I'm tempted to pull out of the show."

My head jerked back, and I shook my head. "You don't want to do that. Your sister and everyone will be here to see it. Aren't your dad and Carla coming?"

He shrugged. "I think I do want to pull out. I don't want to be associated with anyone like that. And yes he might be. Depends on his schedule, but believe me they'd understand and would enjoy the trip anyway."

"It was pure schoolgirl antics. I think we should move on and make it look like it didn't bother us one way or the other."

"I'm not sure I agree."

"I have to say it took me aback, but once she left, and I managed not to knock her out, I felt completely empowered. You know how I had a sudden interest in law again?"

Sitting up, he nodded.

"It was because of this situation. I was so infuriated; somehow things just realigned in my head."

"Your feistiness had seemed to take a hiatus..." his voice trailed off.

I grabbed a pillow and slammed it over his head. "Well, it's back now, and I say we follow through with the exhibit and show how we're the better people in all this."

Aaron tackled me, and I couldn't help giggling as he tickled me and I smacked him with more pillows.

"We're way more refined than those guys," I chuckled, gasping for breath. "We'll show them how it's done."

"Will we now?" Aaron hovered his mouth over mine, and I raked my fingers through his hair, pulling his lips to mine.

France was starting to redeem itself.

CHAPTER EIGHTEEN

Aaron had finished assembling two sculptures and had a surprise planned for our afternoon. He told me to meet him at the stables and that was where I was headed. I was dressed in jeans and a t-shirt, and I hoped that would be okay. The pathway wound along a large herb garden near the back of the house. About a hundred feet in front of me, the stables were nestled in between some trees. I hadn't seen him all morning and I missed him. It felt like things were back on track, and I couldn't wait to spend some quality time with him in France. After our confessional last night, we were ravished and ate every single item the chef had cooked. The dessert should have lasted several nights, but we managed to polish it off too. I could still taste the buttery crumbly crust of the salted caramel mouse.

I saw some movement behind one of the trees and my heart rate increased. I couldn't wait to see what he had arranged.

"I'm here." I hopped over to Aaron, and he spun around, holding two champagne glasses.

"Yes. You. Are." He kissed me, and his lips lingered, making me rethink whatever he had planned. Spending the day in the bedroom sounded just as perfect.

"For you." He handed me one of the glasses, and I took a sip as I scanned the area, looking for any clues.

"So what have you been up to out here?" I asked.

"I thought we could go riding and have lunch. You said you used to ride when you were growing up." He smiled.

"You remembered?"

"Of course."

Completely exhilarated at the thought of getting to ride this afternoon, I sipped the last of the champagne. He took the glass and set it down on a wrought iron table right behind him. I spotted several bags with prepared meats and cheeses and fruits that he'd been stuffing into a sack.

"Geoff, an equerry for the stables, will be riding with us for the first hour," Aaron said. "If we want him to stay with us he will or whatever. I wasn't sure what your comfort level would be."

As he spoke, it hadn't even hit me. I hadn't been on a horse since my bike accident. I had no idea how my body would respond; how the muscles would react after such trauma. My stomach twisted in disappointment as my mind wandered to yet another thing that was forever changed, thanks to Derek.

Derek. Good old Derek.

I'd been so preoccupied since we arrived at the villa that I hadn't even checked to see if we had wireless. I knew I should be finding out what was going on with the trial, but part of me didn't want to know.

"You okay?" Aaron asked, touching my chin softly.

"Sorry. I spaced. I've been trying to forget about the trial and it popped in my head again."

"That's completely understandable. You heard anything more?" he asked.

I shook my head. "I forgot to ask you about wireless. I haven't been able to get any phone reception since we got here. The messages I told you about must have come over on our way here."

"I can hook it up right now if you want to see what happened while we were sleeping. Geoff won't mind waiting."

I reached for Aaron's hand and squeezed it. "I don't want to know. We can check later, after I enjoy our day together. No good can come of it."

"You sure?"

"Completely. It's like what? Three in the morning there?" I asked.

"Something like that."

"Yeah, so if I see something that upsets me, I

don't want to wake my poor mom up. I'll wait. By the time we get back to the villa this evening, the trial will be underway, and I can see if she has any new news."

Aaron looked like he wasn't sure that was the best idea, but as I pushed him toward the stables, he got the message.

"We need this," I told him as excitement pounded through my veins.

It had been so long since I'd ridden, I couldn't wait to get on a horse. They were such kind and caring animals. I'd always wanted one as a little girl, but it wasn't exactly in our budget so I rode my friends' horses, or my parents would rent a horse by the hour for lessons.

A gentleman in his mid-fifties walked out of the stable and gave a quick wave to Aaron before turning his attention to me.

"Vous êtes magnifique," Geoff exclaimed, taking my hand and kissing it. I had no idea what he said but hoped it was good. It sounded like something was magnificent. I just didn't know what in particular.

"Merci," I replied, glancing over at Aaron who was beaming.

Geoff led us into the stable and handed us each a helmet. I fastened it on tightly and followed Geoff to the first stall where a beautiful palomino stood. She was caramel colored, and her flowing white mane was gorgeous. She looked like the perfect size for me, around fourteen hands.

"Son nom est Sasha," Geoff said, opening the

gate and leading her out by her reins.

"Sasha," I repeated, as he walked her in front of me. "Beautiful name for a beautiful horse."

He tied her up in front of me and walked over to grab a saddle. I glanced at Aaron and he was watching me as I rubbed Sasha's neck.

"C'est magnifique." Geoff winked and put her saddle on.

I nodded and continued to run my hands along her neck. She loved the attention, and I was falling in love with her. Sasha's doe eyes were so expressive, and I knew our connection went both ways.

Geoff finished securing the saddle and walked over to another stall and opened the gate, bringing out a beautiful chestnut colored horse.

"French Trotter," Geoff said, and I couldn't help but laugh.

Of course he spoke English.

"He's beautiful," I said, looking over at Aaron.

"He is," Geoff agreed.

Sasha snorted as if to remind me that she was standing in earshot, and I quickly turned my attention back to her. I was certain they could understand what we were talking about, and she didn't like the fact that my affections were so easily swayed.

"You're just as beautiful, Sasha," I whispered.

Sasha moved her head up and down in agreement, apparently feeling immensely better at my admission.

"His name is Bob," Geoff said, bringing Aaron's horse in front of me.

"Bob?" I asked, shocked.

Geoff broke into laughter and shook his head. "No. His name is Bruno."

I smiled and glanced at Aaron who was watching Geoff tease me. "Bruno is more fitting, considering."

Aaron's horse neighed as Geoff put the saddle on and Aaron's brows shot up. Aaron looked a little on edge, and I thought it was kind of cute. There were very few things in life that made Aaron nervous, and I think we just found one. Geoff caught Aaron's expression and grinned as he fastened the buckles.

"You doing okay over there, cowboy?" I asked, grinning.

Aaron smiled and cracked his knuckles. "Never been better. Thanks for checking."

We led our horses out of the stable and Geoff followed behind with his. My pulse quickened at the thought of getting to ride Sasha this afternoon. It had been so long and I was really looking forward to it.

Aaron handed Geoff the reins and jogged over to where he'd left the food. He looked so excited about the day he'd planned, it melted my heart. Aaron brought over the sack and Geoff helped him secure it to Bruno's saddle.

Bruno got a little restless and Aaron's lips pressed together and his face paled slightly. I could see his anxiety level raise, and it was hard to suppress my laughter. Come to find out my big, tough boyfriend was afraid of horses.

"I thought you said you've ridden before?" I

asked, smiling.

"Many times," Aaron said.

"Could have fooled me," I teased, checking to make sure the cinch was snug and the buckles tightened. I grabbed the reins with my left hand and lifted my leg, sinking the toe of my shoe into the stirrup as I grabbed the cantle with my right hand and swung my legs up and over the horse. I sat snuggly on my horse and watched over Aaron as Geoff helped him into the saddle. Geoff was holding the horse's reins tightly while Aaron got situated on Bruno. I watched Aaron slide himself in the saddle, trying to get comfortable, and I chuckled slightly.

Geoff glanced at me and winked before giving Aaron some last minute instructions. He handed over the reins and nodded, asking if Aaron had any questions.

Aaron caught me watching him and grinned. "It's been a while."

"I didn't say a word." I smiled.

Geoff mounted his horse quickly, and we began following him away from the stable.

We couldn't have asked for a better day to ride. The temperature hovered around seventy degrees and there was a slight breeze. Following behind Geoff, we rode through the property, discovering a tiny but fertile vineyard and ruins, which Geoff explained was once a small monastery.

As we rode deeper onto the property, the surroundings became even more magical. The property was walled in stone, but it stretched as far as the eye could see. Geoff steered us to a clearing and stopped.

"I thought this might be a nice area for your meal. It seems like you two are doing just fine on your own." Geoff glanced at Aaron for confirmation.

"I think we've got it," Aaron replied, glancing over at me and I nodded.

"You should be able to find your way back to the stables. If all else fails, follow the stone wall and you'll eventually find where you need to be," Geoff said. "There are tie posts throughout the property if you want to take breaks." He pointed at a few behind us.

"Merci," I said, unable to believe we'd already been riding for over an hour.

Geoff gave a quick wave as his horse trotted away, leaving Aaron and I alone. I dismounted and led Sasha to one of the tie posts and tied her up. Aaron was having a bit of difficulty turning Bruno around so I walked over and led Bruno to one of the vacant posts.

"You got this?" I asked Aaron.

He nodded and began dismounting, but Bruno was getting agitated and began the dance.

"Are you digging your toe into him?" I asked, trying to calm Bruno.

Aaron repositioned and tried again, this time dismounting perfectly if you counted tumbling backward as a perfect dismount.

I couldn't help but grin as I tied up Bruno and rubbed his neck. I spun around to see Aaron watching me.

"You're really in your element."

"Who knew?" I laughed.

"How are you feeling? We can always head back if you're sore."

I shook my head and laughed. "Surprisingly, I'm not feeling it at all. I thought my muscles might revolt, but everything feels really good. I think all the PT has helped strengthen muscles I never thought about."

"That's good." Aaron walked over and stood next to me. He reached his hands into the sack that had been strapped to Bruno.

"How about you. Are you getting sore?"

Aaron shook his head.

"You wouldn't tell me if you were, would you?" I narrowed my eyes and he laughed.

"We've only been riding for an hour. It's not like I'm an old man," he teased as I grabbed the blanket that was rolled behind the saddle.

I found a nice place to lay the blanket down and spread our lunch out. I felt like we were worlds away from civilization as I looked around the picturesque countryside.

"This is absolutely beautiful," I whispered, taking a seat on the blanket. "Thank you for planning this."

Aaron sat next to me and stretched out his legs. "I thought it would be a nice change."

"It's perfect."

Aaron slid off his helmet and I did the same, trying to fluff my hair. We sat in a silence for a few minutes while we unpackaged the food. The silence was soothing with only the horses making an occasional sound. I took a piece of bread and placed some meat and cheese on top and leaned back on one arm. Feeling the rays from the sun splash on my skin reenergized me.

"This is delicious," I said, taking another bite.

"I swear it wouldn't taste like this in Washington," Aaron replied.

"Weird how that works. So how is everything coming along?" I asked.

"Just as I thought it would. I'm still debating about pulling out though."

I shook my head. "I wouldn't do that. Tracy's shenanigans are ridiculous, and I think that would feed into whatever weird game she's into. The best revenge is having a successful show and us living happily ever after."

Aaron grinned and his gaze intensified sending a flutter of anticipation through me. "I think I can handle that."

Before I even had a chance to feign objection, Aaron rolled me onto my back and began dusting kisses along my neck. A shiver ran through me as I felt his body press against mine, and his gaze darkened with longing as he brought his lips to mine.

And that's when I realized I'd been mistaking the look in Aaron's eyes ever since I met him. It hadn't been complete arrogance that rested behind his gaze. He'd spent his entire adulthood safeguarding himself from others. He was guarded, and I'd finally started to break through.

CHAPTER NINETEEN

Between the bucolic farmland and rustic vineyard, the ride had felt like we were in a fantastical wonderland. When we returned back to the house, I didn't even think about the trial. We'd had a wonderful dinner and night to ourselves, and there wasn't one moment that my mind wandered to the mess back home. It wasn't until this morning when I was awoken by another nightmare. This time Derek had arrived at our house after being found not guilty. I turned around to flee back inside but had nowhere to run. His followers were inside my house waiting.

I must have said something in my sleep because Aaron had woken me up and held me tightly until I calmed down. I'd fallen back asleep in his arms, but when I woke up the second time, he wasn't in bed.

As I took in a deep breath I understood why he wasn't next to me. He was downstairs cooking breakfast. I stretched under the covers once more and then climbed out of bed. I walked to the bathroom and brushed my teeth, not wanting to scare him away. I thought about brushing my hair and decided against it. That was far too painful of a proposition before conditioner had a chance to work its magic.

I debated about bringing my phone down to have Aaron hook it up to the wireless and decided to take it with me. I couldn't hide from the trial forever. I let out a sigh and reached for the phone. It dropped from my hands and landed on the floor with a horrible thud. I picked it up and flipped it over to see a cracked screen.

"Shoot."

I twisted my lips in frustration and slipped on a robe, tucking the broken phone in my pocket. Maybe it was a sign. My stomach knotted at the thought of what my own destiny might be trying to hide from me. I padded down the stairs slowly to the smell of ham and eggs. The kitchen looked like an explosion went off and I chuckled at the scene. There was a bowl with batter dripping from the sides, a plate with a stack of burned toast, steam arising from eggs on the stove, and ham sizzling on a burner. It was quite the triumph.

"You always outdo yourself," I whispered. "I feel like the luckiest girlfriend in the world."

Aaron laughed. "Well, I have a lot of making up to do."

"No, you don't."

His brow arched and he smiled.

"Maybe just a little."

He laughed, bringing me closer into him, and I rested my forehead against his chest as my fingers trailed down his arms. He'd somehow managed to sneak in a shower between waking up and making breakfast. He smelled of citrus soap and it made me want to stay nestled in his arms.

"I'm just a nosey person, which seems to translate into a nosey girlfriend."

I felt Aaron's body shudder as he chuckled. "Not nosey, Brandy. You deserve to know everything about the man you love. And you said it yesterday... to live happily ever after is the best revenge."

I took a step back and grinned. "Well, you know me. I always like to set goals."

"You look so damn sexy in that robe with your hair all messed up," Aaron nearly growled.

I laughed and narrowed my eyes at him. "You're scoring points left and right."

He stirred the scrambled eggs a couple more times and turned off the burners. "Wanna grab a couple of plates?"

"Your wish is my command." I grinned.

"Can I count on that always?" He wiggled his brows and I groaned.

"I'm not that gullible."

I handed him the plates, and he scooped some

eggs and sprinkled them on my plate, followed by a slab of ham. He opened an oven and pulled out a plate of pancakes or crepes. I wasn't sure which they were, but they looked wonderful regardless.

He slid two on my plate and handed it to me. "There's toast on the counter, but it might have seen better days."

"Looks and smells delicious." I walked over to the plate of toast and grabbed the top piece as Aaron filled his plate up with eggs and ham. I poured some syrup on my pancake crepes and walked into the dining room, feeling absolutely spectacular. France and I really were becoming friends. I set my plate on the table and took a seat.

Watching Aaron walk into the room made my insides warm. There was something so sweet about him. I doubted many saw it, but I was glad I did.

And then I noticed him try to sit and giggled.

He took a seat, rather stiffly, and glanced over at me. "What?"

"You're just too cute."

He rolled his eyes and took a bite of toast. "Might want to skip the toast." He reached for some water to swallow down the burned bread.

I laughed and took a bite of the ham. "Delicious. So how did Bruno treat you yesterday?"

"Doing fine. Great horse." He quirked a brow and, unwilling to concede, flashed a brilliant smile.

"You're not sore at all?" I asked, taking another bite of ham.

He shook his head. "Not sore at all."

"Liar."

"I'd tell you."

"Sure you would." I dropped my napkin on the floor and glanced at him. "Do you mind picking that up for me."

Aaron drew in a deep breath and reached over, letting out a little groan as he snatched it from the floor and handed it to me.

"Guess I was wrong." I smiled and he grinned, shaking his head. "You must not be sore at all."

"You play so dirty."

"Not me." I grinned as we quietly ate and enjoyed our breakfast together, and I thought about the coming days. I really should see what was going on with the trial. There was no such thing as a sealed deal when it came to the legal system. No matter what I did or didn't see, I promised myself not to get my hopes up. One step at a time... Aaron's voice broke me out of my daze and I glanced at him.

"I really wish there was something I could do to Derek to make it all end."

My eyes locked on Aaron's and I nodded. "It's hard to believe when there's this much evidence against him a conviction isn't a sure thing."

"Attempted murder is murder, if you ask me. Just because he did a lousy job or made a mistake doesn't mean the guy isn't a murderer."

I let out a sigh and understood where Aaron was coming from. It was frustrating. Someone wanted me dead, tried to kill me, and yet there was a possibility that he could walk away with not even a slap on his wrist.

"All I can do is hope that justice will be served." I pressed my lips together and thought about what that actually meant. Was justice possible? I'd always be left with reminders of that horrible day.

I reached into my pocket and pulled out my phone with the newly broken screen and handed it to Aaron.

"I did this upstairs. Apparently the screen doesn't like to fall flat onto hard surfaces."

Aaron let out a whistle and examined the cracked screen. "Could be worse." He clicked the phone on and slid the screen on. "Looks like it still works. Might be kind of hard to see detail, but we can get it replaced."

"Here or when we get back to the states?"

"Probably here, but I'm not sure. I'll add the wireless for you though. It might take some finagling to see what you're trying to look at. I'll leave my phone in here for you to use."

"Thanks. Maybe I'll stick with this and miss all of the bad news with a broken screen."

"You never know." He handed me the phone that was now hooked up to wireless, and I felt my chest tighten as I thought about checking my emails.

I set the phone down on the table and decided to wait. Waiting a few minutes wouldn't hurt a thing.

Scooping the last bit of scrambled eggs onto

my fork, I took a bite and sat back in the chair. The breakfast was delicious, but now I was ready to go back to bed.

"I think I'll be able to get another two pieces put together today and that will leave only one more for tomorrow. There's a town, Chartres, not far from here that I thought you might enjoy visiting tomorrow afternoon."

I nodded and watched Aaron's expression soften as he spoke. "It's known for some Gothic cathedral. I thought it would be a nice change."

"I can't wait. I'll probably need it after I spend today finding out about who knows what."

Aaron reached for my hand and squeezed it. "I can push off putting the pieces together. We could go to town today, or I could stay inside with you while you look into things. I'm game for anything."

I shook my head. "That's very sweet of you, but I want to get it over with by myself. I think what you have planned is perfect." I smiled and took a deep breath in as I thought about what I might find. "I'll take care of the dishes. It's the least I can do after getting spoiled with breakfast."

He stood up tentatively and pushed the chair into the table before stretching toward the ceiling. It looked like every leg muscle must be sore, but for the life of him he wouldn't admit it. His shirt rose slightly, and my eyes traveled down his bronzed skin.

Aaron caught me looking and grinned. "Something catch your attention?"

I laughed and realized that he was indeed guarded, but he was also a little arrogant, and I happened to be hopelessly enamored with all of him.

"You are irresistible," I muttered.

"That's what I like to hear." He walked over slowly and draped his arms over my shoulders and gave me a big hug. Feeling the strength of his embrace made me think that nothing was impossible. No matter what I found online, I had Aaron to lean on and that meant more than anything.

Aaron let go of me and set his iPhone on the table. "You know the password. If you need anything, you know where to find me."

I smiled, and he swept a kiss on my cheek prior to heading out to the workshop. I debated about showering before I started the pursuit of information, but I decided against it. The longer I put it off, the worse it would get. I quickly did the dishes and went into the sitting room. I turned on my cracked phone.

Pressing on my email, I waited for the new messages to populate. To my surprise, there was only one update from my mom. I read through the message quickly and was cautiously relieved. She felt the trial was going well and the evidence was convincing. She praised the attorney's clear and concise arguments. She didn't want to give me false hope, but she felt things were looking promising. Her thought was that the trial would be over by early next week. I let out a sigh, thankful that there wasn't any bad news in her email and closed it up. Not that I didn't trust my mom's thoughts on the subject, I went to some of the bookmarked sites and reviewed some of the snippets from the trial.

As I glanced at one of the articles, I realized why my mom didn't say much. They'd called her as a witness. My heart sank as I read the transcripts and journalists' recap. I cringed at the depths of deplorable questioning that the defense attorney had been willing to go to. My pulse raced as I read his accusatory statements about my mother. Somehow the defense attorney managed to turn the entire situation into a condemnation of my mother's legal defense of Derek's mother versus my attempted murder. Several of his questions got stricken from the record, but the jury was still able to hear them. As much as I hated to admit it, Derek's defense attorney was good, but I'd like to think the prosecuting attorney was better. I still didn't know if Derek would be getting on the stand. I guess only time would tell.

A rather uplifting article showed up in a Google Alert I'd set up about the cult link to Derek. It looked as if there would be new charges brought against the person who sent the letter to me. I quickly scanned through the discussion boards and saw some of the followers of Derek sounding off on this latest revelation. It concerned me, but my hope was that if Derek got locked behind bars, they'd find some other bandwagon to jump on. Unfortunately, I'd also seen how once a person was behind bars, they almost achieved a celebrity status.

Ever since I was a kid, I always got the heebie-jeebies when the Charles Manson specials would come on, and I couldn't believe he actually had fan clubs. I shivered at the thought of Derek gaining more recognition and tried to push the thoughts aside.

One step at a time.

I glanced out the window and saw the blue skies completely trading out for heavy clouds. In the distance it looked as if buckets of rain were pouring down. It probably wouldn't be long before the storm arrived here.

Without even realizing that hours had gone by, I glanced at the time and forced myself to stop searching. It got me more nervous. I should have read my mom's email and stayed oblivious to the rest, but that wasn't how I operated. I clicked on my mom's message again and quickly typed a reply, thanking her for everything she did and congratulating her on the snide comments she managed to slide into her answers. I could only imagine the laughter some had to hold in. As I hit send, I saw a message from Ayden with the subject: Lily.

I quickly opened the email and read the first line,

Would you be okay with me asking Lily to marry me while we're in Paris? I bought the ring already... So I hope the answer is yes, knucklehead.

My heart beat wildly as I reread Ayden's

question. Seriously? My best friend and brother were getting engaged? I could barely hold in my excitement. Now I really couldn't wait for everyone to get here. I wondered if she had any idea? I hit reply and filled my message with exclamation points and hearts. This was exactly what I needed to end on today so I wouldn't be all doom and gloom.

I nearly skipped my way into the shower. I made it a quick one since I was so excited and had to share the news with Aaron. This was way too awesome to keep to myself. I rinsed the soap off my body and the conditioner out of my hair as I thought about how Lily was going to absolutely die when he popped the question. Miss anti-love was about to get engaged. She'd talked about them spending the rest of their lives together, but then she would stop herself, worried that it was moving too fast. But I knew how my brother worked. He wouldn't want Lily to slip away.

I turned off the water and stepped out of the shower, drying off quickly and dressing even quicker. I went through the kitchen to grab a glass of water since the ham was making me extra thirsty. I heard Aaron's phone ding and polished off my water before going into the dining room to take Aaron's phone to him.

Sliding the phone on, I looked at the screen and saw Elizabeth's text flash onto the phone. My chest tightened as I saw her words.

Please tell me what it is that I did. I'm sorry for anything I may have done. It wasn't on purpose. If

*you could just give me a few minutes of your time
to explain whatever it is...*

For some bizarre reason I felt bad for her, but
then I remembered Tracy and the guilt left as
quickly as it came. Taking the phone, I walked
out to Aaron's workshop and was caught
completely off guard when I spotted Aaron.
Rather than being dressed in his protective gear,
he had stripped off his shirt and tucked it in the
waistband of his low-hanging shorts. His wide
shoulders and strong legs were stretched as he
reached for something on a shelf. I couldn't help
but be distracted by Aaron's physique as I stood
in awe and imagined myself tangled within his
embrace.

As Aaron managed to pull a box off the shelf,
he spun around to see me ogling. He broke into a
smile. "What do you think?"

"About what?" I asked.

He shook his head and laughed, pointing to
the sculptures. My cheeks heated as I realized I
hadn't even noticed. How horrible of me. I took
another step inside and became completely
mesmerized at the fully formed sculptures.
Seeing them completed in their full size literally
took my breath away. I hadn't expected him to be
done with one, let alone two.

"They're fantastic. I can't even imagine what
people are going to say..."

"I don't care about what people say, only you."
He set the box on a worktable and walked over
to me. "How's the trial going?"

I shrugged as he slid his hands onto my hips. "I'm afraid to say one way or another. My mom went on the stand yesterday. She didn't tell me. I looked it up. The defense attorney was a complete ass, but that's what he's paid to be. Anyway, I came out here to share some pretty exciting news."

Aaron took a step back just as thunder clapped in the distance.

"Well, that's quite the Lily dramatics."

Aaron furrowed his brow in confusion.

"Sorry. That just seems exactly how Lily would want me to tell you the news if she were here... thunder clapping in the distance."

"Tell me what?" Aaron questioned.

"Ayden just emailed telling me he plans on asking Lily to marry him while they're here in Paris."

Aaron's mouth dropped open, and he slid his fingers through his hair. "You don't say."

"Oh, it's happening. He's already bought the ring."

Aaron smiled and brought me into him. "Well, that's a perfect way to end our time here in Paris. Wouldn't you say?"

"Totally. I wonder what my parents think."

"My guess is that they're thrilled."

I nodded and rested my head against Aaron's chest, taking a deep breath in. "I bet they are."

Closing my eyes, I celebrated silently for Lily and hoped one day it would be me.

Chapter Twenty

Chills ran through me as I stared at the 11th century Gothic cathedral directly in front of us. The grandeur of the building was breathtaking. the scale was unbelievable, and to say the steeples reached the heavens would be an understatement. The stained glass windows sparkled even in the cloudy weather. The ornate façade with flying buttresses sweeping around the building and pinnacles projecting into the air were unlike anything I'd ever seen before. The tapered rooflines and jagged towers created an intriguing spookiness. The structure eerily oozed resilience that had somehow withstood centuries of war, peace, love and hate.

Chartres was right out of a picture book with medieval architecture dotting the streets and gothic buildings pushing toward the sky throughout the town. Brightly colored shutters bejeweled the ancient buildings of Chartres and created a charming feel throughout city, but the cathedral was the crown jewel.

"I don't even think a photograph will do it justice," I said, glancing at Aaron.

He wrapped his arm around my waist and pulled me close to him as he placed a quick kiss on my forehead.

"I'm glad we got to see it in person...together," he murmured.

We walked up the steps and went inside the cathedral, which was even more jaw dropping than the exterior. The cathedral was lit by flickering candles and what few rays of light shone through the stained glass from the otherwise dreary day created a sense of tranquility. The bowed buttress supports and spired interior created a haunting space cloaked in mystery and history. I couldn't stop shivering with each step deeper into the cathedral with its endless pointed archways and irregular vaulted ceilings.

I glanced at Aaron who seemed to be in as much awe as I was as we walked throughout the cathedral. The glow of the candles welcomed us further as the warmth of the wooden pews and the harshness of the stone walls provided an evocative contrast.

Stepping into the cathedral's open space, Aaron looked down as he held my hand. We both saw the elaborate labyrinth at our feet with flickering candles outlining the beautiful maze of spirit and soul as we followed the pattern and found ourselves in the center. Aaron held me close as we continued to take in the brilliance of the church setting. We walked slowly out of the labyrinth and meandered through the cathedral. Before leaving the church, I said a silent prayer that everything back home would work as it was meant to and followed Aaron outside into the chilly evening air.

The experience left me oddly numb but somehow full of hope and determination. I couldn't imagine my trip to France without seeing this cathedral, and I'd never even known about it until today.

"Thank you," I whispered.

"Thank you," he replied smiling, as he took my hand, and we walked toward a restaurant that had caught our attention earlier. The storm from the day before still lingered in the air so we sat inside, and each of us ordered a glass of wine.

"We're so lucky," I sighed, feeling a dopey grin on my face, but there was nothing I could do about it. I felt completely relaxed and optimistic.

"We are."

"Can I ask you something?"

He nodded and grinned. "The answer to that will always be yes. I learned my lesson the hard way in the middle of Paris."

"With all your life experience and everything you've been through and seen in the world, why would you want to be with someone like me? I don't mean that in a self-deprecating way, but

I've got so much catching up to do. I mean my idea of a good time is to unroll some party streamers and put a keg in the backyard. Your life is begging to be more glamorous and—"

"Brandy, don't even go there," he interrupted, smiling.

"Oh, I went there," I teased.

"Don't you understand how much I love spending time with you? Getting to experience these things with you brings me more joy than I ever thought possible. There was a time when all I could see for myself was working and working some more. I never imagined finding someone that could make going to a church fun or riding a Jet Ski exhilarating and oh...so much more." He had a devilish look in his eyes and grinned. "And there's nothing better than ice-cold beer and BBQ. Your brothers can attest to that."

"Don't forget the party streamers." I smiled and took a sip of wine that the server had brought over while I was intently listening to Aaron.

"Definitely need the streamers for all occasions."

"With all the excitement about the impending engagement with Lily and my brother, I forgot to mention I saw the text from Elizabeth come over," I said.

Aaron's gaze hardened and he looked away. "Yeah."

"So I take it you haven't reached out."

He took a large swallow of wine and shook his head. "Haven't really cared to do so."

While being partially relieved, I also felt the best thing to do was to have a talk with Elizabeth. While I wasn't a fan of her friend, Cruella De Vil, I understood Tracy's loyalty. As long as I didn't allow the untidy condition of my mind to go into overdrive, things should be okay moving forward no matter the outcome of Elizabeth and Aaron's friendship. Of course, that was contingent on our meeting going well, and I didn't want to believe it would go any other way than smooth without any melodramatics.

"I kind of think it might be the best thing to do. You've had a habit of fleeing and as much as I like the idea of you never talking to them again, I know it's not realistic, and it's better to end things on your terms, not theirs."

"I see where you're coming from," he admitted.

The server took our order and Aaron took out his phone and stared at it for a few seconds. "And you'll come with me when I meet with her?" he asked.

I laughed. "I wouldn't have it any other way."

He couldn't help but crack a smile as he slid the phone on. He quickly typed a text and sent it. He turned off the phone and slid it back into his pocket, and it felt like a weight had been lifted. I never liked being mean to people and even in my own ended relationships wanted everyone to feel at ease.

"Now it's my turn to ask you something," he said.

"Let me have it." I took a sip of wine and

waited.

"How often are you having nightmares?"

I almost spit out my wine. I hadn't expected him to go there. I thought we were keeping things a little more light.

"More than I expected. They've increased since the trial started," I admitted.

He nodded. "Those can take a bit of time to get over."

I stiffened slightly. "Do you get nightmares?"

His eyes connected with mine and a charge ran through me. "I did up until I met you. I think you saved me from my own mind."

"Really?" I croaked. I couldn't ever imagine Aaron suffering from nightmares.

He nodded. "Almost nightly. Some people have a bad day and look forward to sleeping so their mind can reset..."

I nodded.

"That wasn't how my nights worked. I tried everything and nothing worked. Until I met you."

My cheeks warmed with his admission.

"Like you said, I've seen a lot. I've done a lot. Not all of those things were pleasant, Brandy. It took having someone as amazing as you to set me right again. You reset me."

"It couldn't be me," I whispered.

His eyes stayed locked on mine, and it felt like we were the only two in the restaurant.

"It was most definitely you, Brandy. You're like my medicine. The day you left me when you found out I was going to China, the nightmares came back that very night. They stayed with me until I came home to you. I'll never make that mistake again. I only wish I could do the same for you. I wish I could destroy the monster who did this to you." His jaw tensed, and I reached out across the table for his hand.

"I had no idea," I said, his hand squeezing mine. "You never mentioned..."

"Yeah. There were a lot of things I'd failed to mention. They were all connected."

I nodded. "I see that now."

The server delivered our dishes and asked if anything else was needed. We ordered another glass of wine.

"You've helped more than you can imagine, Aaron. I don't know where I'd be without you. You helped in ways my family and I will never be able to repay."

He shook his head. "I did it because I love you. Your family would've done it too."

"They would've gone into so much debt that—"

"I want to spend the rest of my life with you, Brandy. I knew it then. I knew it before the accident." His eyes steadied on mine, and my heart fluttered. "I'd been daydreaming about asking you to marry me before we even took that ride that day. I hadn't bought the ring yet because I wanted to ask your father first, but I was on the verge. It kills me that you thought you were a pity case and then to have Tracy try to throw that in your face... I could never apologize enough. I never should have talked with Elizabeth about such personal things."

"It hurt to hear it again, but I knew it wasn't true. I'm too much work to be one of those pity cases," I chuckled.

"That is a valid point." His gaze fell along my body and he grinned.

"Hey now." I tossed my napkin at him, and he snatched it out of the air and gave it back to me.

"See what I mean?" he chided.

My heart raced as his gaze steadied on mine, and I wondered how close we were to that next step. With me going back to school and Aaron heading back to the corporate world would priorities change and expectations shift? After this trip, it felt like things could change on a dime.

"So what do you think about visiting the catacombs when we get back?" Aaron asked, his eyes wide.

"I think that sounds beyond awesome."

"It's a date. That first day we get back." His phone buzzed, and he took it out of his pocket as I had my first bite of filet mignon. It literally melted in my mouth and all my worries drifted away.

"Did you just have an out-of-body experience?" Aaron laughed.

"Possibly."

"It's Elizabeth. She'd be more than happy to meet with us both."

"How about the day we get back? Then we can go to the catacombs after."

"Are you sure?" he asked.

"Totally. I might not feel like the living after

coffee with her."

He flashed a wry smile and sent a text back to Elizabeth as I took another bite. This trip to France had been far more than I bargained for, but I'd grown as a person and our relationship had elevated to another level, and I'm not sure any of that would've happened if it hadn't been for the chance encounter with Elizabeth.

In all relationships, I've always had the upper hand. That all changed once I met Aaron. He turned my world upside by challenging beliefs I had and opening my eyes to a new way of looking at life. I was no longer skeptical of reaching for the stars or trying new things. In fact, I seemed to thrive in both circumstances, and I had Aaron to thank for that.

"Well, I don't know about you, but at least I found what I was looking for in life."

"And what was that?" I asked.

"You."

I did my little happy dance inside and pushed aside the fear that things were getting too good.

CHAPTER TWENTY-ONE

It was our first morning back in Paris, and it felt like a new city. None of the negativity that had infiltrated the first time hovered around us this time.

That was until I opened the email and saw a new Google alert about myself with a picture of Aaron. I read the article and groaned as the one thing Aaron tried to leave behind was trumpeted on the front page of the Times, all because of the trial. One of the journalists dug up the information about Aaron and his time serving overseas as well as the shooting and ran with it. The story explained how a national hero was by my side helping me through the devastation and healing of the accident. I winced at the thought of how Aaron would react as I read the last statement about Aaron's story that was now forever mingled with mine.

I let out a deep sigh and turned over in bed. Facing Aaron, I slowly handed him my phone.

"Oh, no. What happened? Your face looks like you saw a ghost." His brows shot up as he read my phone and then anger began tingeing his expression.

"Did you say something in one of your interviews?" he asked.

I shook my head. "Absolutely not."

"You're sure?" His gaze darkened.

"A hundred and thirty percent," I countered, angered he'd even question my loyalties.

"Someone had to have tipped them off," he said.

I sat up in bed and grabbed my phone back. "Well, you better get your facts straight because it sure as hell wasn't me, mister."

Aaron reached for his cell and turned it on. His phone was blanketed in messages and texts. If I hadn't known about his past life, other coworkers and friends certainly hadn't either, but now they did.

I watched as he shook his head slowly, scanning message after message asking him if it were true. I walked around to his side of the bed and rested my hand on his leg.

"I'm sorry for saying any of that. I know it's not you. I just—"

"I know. I can't believe it either," I interrupted.

"You don't think it was my sister, do you?"

I shook my head. "No way. That's not Gabby's

style. She's as protective as you are when it comes to privacy, especially with Katie. Besides, can you imagine that going over with Jason in the house?"

"Good point. I don't even know what to say. This shit's messing with my mind." He tossed his phone onto the comforter and let out a sigh.

"It's going to be okay. We'll get through it."

"I don't know who would've done this," he muttered, and it hit us both at the same time, except he muttered Elizabeth and I muttered Tracy.

"Why would they do this?" I asked, bewildered.

"I can't even imagine."

"Unless it's only to hurt you..."

Aaron nodded. "Could be as simple as that. Well, we'll certainly get to the bottom of it soon."

I glanced at the time on my phone. "We've got thirty minutes to get to the café. Think we'll make it?"

"Without a doubt." He shoved off the covers and stretched. "I can't wait for coffee though. Not with this news. I'll go make some while you're in the shower."

I nodded and gave him a kiss before turning to grab some clothes.

My anger at those two went through the roof, but for some odd reason it helped me calm down because either today or tomorrow a verdict was expected in the trial. At least, I could focus on those two instead of my problems.

I turned on the shower and waited for the

steam to roll out before I stepped in and took a quick shower. I heard Aaron whistling as he walked down the hall, and I shifted my attention to what was important; attempting to look drop dead gorgeous for my coffee date with the naturally beautiful Elizabeth. Sorry! I knew it was petty, but I at least had to try to put her to shame.

~

Aaron pulled on the door to the café and we walked in, hand in hand. We both spotted Elizabeth tucked in the corner of the dining area, reading a book. There was something that was so difficult about being mad for long at this woman. Aaron squeezed my hand and pulled me along through the café. He was clearly still angry and judging by Elizabeth's expression, she saw it in his eyes immediately.

Elizabeth closed her book and stood up quickly. She reached her hand out to shake mine and Aaron shook his head. "Let's cut the crap."

I was shocked to see this side of Aaron. I knew it existed. I'd heard about it when he was working for his father's company, but I didn't expect to be around when it appeared.

"Aaron, I had nothing to do with it," she said, taking her seat and stuffing her book in her bag.

Awkward.

I glanced at the counter and wondered if I could escape and go place our orders. No. That was wrong of me. I needed to stay by his side, but the cappuccinos and croissants were calling. I could literally hear them singing...

"Do you really expect me to believe that?" he asked, his voice so quiet, it was barely audible.

"I would hope you would," she said, glancing at me.

Aaron took a seat across from Elizabeth and leaned over the table. "Why? Between the threats and doubts that Tracy so keenly placed in Brandy..."

I was still standing, unsure of whether I should sit, stand, order or what when Aaron went right for the throat, which was exactly what he said he wasn't going to do.

"Maybe you should get something to drink first and then we'll discuss," Elizabeth said, noticing my unwieldy shifting of weight from one foot to the other.

Aaron shot back up and grabbed my hand, spinning me toward the counter so quickly I almost lost my balance.

"Whoa, cowboy," I whispered, as we stood in front of the pastry case. "What happened to calm, cool, and collected?"

"It flew out the door with reason and empathy."

We ordered two cappuccinos and croissants and Aaron managed to calm down slightly before we returned to the table. I sat down this time, followed by Aaron.

"Anyhow," I said, taking a sip of my cappuccino. "As you were saying?"

Now that I had a place to sit and a coffee, I felt far more in control. I centered my gaze on Elizabeth and tried to gauge her response to Aaron. There was no doubt she was in love with him, but I couldn't tell if she was a woman scorned or what. Her expression was misleading.

Elizabeth looked at me. "I should never have put my nose where it didn't belong. I'd be lying if I didn't admit there was a part of me that wanted to cause a rift between the two of you. Not to mention having Tracy in my ear didn't help. But I'm not making excuses. I'm a grown woman, responsible for my actions."

She looked at Aaron. "I never should've passed on any information to Tracy. I knew she was fiercely loyal, but I misunderstood the lengths that she would go to. I didn't know she would turn it around or ever use it against you. I treated her as a confidant and I shouldn't have. When you stopped communicating with me, I began pressing Tracy since she was still in contact with you. I never imagined that she would have done what she did. I'm deeply sorry for that, and I can understand why you cut off contact with me. I didn't find out what she did until yesterday when I told her I was meeting with you both."

Elizabeth took a deep breath in and looked over at me. "You've been through enough, and I didn't mean to make things worse on either of you, but I did. I hope you can forgive me."

Completely shocked, I stared at her as I tried to find my voice. Either she had supremely elevated acting skills or she was the most sincere person I'd ever met. I could see why things might just roll off of Aaron's tongue around her.

"Unfortunately, last night while Tracy and I were arguing I found out she'd gone to the press about your story, Aaron. I'm absolutely sick about it," her voice trembled and strangely, I wanted to comfort her.

I reached my hand across the table and touched hers. Her eyes connected with mine, and I realized she wasn't a woman scorned. She was a woman who fell in love with the wrong man, and she had no power over it. There was something about Aaron that drew people in.

Aaron glanced at me, and I saw a slight curl of his lip as he shook his head perplexed by the scenario unfolding in front of him.

"I accept your apology. Sometimes even with our best intentions, things can go seriously haywire. I'm sure Aaron can attest to that," I said.

Aaron furrowed his brows as I released my hands from Elizabeth's.

"You know talking about emotions and feelings is not a strong point of mine," Aaron said, shifting in his seat. "But I'm beyond angry with what has transpired. It could have cost me a relationship that I cherish more than life itself."

Elizabeth nodded and blinked back tears. "I realize that and I know that my words aren't enough."

I slid my hand to Aaron's knee and pressed my fingers into his flesh so he'd take it a little easy on her. A twitch of his mouth signaled he'd received the message, and he let out an exasperated sigh instead of the bottled up words.

"You know, Elizabeth. You're just lucky Brandy is here with me, and that she's such an amazing woman because there are a lot of unkind things I wanted to say to you, but the woman sitting next to me is stopping me."

I blushed at the compliment but also reveled in it.

"I know, Aaron. You've found your equal, and all I can hope is that I'll find mine one day." She smiled faintly. "I wanted to tell you in person that I've found a buyer for my company. You'll be receiving your investment back, along with the percentage that we spoke about when you tried to convince me to sell it years ago."

So Aaron was telling the truth.

"Are you sure that's what you want to do?" The words rolled out of my mouth before I could even stop them.

"I wasn't meant for that world. I detested it, but I also kept holding onto it, thinking that I could win a man's heart that was never meant to belong to me. Brandy, I don't know what Aaron has or hasn't told you about us, but I can assure you there never was an us. That ideal only existed in my imagination, and unfortunately that version was what I told Tracy about. She's not a bad person, just misguided."

"You had me until there," Aaron said, laughing. "You've really got to reevaluate your friendships."

Elizabeth smiled, and I saw her beauty fill up

the room. "You're probably right about that. But at least something good came out of it."

"What was that?" he asked.

"The world gets to see your work."

I wanted to hate Elizabeth, but for the life of me I couldn't. I sat quietly and debated what to say and decided nothing was probably best.

"I don't want to beat the subject to death. All I can do is apologize and move on, but I wanted to warn you that she went to the press here in France too. She thought it would be good publicity for the show."

I saw the vein throb in Aaron's forehead, and I knew Elizabeth caught it too.

"Thank you for letting us know," I said.

"Well, I think you just gave me the final reason to back out," Aaron sighed.

"Final reason?" Elizabeth asked bewildered.

I nodded. "Since Tracy so aptly defined conditions of my relationship with Aaron, she threatened many things and Aaron wanted to pull out. I convinced him not to, but maybe I was wrong."

Elizabeth looked stunned, but anger quickly replaced it. "I'm so sorry."

Aaron shrugged. "I doubt anyone in Paris will give two shits about it. It'll be fine."

I glanced at Elizabeth and our eyes connected. She knew as well as I did that the press would eat this up, especially if Tracy put a spin on it to sensationalize it.

Elizabeth stood up, lifted her bag up and slung it over her shoulder.

"You'll be at the opening?" I asked.

Elizabeth shook her head.

"Oh, no you don't," Aaron laughed. "You can't drop a bomb and run away."

"I thought that was the Aaron way," she retorted.

"Ooh," I whispered.

"Seriously, I would appreciate it if you would come. You might be able to handle Tracy so that we don't have to," Aaron eyed her and she nodded slowly and glanced at me.

"I guess it is the least I can do," she sighed.

"It would be nice," I admitted.

She nodded and looked like she was about to burst into tears, but instead she gave us a quick wave and left the café quicker than I could turn around.

"Well, I guess we're back in the Twilight Zone," I whispered.

"I didn't know we ever left."

CHAPTER TWENTY-TWO

*R*egardless of what Aaron felt about his future in the art world, he'd been pouring himself into his work and what he created was sensational. Having the time away in the country centered us both and solidified our future together. The peace of the chateau quieted our minds and allowed us to focus on what mattered to us. We knew when we got back to Seattle, our lives would be going in several different directions, but we understood no matter what was thrown at us, we had one another to lean on. Talking with Elizabeth only finalized that. We were united and there was no tearing us apart. After meeting with her, we wandered over to the catacombs and got in line only to have Aaron's shoulder tapped and a couple of workers explained that the wait was too long in the line, and we wouldn't make it inside. They assured us if we came back about an hour earlier the next day, we'd be able to get in. Well, that didn't happen either. We'd gotten there at ten o'clock in the morning, only to have the same guys tells us that the line was too long, and we wouldn't make it in by closing time. I wasn't sure if I believed them, so I made Aaron hang around to see if they told others who tried to get in line the same thing.

They did. So we wandered back to the apartment and that was where I left him so I could do some shopping.

Everyone was arriving tomorrow and in a couple days his exhibit would open. I wanted to treat him to a peaceful night in with a home-cooked meal before the group arrived. I'd been planning the meal for days and was excited to scout along the Parisian streets on my own. I'd gotten pretty familiar with the blocks around our apartment, but I wanted to snoop a little farther out and this gave me the perfect excuse. Not to mention I needed some fresh air. Another nightmare woke me up, and I'd been shaken ever since. With the verdict expected today, I suppose it was too much for my subconscious to handle. Waking up to the thought of Derek being a free man was beyond chilling.

Aaron was finalizing details for the show with Gregory Sennet. Gregory was a nice man, and Aaron and I decided not to hold his daughter against him. I was just praying the showing would go smoothly despite the pending onslaught of media.

I walked down the cobblestoned alley, sipping on a Starbucks, which gave me that little taste of home I craved and brought a sense of normalcy to my otherwise peculiar reality. It was hard to believe Aaron had been in France over six weeks, and I'd been here for three. I figured by the time I got used to being here, we'd be heading for the airport. But until then, I was seeing and experiencing as much as Paris had to offer.

The 6th arrondissement was absolutely enchanting with its galleries, quaint shops, patisseries, and cafés. There was such vitality to this district, and it stirred something inside of me every time I stepped outside. It had been the perfect distraction, but I longed for the villa we'd left behind. Aaron and I had shared so much while we stayed there, and it felt like something that no one could ever take away from us. I didn't understand why that was important to me, but it was. I would treasure those memories for the rest of my life.

Exploring the rickety, green booths along the Seine had become a favorite hobby of mine, and today was no different. I had no idea how much time had gone by as I flipped through the pages of the used books and magazines. The yellowed pages and feel of the thick sheets carried me to another time. Most of the books I'd flipped through were in French, but it didn't matter.

"Bonjour," a man said.

I looked up from the bin to see a handsome

man standing next to me. His blond hair was disheveled, and his expression beguiling. The man matched my idea of a Parisian Professor. He was clasping a copy of Les Fleurs du mal, The Flowers of Evil. Baudelaire was one of the few French poets I recognized, and I appreciated this stranger's taste in poetry.

"Bonne journée à vous," I replied, glancing at the book.

And then I went for it. I attempted an entire sentence.

"Je adore ce poète."

The man grinned and nodded. "I do as well."

I chuckled, relieved that he spoke English because I'd gotten about as far as I could in French.

"This is for you," the man said, handing me the book.

"Oh, no. I can't accept this," I replied, shaking my hands at the man.

"It would be bad form not to accept my humble gift to you, mademoiselle. I see something in you. This book calls to be in your hands. Remember that no matter what people try to take from you, they can't take your truth. Your memories are your own and so is your future."

Before I had a chance to refuse, he shoved the book in my hands and turned around and walked away. It was one of the oddest interactions I'd ever encountered; yet I felt there was something more to it than chance. I held the book tightly and went on my way, as I searched for a place to sit and browse through the pages.

Finding an empty bench under a shade tree, I sat down and placed my bag next to me. I opened the book and a pressed rose marking a page fell to my lap.

I Have Not Forgotten Our White Cottage

I have not forgotten our white cottage,
Small but peaceful, near the city,
Its plaster Pomona, its old Venus,
Hiding their bare limbs in a stunted grove.
In the evening streamed down the radiant
sun,
That great eye which stares from the
inquisitive sky.
From behind the window that scattered its
bright rays
It seemed to gaze upon our long, quiet
dinners,
Spreading wide its candle-like reflections
On the frugal tablecloth and the serge
curtains.

~Charles Baudelaire /Trans. William
Aggeler

A shiver ran through me as I stared at the poem that was marked specifically for me. I didn't know what to make of it, and maybe that was okay for now. I didn't need to have all the answers in order to accept this mysterious message from a stranger. I reread the poem and closed my eyes, thinking about where my life had led me. I smiled internally as I realized it led me right to Aaron. My mind drifted back to our time at the chateau, and I couldn't help but feel at peace no matter what was waiting for me later tonight.

The summer breeze swept through my hair, and I took a deep breath in as I thought about a new beginning using my old dreams. The dreams I'd let someone rip away from me as if they'd meant nothing. Regardless of what the verdict was today, I had things that Derek could never take away from me. I had the villa with Aaron and I had me.

I read the poem one last time and placed the rose back inside before closing up the book and tucking it in my bag. I hopped off the bench and was ready to begin my mission. One of the stores I wanted to hit wasn't actually in this arrondissement. Theoretically, I could hop on a train and be where I wanted in fifteen minutes. I wasn't sure I believed that any longer because fifteen minutes seemed to be the standard answer whenever we asked how long it would take to get somewhere, and most of the time, it took far longer. Feeling completely determined, I spotted the Metro sign that stood tall across the street, and I decided to brave the trains on my own. It couldn't be that hard to figure out where I wanted to go.

I jogged down the stairs leading into the tunnel and got my ticket. When Aaron and I came back from the catacombs this morning, rather than walk, we took the train and all went according to plan until I fed the ticket through the machine and didn't move quick enough through the bar. The gate locked and Aaron was on one side, and I was on the other. I panicked as I tried to push my way through, but it wouldn't budge. Aaron was laughing, which didn't help and I just got exasperated. Between that and not getting to see the catacombs two days in a row, I was extremely annoyed. Thankfully, one of the volunteers led me over to a window where they exchanged my ticket for a new one that would let me through. I had no idea what would happen if this happened in a terminal that wasn't manned. I guess a person would just be out of luck.

I prided myself on getting through the system and hopping on the appropriate train in time. I sat with my bag pinned to my side so no one would steal what little I had and mentally calculated which stop I needed. Every time the train slowed my nerves ignited, worried that I'd miss my stop. Finally the correct stop flashed on the screen and even though the automated voice didn't sound quite like I imagined the stop to be spoken, I hopped off the train and made my way through the busy terminal and back up the stairs to daylight. This store better be as good as the reviews said.

Wandering down the street, I stared at the dangling signs as I tried to find the correct one. Seeing the sign, Une épicerie fine pour vous made me victorious against the city that had tried to claim me time and again. I swung open the door and complete jubilation spiked through my veins.

I'd made it. I was on my way to conquering this city yet!

I picked up a bag and wandered down the nearest aisle, picking up olives and toasted Grenoble walnuts, along with a little wine. A line wound along the case as people peered into the glass staring at the different meats and cheeses spread along the silver trays. My mouth watered looking at the different types of Brie.

When it was my turn to place my order, I fumbled my way through French and the shop owner seemed really happy that I at least tried. I paid for everything at once and walked out of the store triumphantly.

I decided to find a bakery nearby so I didn't have to bother with shopping when I got back to our arrondissement. I could just hop on the train, hop off, and head right for our apartment. I had no idea how long I'd been gone and didn't want Aaron to worry.

As I moseyed along the Parisian streets, I stopped every so often to look into the boutique windows and ogle at the shoes, bags, and clothes that beckoned me. I was grateful I was hauling around a bag of meat and cheese so I wasn't tempted to go inside.

With what seemed like far too long, I stopped and tried to figure out where in the world I was. I think I made enough turns that I was actually headed back in the direction of our district, the 6th arrondissement, but I wasn't certain. Spotting a bakery down the street, I made a left and beelined there.

I walked into the bakery and could smell the fresh baked bread. It made me want to stop where I was and eat every type of roll and loaf they had to offer. After scanning the case, I picked out four different rolls, names of which I butchered and happily paid. I strolled down the street making my way over several blocks, feeling more confident about where I needed to be with each step. At least, I would work up an appetite. Ambling along the sidewalks felt so French, and it helped that I was certain I was headed in the right direction. I stopped at a city map and glanced at where I thought I was headed. A big, red circle with the words vous êtes ici fooled me into believing I had this down.

After around four hours of aimlessly wandering around Paris, I realized that I was lost. I didn't want to admit it. At first, I was content with lying to myself. I assured myself that I truly wanted to see some of the tourist attractions I happened to drift by. It wasn't until the last ten minutes when I had actual arguments with myself that terror struck and so did hunger—not to mention thirst.

I stopped and took in a deep breath. I could handle this. I opened my phone and attempted to connect to the app I'd downloaded for emergencies like this, but I had no cell service on my broken phone.

None.

Zero.

Zip.

I stuffed my cell phone back in my bag and adjusted it in front of me. It didn't help hearing all the pickpocket rumors floating around endlessly. By this point in my day everyone was suspect in my book: the cute little kindergartener with the pigtails, lying in wait; the cute teenager flirting with his girlfriend, probably a ruse; and the sexy man who winked at me, just trying to distract me. It was definitely time to get my paranoid self home. I stared directly in front of me and started walking more briskly. Spotting what I'd hoped was a Metro station, I booked toward the sign. It wasn't until I arrived that I realized it wasn't a train station entrance, but there was a map.

I stared at the unfamiliar plotted course in front of me with the familiar large, red circle and the words, vous êtes ici sprawled on the map again. I'd come to know that phrase well.

You are here.

I sighed.

"Yes, I know I am here, but I don't know how to get there," I muttered, staring futilely at the map.

Unsure of how many hours I'd been wandering around, I began to feel a sense of panic take over. My stomach growled, and I laughed aloud as I found a bench and sat down. Plopping my bags next to me, I'd vowed not to touch the food I'd bought for dinner.

But my stomach sounded like a herd of elephants, and my feet were aching. I glanced up and down the street amazed that I'd somehow found the one street in Paris without any patisseries or cafés. There was not a single person on the street.

I wiggled my toes and attempted to get the blood flowing again as I glanced at one of the rolls sticking out of a bag. I was better than that. I wasn't going to eat our dinner. I was going to find a Metro station, figure out what trains to take, and find my way back to our apartment. That was going to be the plan.

I licked my dry lips and let out a sigh. This was torture. I was exhausted, thirsty, and hungry all while being lost in a city that prided itself on glorious food and drink, and somehow I managed to get lost in the one part of the city that had neither. Straightening out my legs, I let my feet float in the air as I figured out what to do. The blisters started throbbing and I knew I'd had it. I was done. I needed someone to pick me up off the streets of Paris.

The city had won.

I didn't have enough money for a cab since I'd used all my cash to buy the food, and I had no idea where a cab stop was anyhow. Hopefully, I had enough cash to ride the Metro. That couldn't be much... Could it? I guess it depended on how far away I'd gotten myself.

I glanced around the neighborhood once again and seeing no one, I lifted out the bottle of wine and untwisted the cap. Feeling completely dehydrated and hopeless, I took several big gulps, allowing the wine to wet my whistle just enough. I sighed and placed it back in the bag, propping it up enough so it wouldn't fall over. I grabbed a roll and ate it so quickly that by the time I was on the third one I was ashamed. It didn't help that I took a couple more sips of wine to wash it down.

It also didn't help that only bread and wine weren't a good mixture so I opened the jar of olives and began nibbling them to settle my stomach. Not wanting to eat them all, I put the lid back on and went in for the meat. I glanced around the street again and went in for the wine. I was starting to feel human again. Granted, I couldn't walk, but at least I wouldn't die of dehydration or hunger. I shoved everything into the bags and sat back on the bench. Without realizing it, my eyes had closed and it wasn't until I heard his voice that I realized I'd fallen asleep.

"Bonjour."

Hearing Aaron's voice made my world come absolutely alive. My eyes flashed open, and I no longer felt defeated and exhausted as I sprang to my feet.

Aaron stood on the sidewalk, grinning as his eyes traveled along my body, taking in the mess I'd become while walking around aimlessly for hours.

"How did you find me?" I asked.

"I tracked where your phone last pinged. When I came downstairs and saw that you still hadn't returned, I figured something might be wrong."

"Nothing's wrong," I lied. "I was getting to

know the city better."

His brow arched, and even he couldn't help the smile that landed on his lips as he reached over and dusted the breadcrumbs off my shirt. It only took another step for him to bring me into his embrace and press his lips to mine.

"You taste like wine," he murmured.

"I was thirsty."

"Did you see the verdict?" he asked, stepping back. His expression was solemn and my entire body became rigid with fear.

"My phone isn't working. Should I sit?"

Aaron nodded, and I knew my world was about to be forever changed.

Chapter Twenty-Three

Aaron and I had ridden in a cab back to the apartment the night before. It turned out I'd been wandering the streets of Paris for over five hours, and my feet had the proof to show for it. I was barely able to sleep as I waited anxiously for the sentencing. I woke up early and Aaron rose with me to hear the news. I quickly scrolled through my messages and found the one I'd been waiting for.

"He was sentenced to three-hundred and twenty months," I said, shaking my head in disbelief. The maximum sentence for attempted murder in the first. I expected to feel glee and relief, but I think I was still in shock. I handed Aaron the phone, and he read aloud the same words, and it didn't seem any more real coming from his lips.

I'd spent so long not getting my hopes up, that now I couldn't wrap my mind around the fact that Derek was going away for a very long time. There was no resolution with his accomplice on the outside, but my hope was that his cousin would plead guilty and get it over with. I doubted it would be that simple, but I could hope.

"You're handling the news really well," Aaron said, rubbing my back.

I shook my head, my hair falling out of my ponytail. "I don't think I believe it's really over. I've been waiting so long for something to go wrong that now that it has gone right I don't know what to do."

"Well, I think a celebratory dinner is in order," Aaron said, smiling. He looked so reassured and at ease with the news and I still felt wound up tight as a rope.

"I think that sounds like a wonderful idea. I wonder if Ayden or anyone even knows. They might have gotten on the plane before the verdict or sentencing was read."

"Yeah. I don't know. You better write to your mom so she knows you got the good news," Aaron said, pulling a shirt over his head. "I'm going to go make us breakfast."

I sat up and let the feelings of ease replace the torment I'd gotten so used to.

"We only have two hours before we meet them at the airport," I called to Aaron as I crawled out of bed. "I can't believe they're actually going to be here soon, and my brother's going to be engaged."

Aaron laughed. "You're assuming she's going to say yes."

"Hey, she'd be crazy not to marry him."

I slipped into my terrycloth robe and wandered into the kitchen where Aaron was slicing some of the leftover ham from the night before and scrambling eggs.

"I'm making us some breakfast sandwiches."

"You're getting pretty clever with breakfasts," I teased.

"Better enjoy it while we're here. I have a feeling once we get back to Seattle, there'll be no rest for the weary or wicked or both."

"However that goes," I laughed, taking a seat at the table as Aaron brought over a cup of French-pressed coffee. I took a sip and let the warmth trickle down my throat. "Can you believe tomorrow is your show?"

He shook his head. "Not really. I've got to go over there this afternoon."

"Well, I'm sure no one will mind. They'll probably need rest after the flight anyway."

Aaron grabbed a plate and made a sandwich out of the bread, cheese and warm slices of ham. He cut it in half and brought it over to me.

"Looks absolutely delicious."

He walked back into the kitchen and prepared a sandwich for himself before coming over and taking a seat next to me.

"Not that this trip hasn't been absolutely thrilling," he teased. "But I'm really looking forward to going home early."

I threw my head back and laughed. "Me too. I think I'm set for traveling for a while. Not that I didn't love every second of being here."

"Oh, of course. How could a person not love Paris?" he teased.

"So I still need to see the damn catacombs and the Eiffel Tower," I mused, wondering if we'd be able to fit them in with our company or if it would be by ourselves.

"Definitely."

"And we only got through a quarter of the Louvre…"

Aaron smiled and nodded. "We'll definitely make it through the rest."

"Promise?"

"Promise." He took a bite of the sandwich, and so did I.

And that's when I realized the weight that had been hanging on my heart had finally started to flutter away. The thoughts of a mad man were slowly drifting to another place and becoming a distant memory. Things were going to be okay. I was going to be okay and law school was going to be okay. And we were going to be more than okay.

Aaron leaned back in the chair and studied me as I chewed the last bite and I scowled at him, not enjoying the attention. I swallowed and waved my hand in front of him. "Not when I'm eating."

"You're just so beautiful." His eyes twinkled, and I hoped he'd never stop believing that.

I couldn't believe it. Ayden, Lily, Gabby, and Jason were right in front of me in Paris. The girls wrapped their arms around my neck, crashing into one another. They, no doubt, had heard the news.

"We're so happy for you," Lily gushed. "This is huge. That scumbag deserves life if you ask me, but I guess we'll take the maximum."

She stepped back and Ayden gave me a great big hug. "So happy to see you, knucklehead."

"Still with the knucklehead?" I groused.

"Yup. It might change to aunt knucklehead someday, but it'll still be there."

I narrowed my eyes as Jason gave me a hug. "Congrats, hun. You deserve it. You've been to hell and back."

I smiled and blushed. "We've all got something."

Aaron squeezed my shoulder and was beaming. I caught him trading looks with Ayden, and I loved that I was in on the secret. By the looks of everything, Lily was completely oblivious and I planned on keeping it that way. It was pretty easy, considering I had no idea when Ayden was going to pop the question.

"So your hotel is literally one block up from our apartment. You're going to love it," I gushed. "Aaron has to go to the gallery to check on things this afternoon, and I wanted to go with him because I'm just too nosey, but I thought that would give you guys some time to rest before we go to dinner."

"Totally," Jason said. "Between leaving Katie with Carla and the flight, I'm exhausted."

I glanced at Gabby. "She didn't want to be left?"

"No way."

"That's still too bad about everything. I thought you started the whole process soon enough so that she was allowed to come," I said, helping with Gabby's luggage.

Gabby blushed and dropped her gaze. I wanted to ask, but I kept quiet as we walked to their waiting car.

"So here's our address. Aaron thinks we'll be back to the apartment around six o'clock. Beep us and we'll let you up. We're on the sixth floor."

They shoved all their luggage into the car and piled in. I wasn't sure they were going to fit, but they made it and we sent them on their way.

Our car was still waiting for us, and we slowly walked over to it. "Well, that was a whirlwind. I feel bad for shoving them in the car and ditching them."

Aaron laughed and opened the back door of our car and I slid in. Aaron gave our driver the address of the gallery and we were off.

It was a short drive, about fifteen real minutes, until we arrived at the door of the gallery. I saw a few people hovering around and didn't realize what was going on until it was too late. As soon as we stepped out of the car, the flashes were going off and bits of English and French were being shouted at Aaron and I as we walked to the gallery. It was the most bizarre sensation I'd ever encountered. Since I had no idea what they were saying, it made it easy to ignore them as we bolted inside. The moment the door shut, the shouts went silent, and I was awestruck by what was directly in front of me.

Aaron's sculptures belonged here. They stood impressive in size and expression. The pieces were astounding, and it was empowering seeing Aaron's manifestations of temperament and art tower over the otherwise dull room.

Mr. Sennet walked into the space, offering apologies about the press. I doubt he knew who was behind the tipoff to the paparazzi, but regardless, I was still shocked any showed up. I don't think either Aaron or I really thought they would.

"So what do you think?" Gregory asked, clapping his hands as we walked around the first sculpture.

"Gorgeous," I whispered.

"They're certainly a commanding presence," Aaron said.

"We had a private showing for some of our top collectors. They bid on every single piece. We'll see how much higher we can get them after the opening." His eyes almost sparkled with dollar signs, and I realized he very well might have known about his daughter's antics with the paparazzi.

We spent the next several hours going over the setup and timeline for tomorrow night's events. When we finally left, the paparazzi were no longer waiting outside, and we were able to climb right into our waiting vehicle without hassle.

We made it back to the apartment barely in time to get settled before my brother and friends buzzed their way into our apartment.

Lily was beyond excited and Gabby was a close second. They rushed into the apartment thrilled to tell me something, but they stopped short when they saw the place.

"Wow. So this is where you've been spending your time?" Lily gawked.

"Most of it," I confessed. "But Aaron rented a chateau outside the city last week for us. We even went horseback riding."

"Showoff," Jason muttered, as he slapped Aaron on the back. "You're making the rest of us look bad."

Aaron's laughter filled the room, and he shook his head. "Believe me, I need all the victories I can get."

I rolled my eyes, but placed a kiss on his cheek as we walked into the living room and everyone took a seat.

"So something tells me you didn't rest in your hotel rooms," Aaron said, glancing at Jason who looked exhausted.

"Nope. No rest for the weary," Lily said.

I eyed Aaron and we couldn't help but laugh.

"What's so funny?" she prodded.

"I don't even know. So come on spill the beans. What did you manage to fit in this afternoon?" I asked, eager to hear about their first day in Paris.

"You're not going to believe it," Gabby gushed. "It is the coolest thing I think I've ever seen, like ever."

"Come on," I said, laughing.

"The catacombs. We got to see the catacombs," Lily exclaimed. "Have you seen them yet?"

"You're kidding right?" I asked.

"Yeah. You've got to be joking," Aaron said, grinning.

"Why would I joke about that?" Lily asked confused.

I let out a groan and threw the first pillow I could find right at her.

Aaron was cracking up, and I just kept tossing pillows at poor Lily while Gabby started chucking them back.

"Do you realize how many times I've tried to get into see those skulls?" I asked.

"I have no idea," Lily said, laughing in between breaths. "But they're really cool."

CHAPTER TWENTY-FOUR

The night was absolutely magical. Our friends came over early to have a celebratory cocktail before we all went to the gallery. It was so much fun to be with my best friends, dressed in cocktail dresses and playing pretend for an evening in Paris.

I was holding up my martini and toasting Jason, Gabby and Ayden as Lily ate some of the leftover olives from my afternoon out on the town. Aaron was standing behind me dressed in a tuxedo that fit him in all the right places. I was dressed in a sapphire blue dress that hugged my curves and made me feel like I was royalty.

"Hate to break it to you, but we should probably get going," Aaron said, wrapping his arm around my waist for one last squeeze.

"Wait until you see everything, guys," I started, but Aaron cut me off.

"No...no...no. That's not how it's done. Set the bar low so they're surprised." Aaron grinned and gave me one last peck on the cheek.

Jason laughed and shook his head. "We already know your work is amazing, brother. You don't have to sell us on your brilliance."

"True. Not many people I'd travel halfway across the globe for," Ayden teased and Lily bumped him with her hips. Ayden wrestled her into an embrace, and my heart warmed to see them together like that. I caught Ayden's hand resting on her stomach, and I almost choked on the last drop of my martini.

"You okay there?" Aaron asked, slapping my back.

"Yeah. Sorry. Got too excited."

Ayden flashed a peculiar grin as I followed them out of the kitchen, turning the lights off as we went.

The SUV was waiting for us at the curb, and we all managed to crawl in, but I was obsessing over my brother's hand placement.

"You okay?" Aaron whispered next to my ear.

"Yup. I'm just sleuthing."

"I'll let you be then," he laughed, and our vehicle began its journey to the gallery.

The streets were so narrow and the vehicle was so large that I decided not to look out the window. Instead, I kept my gaze focused solely on my brother and Lily. I didn't see any other suspect gestures or movements. So by the time we arrived at the gallery, I'd pretty much dismissed my musings.

A huge line had wrapped around the building and several paparazzi had lined up.

"Seriously, dude? Paparazzi?" Jason laughed.

"It's a long story," Aaron said, shaking his head.

"And one we'd like to forget," I chimed in as Aaron helped me out of the SUV.

"Leave you two alone in another country and you get into all kinds of trouble, huh?" Jason grinned as he stepped out of the vehicle and helped Gabby out onto the sidewalk. She was dressed in a pale pink chiffon dress. The neckline was dazzling on her, dipping low enough that ample cleavage mesmerized Jason with just about any movement.

As Ayden helped Lily out of the vehicle, I watched his careful movements with her and wondered, just wondered...but it was quickly squashed once people began hollering our names, and my cheeks flushed with embarrassment as we walked quickly down the carpet that had been rolled out in Aaron's honor.

Feeling like we'd never make it inside, I was relieved to feel the stuffy air touch my skin just as I heard the broken English call out hero and shooting. I hoped Aaron heard neither and he didn't show a reaction one way or another. The gallery was already filled with people admiring Aaron's pieces, and my chest felt like it wanted to explode with pride. Gabby and Lily hugged me as they watched Aaron wander through the crowd, answering questions and discussing each piece. This might be his last showing, but it certainly was an amazing one to end on. Not that I totally believed he was giving it up.

"I'm really proud of my brother," Gabby gushed, and I squeezed her hand.

"Me too. He's an incredible man."

Gabby nodded and smiled, and I swore I saw a glimmer of tears come and go as quickly as I spotted them.

"We're all so lucky," she said, hugging me and Lily.

I spotted Tracy and my body stiffened. Lily immediately felt it and followed my gaze to the woman scowling at us all huddled together.

"I've been waiting for this story," Lily said.

"Me too." Gabby nodded. "Let us have it."

Elizabeth came up behind Tracy and escorted her out of view, and my heartbeat quickened when I couldn't find Aaron in the crowd. I stood on the tips of my toes as I scanned the people moving between the pieces, and relief immediately flooded through my system the moment I spotted him.

Jason and Ayden were making their way around the backside of the room, studying the pieces, and Lily, Gabby, and I were weaving through the two tallest ones in the middle of the room as I proceeded to fill them in on the first couple weeks of my French experience. Between horror and fits of giggles, it didn't take much before I realized it was all a distant memory. As I relayed the Tracy details, I actually felt sorry for her. Anyone who got joy out of meddling in such a vicious way had to be absolutely miserable in their own life to spread the evil so to speak.

Aaron waved us over, and I wandered through the room, which was really crowded now. I stood next to him as he introduced me as his fiancée. I was startled at the slip of his tongue but loved the way it sounded as I shook hands with the man who was admiring Aaron's scion piece.

Jason found Gabby and they drifted into the crowd just as Ayden and Lily walked toward the front of the gallery.

The man thanked Aaron and continued studying the piece as we slowly walked away. Aaron's arm was wrapped around my waist as we strolled through the crowd. He'd stop every so often to converse with one of the attendees, and I swear if he let go of me, I might actually float away. I was so happy that so many were recognizing the brilliance that was my boyfriend and proving Tracy wrong. That was one comment I'd take to the grave with me.

Aaron guided me to a quiet corner and sat me down on one of the only empty chairs. For some reason, my pulse started pounding as I watched him kneel in front of me, but he quickly readjusted, and I realized I was way too ready for that, especially once I heard him say the word fiancée.

"I've been working on something since we went riding," Aaron began and my heart sped up again, not knowing what to expect.

"What would that be?" I asked.

"It's not much, but I saw this property and thought of you immediately. It's just east of the mountains in Washington. There's a small vineyard on the land and stables. When I saw the home, I knew it was meant for us. I mean I know not right away. You have law school to finish, I'll be busy in Seattle, but it'll be perfect for the weekends..." He grabbed his phone out of his pocket and slid it on, revealing a photograph of a small white cottage, eerily similar to the chateau we'd recently stayed at.

"I thought someday you might like to raise horses and teach our kids to ride. But in the meantime, it could be our little taste of France in Washington." His eyes connected with mine, and I couldn't help but fall in love with this man one click further.

He never ceased to amaze me, and I couldn't believe that Aaron had done this while we were in Paris. My mind drifted back to the strange fellow who'd given me the book of poetry, and my body tingled at the lack of coincidence. Nothing was beyond chance in this world. Everything happened for a reason. It was just a question of being open to the world's possibilities, and as we stood in a Paris gallery with my boyfriend's sculptures being praised by art critics from around the world, I knew that I'd never be able to imagine what life held for Aaron or me. It also occurred to me that I never told Aaron about my chance encounter. I'd have to do that someday.

"I don't even know what to say," I whispered.

"It's absolutely breathtaking and beyond thoughtful."

Aaron's eyes ignited with carnal desire, and I wished us to be somewhere else as he pressed his lips to mine. The bulbs of the cameras flashed in every direction. Even with my eyes closed, I saw the lights reflecting through, but I didn't care. I loved this man with all my heart and couldn't wait to get back to Washington and continue our lives together.

He slowly broke his lips from mine and smiled.

"Well, maybe that will give the paparazzi enough of the story they wanted," he said, standing back up and lifting me to my feet.

"Maybe so," I laughed, feeling like I was in another world.

The rest of the event floated by in such a dreamy state, I was surprised when it had actually ended. We all climbed into the SUV when Aaron announced a surprise detour.

We were finally going to the Eiffel Tower. I was so excited I almost jumped out of my seat.

Gabby was grinning from ear to ear and Lily slapped Ayden's knee. "Did you know about this?"

"Maybe. Maybe not." My brother grinned, and I knew he had this planned to perfection.

The drive was relatively quick and the SUV got us quite close. The area surrounding the tower was eerily still, and I held onto Aaron's hand a little tighter as we were ushered right into the elevator without even a wait or hassle.

Something seemed planned really well. Like perfectly so. I glanced at Ayden and tried to gauge his expression as we all waited in the elevator. Besides the operator there wasn't another person in sight. The doors closed and Lily and Gabby were babbling away as I eyed the men in the carriage. Every so often they'd trade glances, which only made me more excited. This had to be it. Ayden was going to pop the question.

Aaron slipped his arm around my waist, and nuzzled his chin into the crook of my neck as the elevator glided up the Eiffel Tower, the lights of the city sparkling below. The elevator came to a slow stop, and the operator instructed us to step off the elevator and follow the signs.

The platform was empty. Not a tourist to be found. Boy, talk about raising the bar high. I squeezed Aaron's hand as we walked along the platform and my heart rate began to increase. Not because of the excitement for my brother but because we were up so damn high. I slowly made my way over to the edge and looked below.

My fingertips pressed against the wire cage as I peered out over the city. Everything was so tiny, but glittered it like gold across the city. A chill dashed over my skin as I took in the beauty of this city. Finally, Paris had accepted me and I respected her. My skin tingled with excitement with what was awaiting my brother and Lily. I wondered how long we'd be up here before he popped the question.

"Brandy," Aaron whispered, draping his arms

over my shoulders.

"Mm..." My body melted into Aaron's as my eyes canvassed the beautiful city below.

"I don't ever want to lose you." His voice held something I didn't quite recognize and my body stiffened slightly.

"You never would."

"That makes me a very happy man," Aaron murmured as his lips skimmed along the crook of my neck, sending a spike of electricity through me. As quickly as the pleasure came, it left when he took a step away from me.

I spun around and noticed that everyone except Aaron had vanished from our lookout point. Gabby, Jason, Lily and Ayden were nowhere to be found. I craned my neck slightly trying to find the slightest hint of movement, but I saw none. My eyes flashed to Aaron's, and that's when my entire world went into slow motion. A violinist stepped from the shadows and began serenading us as my head began to spin. Aaron's expression turned to sincere contemplation as he reached into his tuxedo jacket.

I heard a sniff from behind a tower wall, and my heart raced into infinity and back as I watched the man I loved with all my heart get down on bended knee and remove a ring box from his jacket. My breath caught and my world spun out of control.

"Without your love, I'd be nothing, Brandy Rhodes. You make me whole. I know life hasn't always taken us where we thought we'd go, but we certainly can't complain that it's been boring..." Aaron's eyes locked onto mine and my lips parted, but I couldn't say a word. I was in a trance, frozen in front of him as he opened the ring box. "Will you make me the luckiest man in the world? Will you become the missing part of me? Will you become my wife?"

"Yes." I nodded as my hands trembled as Aaron slid the ring on my finger. I was in complete shock as Aaron stood up and wrapped his arms around me, pressing his lips to mine. Cheering erupted behind Aaron, and I realized there were far more voices than just Lily, Gabby, Jason, and Ayden. My mom whooped from the shadows as Aaron's mouth broke from mine.

"I love you, Brandy Rhodes. I told you that you were mine forever and I meant it."

I dabbed the tears that threatened to spill down my cheeks as I watched my mom, dad, Mason, Aaron's parents, and Katie come from the shadows. My mom threw paper confetti at us and I had to laugh. If you can't take the party streamers out of the girl, you bring the party streamers to Paris like only the Rhodes family could.

"I love you Mr. Sullivan and I have no idea how you pulled this off."

"The fun's not over," he whispered. He pointed at Ayden and I watched as my brother went down on one knee and asked Lily to be his wife. Lily nodded and cried as Ayden slipped the ring on her finger.

That was my breaking point. The tears fell from my eyes just as my mom began to wipe the wetness from hers. Mason walked over to me and hugged me.

"Congratulations, knucklehead." He turned and shook Aaron's hand. "You better take excellent care of her."

"Without a doubt."

"I thought you couldn't get off to come over here?" I narrowed my eyes at my brother.

"It was all part of the master plan," he laughed. "I just do what I'm told."

I turned and stared at Aaron. "How long was this planned?"

"A very long time. I asked your father for your hand in marriage before I even knew we'd be coming here. The rest was the easy part," he laughed as my father and mother made their way over, congratulating us both and hugging me like never before.

"I guess you're not my little girl any longer," my father whispered.

"I'll always be your little girl," I said, tearing up again.

"You've got yourself a wonderful man, Brandy. I couldn't have chosen better if I tried," my dad said, turning to shake Aaron's hand as my mother came in for another hug.

My dad turned to Ayden and gave him a huge hug just as I squealed with delight and hugged Lily. "I can't believe this."

"I can't believe this either," Lily said, sniffing in between breaths. "Ayden told me Aaron was going to pop the question and it took everything I had to keep it in."

"You've got to be kidding. Aaron told me Ayden was going to pop the question."

Ayden and Aaron both laughed and pointed at each other. "We knew we had to throw you both off somehow. You're far too suspicious for your own good."

I couldn't deny that. Gabby gave me sly grin and hugged Jason. "Guess who knew both of you were getting the question popped. This girl." She pointed her thumbs at her chest and Jason picked up Katie and walked over so she could give me a hug and look at my ring.

"Pretty," Katie said, before resting her head back on Jason's chest.

My night couldn't have turned out anymore magical. I was with the man I loved with all my heart and family and friends who would do anything for me, and I had a sneaking suspicion I might be an aunt soon. Or I could be fiercely wrong. Only time would tell.

But one inarguable fact was that I was deeply in love with Aaron Sullivan, and I couldn't imagine my life any other way.

Note from Karice:

Thank you for taking the time out of your busy schedules to read the Beyond Love Series. I hope you've fallen in love with the characters as much as I have. I'm excited to announce the Island County Series, debuting in 2015.

The first book in the series will follow Mason Rhodes as he finds love in an unexpected place. I'm absolutely thrilled about linking these two series together and starting off the first book with Brandy's single brother is a dream. For more information, be sure to join my mailing list at www.karicebolton.com.

And don't forget to follow Lily and Ayden as they head down the aisle in Beyond Promise, but nothing is as it seems...

AVAILABLE 2015

Beyond Promise
and
Beyond the Mistletoe

And the Island County Series featuring Mason Rhodes from the Beyond Love Series.

Keep reading for an excerpt from Hidden Sins and Beyond Chance Recipes...

Recipes

Croissant French Toast

6 eggs
2 tbl honey
1/3c milk
1 tbl vanilla
1 tsp cinnamon
butter for frying
5 croissants

Whisk together eggs, honey, milk, vanilla, and cinnamon. Slice croissants in half. Melt butter in skillet on low. Dip each side of croissant in prepared liquid and place as many slices as will fit in the skillet. Cook for about four minutes (until golden brown) and flip and cook on low until warmed through center.

Ham Strata

9 eggs, whisked
3 c milk
1 c ham, cubed
1 onion, chopped
1/2 pkg frozen spinach, chopped
1 tsp salt
2 tsp pepper
4 tbl butter
2 c cheddar
1 loaf of French bread, cubed

Sauté onions in 2 tbl butter until golden. Add spinach, salt, and pepper and cook for five minutes on medium heat and remove from burner.

Coat casserole dish in remaining butter and layer bottom of dish with 1/3 of cubed bread and ham. Pour 1/3 of egg and milk mixture of bread, sprinkle with cheese and repeat until all ingredients are gone.

Cover and refrigerate overnight. Allow strata to sit out for twenty minutes. Preheat oven to 350 degrees and cook strata, uncovered, for 40 – 50 minutes (until it's golden brown).

Hidden Sins

Karice Bolton

Prologue

Hannah

*"H*ave you found her yet?" The male voice cut through my soul as I peered down from the hayloft. It was Miles, the father of the man I was supposed to marry. It was an arranged marriage. One that I couldn't accept, but I never would've guessed that his father was involved in this. Then again, for the first twenty years of my life, living here had seemed like an amazing gift, not a horrific nightmare that I couldn't wake up from. I steadied my breathing to ensure I wasn't heard as I watched the two men below me. I needed to stay in control. I had planned too long to fail now.

"No. It looks like she took off. Maybe two days ago. She left most of her belongings behind, but I'd say enough was missing to indicate that she's on the run. Her mother went through the house to confirm that there were items missing," the younger man said. There was something about his voice that was familiar, and I tried to focus on his features, but I couldn't place him, which was odd. The community I grew up in wasn't huge, but it was large enough that people could blend in somewhat. I guess a face could be missed here or there.

"She knows too much, Eric," Miles said, rubbing his temples.

Eric! I knew an Eric in high school, but we

were told he'd left the community. Obviously not.

"Just like her sister," Eric responded. I saw a trace of a smile touch his lips as he shook his head. "But we took care of that problem, and we'll take care of this one."

What about my sister? I'd been told she left the community, ran away. My stomach turned into itself as I thought about my family. Did they know what was going on here? Was my mom actually concerned about my safety or only helping to lead them to me?

Miles took a seat and propped his elbows on the desk, glaring at Eric. "We don't actually know that you took care of Hannah's sister. Now do we?"

"I watched her fall from the cliff," Eric argued.

"No body was ever recovered."

"The authorities said that with the currents, it might never be." Eric stood his ground.

Miles shrugged as if to dismiss the argument that couldn't be won. "You're sure Hannah saw something? Two in a family calls too much attention..."

Eric paced across the floor. "We found her in the bushes close to where the other issue had been taken care of. If Hannah didn't see what unfolded, the gunshots and screams surely would've alerted her. From her vantage point, she could've seen everything. And the wild look in her eyes..."

I know more than you bastards could ever imagine.

"Enough said. Add that to the fact that she'd

already gone to the authorities about Tina," Miles shook his head. "And we've got a big problem on our hands. A problem you were supposed to take care of. We're just lucky that Mark was the officer on duty when she went to the police station. We don't run our organization on luck, Eric."

My heart was pounding as I listened intently. One of the nails in the wood beam poked my ankle something fierce, but I didn't dare move.

"She couldn't have gotten far. We'll find her. My guess is she's headed to Florida, and I've got people already headed that direction," Eric said.

"What makes you think Florida?"

"I found some notes on different cities in Florida. They were tucked under her mattress."

"If this woman is smart enough to vanish without a trace, do you really think she's going to forget or leave behind a few key pieces of information? Come on. You've got to be kidding me. She's just sending you on a wild goose chase." Miles pounded his fist on the desk. "I'm taking this over. You're done. And don't tell my son any of this. You understand?"

Eric balled his fists together at the commandment. "Wouldn't dream of it."

Did that mean Brandon, my fiancé, wasn't involved? I pushed the lump down in the back of my throat as I thought about my entire life being highly orchestrated for some cause I didn't even understand.

Miles stood up, obviously agitated, and both men walked out of the office. It would take them several minutes to walk through the stables that the office was connected to, and I had no plans to come down from my perch until well into the midnight hour. I'd gotten what I came for; the last of the documents were securely tucked into my waistband. It was just an added bonus to catch Miles here, discussing my fate. At least my hunch was right. If they caught me, they'd kill me.

I shifted slightly, moving my ankle away from the nail, as my mind drifted to my sister. Four years ago she had vanished without a trace. My mother was in hysterics, but my father and brother had been completely stoic, dismissing my sister's disappearance as if the cat never came home for the night. Eventually, they had convinced both my mom and me that she had chosen to live a life outside the community. It wasn't unheard of so I was willing to blindly believe that assumption, even though my sister never gave me any reason to believe that she wanted out. In hindsight, that was my tipping point.

With every passing minute that I was stuck in the rafters, I began to doubt my plan that I'd worked on for months. I was only buying time, trying to save enough to get me out of here without looking like I was doing anymore than usual to earn money. Everything was going according to plan until three nights ago. That's when everything changed in my world. Instead of just wanting to escape, I wanted answers.

When I saw her eyes—my best friend's eyes—

filled with terror, I knew I couldn't just walk away so I followed. She asked me not to, told me to stay away, but I followed her from a distance as she walked through the pasture toward the woods. I didn't know if she knew I was following until it was too late. I watched her trembling hands as she covered her face, and she sank down into the dirt, crying. She had told me that she'd been having troubles with her husband— another arranged marriage, and another reason I had no intention of following through with mine. I halfway expected to see him meet her in the woods.

Instead, two men came from nowhere, wearing masks. She didn't fight, and I didn't know what to expect. I closed my eyes quickly and took a deep breath as I readied myself to run up on them. When I heard the first shot, my eyes flashed open as her gaze landed on mine. She knew I'd followed her. Another shot echoed into the air followed by laughter from the one I could now identify as Eric.

My body trembled as the images flooded through me, and I knew if I was going to survive long enough to expose everything, I needed to create a new life. I had to forget as much as I could about this old one, until the time was right.

Chapter One

Hannah

I let out a sigh as I sat in the dusty, blue truck that had miraculously managed to make it across the country. Between the funny interior smell, the engine knocking at speeds over fifty miles-per-hour, and the tricky method for locking the driver's door, I hadn't even been sure I'd actually make it out of my hometown. I found a '99 GMC Sonoma for only eight hundred dollars, and I bought my way out of a life that wasn't my own. Or at least, I hoped I had. Only time would tell. I turned off the radio and watched a family wander into the Starbucks. My chest tightened as I thought about who I'd left behind. But it had to be done. I couldn't second-guess my decisions now. There was no turning back.

I grabbed my wallet and slid out of the truck, feeling the warm California air kiss my skin as I slowly walked across the parking lot toward the coffee shop. I wasn't used to temperatures like this in March, but I was certain I'd quickly learn to love the weather. From what I'd read, Southern California skipped over the entire winter season, which sounded perfect to me. New England winters were brutal and long— really long.

My stomach growled as I pulled the door open

and smelled the aroma of coffee and pastries waft through the air. I hadn't eaten anything since the night before and desperately wanted a big cup of coffee. I'd tried not to spend much money on the long road trip in case I needed any extra cash for emergencies. Lucky for me, I'd made it to my destination without one hiccup and could splurge on a measly cup of coffee.

Yay me!

The family from outside was still in front of me, placing their order as I stood in line. The mom's latte order had so many components I lost track. It was no longer just a drink with coffee and milk. I watched her movements carefully, noticing every blonde hair was in place and her suit flawless. She seemed so in her element, and for some reason that made me feel completely out of mine. Her husband was put together just as impeccably, and I found myself running my hands along my sweatshirt to press out the wrinkles that had formed from the countless hours of driving. I was in yesterday's yoga pants, which were now technically today's, and my blonde hair desperately needed to be washed so it was piled on top of my head in a clip. I glanced around Starbucks and noticed that the family in front of me wasn't the anomaly. Everyone looked put together and ready to conquer the world. I was the odd one with tired brown eyes.

There was a brunette in the far corner who wore Hollywood shades, and her khaki capris showed off her model legs. The guy at the next table over looked like he'd just stepped out of the pages of a Men's Fitness magazine as he intently stared at his iPad. This had to be the best-dressed coffeehouse in America.

"Miss, I can take your order," the male barista said, as the family walked to the drink counter.

I snapped my head to see a friendly guy about my age, motioning for me to step forward to the counter.

"Oh, sorry," I said, nearly tripping to the register.

"Take your time."

"I'd like a large coffee," I said, smiling.

The guy's blond hair was shaggy and his blue eyes playful as he grabbed the white cup. "Pike Place or French Roast?" he asked.

"Pike I guess," I muttered, unzipping my wallet.

"A Venti Pike Place, and can I get your name?"

"Hannah," I said, feeling a breeze from behind as the door swung open.

A wave of shivers ran across my skin, and I started to laugh at how quickly I became acclimated to the warm weather. The barista wrote my name on the cup and called out my drink as he rang it up.

"Two-eighty," he said, as I felt someone come up behind me in line.

"Can I add a blueberry scone too?" I handed him my debit card as he nodded.

Taking my card, he quickly added the scone to the order and swiped the debit.

"So how's your day been?" the barista asked,

waiting for the transaction to complete.

"Really good. Yours?" Another wave of goose bumps ran along my body, and I glanced around, unsure of the source this time. There was no breeze.

"Been great." His eyes landed on the screen, and I saw his jaw tense as he swiped the card again. "Do you by any chance have another form of payment?"

My heart sank and my body felt like it was on fire. I had no other cards, and there should be plenty of money to cover a scone and coffee.

"Can you try it again?" I barely squeaked out. "Third time's a charm."

The barista gave me a sympathetic grin and swiped the card once more.

"Sorry. Same result." The barista handed the card back as my entire body turned into a hot mess. I was absolutely mortified. It wasn't like I was trying to buy a television. I just wanted a lousy cup of coffee. And what was worse was that the money in the account needed to get me by until I could find a job in town. So where was the money?

"Umm. I'm sorry. Can you cancel my order," I whispered. All I wanted to do was run out of the coffee shop and hide in my truck. I wasn't supposed to meet my roommates for another hour, but maybe they wouldn't mind if I showed up early.

Just as the barista was about to key in the cancellation, a male voice interrupted my mini-hell of humiliation.

"I've got it covered. Technology can be such a pain." The guy from behind me took a step forward, and a surge of warmth flooded through me. His voice was gravelly, sexy, and didn't relay a bit of sympathy for my predicament. His immediate dismissal of the crisis at hand actually made me feel immensely better, like this sort of thing happened all the time. And then I felt him, his energy, wrap around me.

He was intense.

"You don't have to do that," I said, turning to see the guy take a step next to me, handing the barista his card.

My heart nearly stopped when I saw how good-looking he was. All six-foot-something of him towered next to me and I felt abuzz with delight. He was dressed like everyone else in this mystical coffee house. But on him, the black suit stretched across his shoulders in such a way that I could almost imagine what lay under his jacket. After all, I was in the land of mirages. Men like this didn't exist in my world. His wavy, dark brown hair framed his chiseled features, and his green eyes were beyond striking as he smiled at me briefly.

"Add a Venti Iced Coffee and an oatmeal cookie to the order," the man said, ignoring my statement as he placed a hand on my shoulder, sending an impossible charge through me.

His eyes connected with mine, and my entire body responded to him in a way that I'd never experienced before. I dropped my gaze and felt a warmth swell deep inside me as he continued to watch me.

"Thank you," I said.

"Anytime." His hand slipped off my shoulder.

"I'm not sure what happened. I should…"

"No need to explain. Banks screw up all the time." He smiled at me and I nodded, thankful for his ability to put me at ease.

"Well, thanks again," I said, turning to walk toward the counter where the drinks were called.

I felt his gaze on me and didn't know what to do. I felt extremely self-conscious as I thought about my day-old wardrobe and messy blond hair. I really didn't fit in here, but I better start learning how to do so.

"Scone and Venti Pike Place for Hannah," a female barista with red, spikey hair called out.

"Thank you," I said, quickly grabbing my food and drink, hoping for a quick escape.

Reaching the door, I glanced behind me and saw the guy grabbing his own drink before looking over at me. My heart stopped as his eyes locked on mine, and I knew I needed to get out of here.

"Hannah," his throaty voice stopped me in my tracks. "It was nice meeting you."

He looked so damn charming, and it was really nice of him to cover my order, but I didn't want to start calling attention to myself. Yet, I was doing that every moment I stood in the coffee house with a dopey smile on my face. I was counting on California to provide the anonymity I needed, and I was also counting on my bank account to be fuller than it was, which had me extremely concerned. I most certainly had enough funds in there to buy a cup of coffee. I couldn't do what my heart wanted me to do so I waved with the hand holding my scone bag and left the coffee house in a dash.

My truck looked like a refuge as I neared the driver's side. The fancy car next to me was parked incredibly close to my truck, and I found myself juggling the coffee and scone as I opened my door. Just as I snuck in between the door and seat, my coffee cup took a nosedive, spilling on the pavement below.

"Shoot." I tossed my scone onto the console and sat in the driver's seat, closing the door behind me. This wasn't how I'd imagined rolling into my new town. It had to get better from here, right? Opening my window, I let the warm sea air fill the car as I munched on my scone. I'd have to wait until the car next to me left so I could clean up my mess outside before taking off. Thankfully, I had some water in my car to help wash down the somewhat dry scone that kept sticking in my throat. As I looked around the parking lot and over to the beach, a deep sense of loneliness crept through me. It was a familiar feeling, but this time it was different. I had nothing to hold onto in my new surroundings. There was no one to commiserate with. There was nothing around here that provided grounding or old memories for good or bad. There were palm trees dotting the edge of the parking lot and tiny orange flowers sprinkled along curb. It was quite different than a foot of dirty snow. I could get used to this.

I heard footsteps behind my car and glanced in the rearview. My heart sped up as I spotted the guy from inside the coffee house. It was definitely my time to exit this parking lot. I quickly put the key into the ignition and turned it, hearing nothing more than a chug and a whir. No turn of the motor. No rev of the engine.

Great!

I saw movement out my driver's window and saw the man walking along the driver's side of the car that was parked next to me. So that was his car, seemed fitting. I didn't even recognize what type of car it was. It just screamed expensive. I twisted the key in the ignition once more, and this time I was met with silence. I didn't even get so much as a grunt from the engine.

Figured!

Letting out a sigh, I thumped my forehead onto the steering wheel and began to laugh in disbelief.

"Excuse me, Hannah?" The man's bold voice interrupted my internal comedy hour, and I lifted my head to see his concerned gaze.

"Hey," I said, pressing my lips together.

"Do you need a ride somewhere?" he asked, placing his hands on his car roof.

"No. I've got it," I said, smiling.

"Do you need me to call a tow truck?" he offered.

"Nah. I think that would go about as well as

my coffee venture."

"Oh, I see." He glanced across the street toward the beach and back at me. "I saw your plates are from New Hampshire. Here on vacation?"

"Um. Kind of. No. Not really."

I didn't need to be having this conversation with him or anyone.

"Are you sure I can't help get you to where you're going? I don't feel right about buying a woman a cup of coffee and then leaving her stranded in a parking lot." His smile was dazzling and it was everything I could do not to take him up on his offer. But I couldn't afford to owe anyone anything else, let alone having him know where I was going.

He walked around the front of his car and inched his way between our two vehicles before his eyes landed on my coffee on the pavement. He was now standing directly next to me, and the breeze carried the soft scent of his cologne into the car. God, he smelled good. It was like a mixture of ocean and something else wonderful.

"Today has not been your day, has it?" A slight smirk appeared on his lips as he reached into his suit jacket, grabbing his wallet. "Listen. Here's my card. If you need anything, give me a call. California's a huge state. One wrong turn and you're in a place you really don't want to be."

I took the card from him and he smiled.

"Thanks," I muttered, glancing at the card.

Luke Fletcher

Fletcher Security
Private Security, Risk Management, and
Counter Terrorism

"You know," he began, bending over and picking up the empty cup. "I can't, in good faith, let you leave here without a cup of coffee. I'll be right back."

"No," I called, but it was too late. He was already out of earshot on his way back into the coffee shop.

I leaned my head against the headrest and let out a garbled groan as I thought about how screwed up things were. How could things go so wonderfully well over the last several days only to end up in the worst possible scenario, without a running car and no money? I needed to get out of here before he came back. He was too much. All of it was too much. I turned the key again and this time the engine almost turned over. I counted to ten and tried again.

"Come on," I muttered.

"Trying to escape?" I heard Luke laughing as he brought me my cup of coffee.

"Uh, no. I mean," I laughed. "Maybe. That was faster than I thought."

"They remembered me and gave it to me free of charge." He smiled.

I took the cup of coffee from him and placed it in the coffee holder. I might've been sheltered for the last twenty-two years of my life, but I wasn't stupid. I wouldn't be drinking something from some strange guy, no matter how appealing he was. The more I looked at him, the closer I felt to him, which was just as dangerous.

"I've got to get going," I muttered, waving him away, but all I was met with was deep laughter.

"Are you planning on Flintstoning it out of here?" he asked, his brow arching. "I really don't mind giving you a ride."

"That's not what I meant," I said, glaring at him, but I couldn't help but laugh. "But no thanks."

"Oh, right. That was my cue. Listen, you have my business card. I don't want to make your day any worse so I'll let you do what you think you've gotta do, but if you change your mind... Call me and I'll get a cab to come for you."

I nodded and watched as he walked away from my window. He was distracting enough that the loneliness had somewhat dissipated until I realized he was leaving. Then it slowly seeped back in.

I was stranded in a parking lot twenty minutes away from where I needed to be. I had a debit card that was completely useless, and a guy who was willing to help me out. Was I determined to make my life difficult?

"Umm. Maybe, I'll save the call and say I'd love a cab ride, and once I'm on my feet, I'll be sure to—"

"You owe me nothing." He shook his head and smiled, grabbing his phone out of his pants. I watched him as he called for a cab and wondered how I'd gotten so lucky to meet such a kind soul. I had flown past embarrassment a long time ago, and I was just hoping nothing more would go wrong.

"I'll wait until the car shows up, and I'll help you haul everything from your truck into the vehicle. You don't want to leave anything in the open, even if it's tied down. What we can't fit in we'll put in the cab of your truck," he said, his eyes meeting mine.

"Thanks." I bit my lip and thought about what to say to this stranger who'd shown me more kindness in the last thirty minutes than I'd encountered in a long time. "This is really nice of you."

He shook his head, stripping off his jacket before walking over to the truck bed. I gently maneuvered between our two vehicles and stood next to him, my eyes dropping to his chest. I could literally see the ripple of the fabric from the definition of his muscles. I couldn't even imagine what that must look like underneath.

He caught my gaze and a tiny curl of his lip surfaced before I turned away, feeling the flush roll up my body.

"You like to park close to things," I teased, as I worked on untying one of the ropes.

"It's a bad habit. I tend to get wrapped up in my own world." He loosened a knot and began on another one.

"I find that incredibly hard to believe," I said, glancing at him. His awareness and willingness to help me out of my predicament told me otherwise.

"Well, there's always exceptions to the rule, I

suppose," he said, letting the first set of ropes fall to the side of the truck bed. "Especially if someone is as eye-catching as you."

I laughed and shook my head. I knew he was only being kind, considering what I looked like compared to the rest of the microcosm. My cheeks warmed as I worked my fingers against the knot, finally loosening it enough to let it fall.

Luke was on the other side of the truck bed, untying the last of the rope when I saw a black Escalade come up behind him and park.

That was odd.

"Your chariot awaits," Luke said, smiling from across the truck bed.

"That's a cab?" I asked.

"It's umm a car service I use and trust," Luke corrected, his gaze dropping away from mine. "I thought we'd have a better chance of fitting everything inside. Less hassle for you that way."

My chest constricted with the idea of leaving this kind stranger behind. His compassion was the first genuine gesture I'd experienced in a very long time. But maybe that was how it was in the real world. Maybe my new beginning would be full of Lukes.

"So it is," I said, nodding. "Thank you."

There were only five boxes and a suitcase in the truck bed, along with an old wooden chair I couldn't part with, which in hindsight, seemed pretty odd.

Luke grabbed the first box I pointed to as the driver appeared, ready to help load his SUV with my belongings. The driver was a portly, older man with dark hair, graying around the edges, and he was dressed in a black suit.

I grabbed my suitcase and pushed it into the vehicle. I went back to the cab of my truck, grabbed everything off the seat and inside the console and shoved it into a bag. It felt odd leaving the truck behind. It had become home over the last week and it was mine; one of the few things that was. The moment I figured out what happened with my bank account, I'd get my truck, but for now, I needed to get to the house and internet. I shoved my bag and purse onto the floor of the front seat.

Everything had been transferred to the SUV and relief spread through me, knowing I wouldn't have to leave anything behind in the truck. I climbed into the SUV as the driver did the same.

Luke walked over to me and stood next to the open door. "Remember, if anything else comes up, you have my number."

"Why are you being so kind?" I asked softly.

His eyes locked on mine and he smiled.

"You looked like you could use a little kindness in your world. Welcome to California." Luke closed the door and took a step back, waving as the driver turned on the ignition and stepped on the accelerator.

"Where to, Miss?" the driver asked.

I gave him the address and his jaw tensed. "Are you sure about that address?"

"That's the one I was given. Why?" I asked.

"It's not a good part of town. That's all."

"Oh. Well, that's where I'm headed."

"Very well," the driver said, turning the vehicle onto the main road.

I looked out the window and saw Luke still following the vehicle with his gaze. I gave him a quick nod and prayed that whatever was waiting for me wouldn't be worse than what I left back home.

ABOUT THE AUTHOR

Karice received an MFA in Creative Writing from the U of W. She has written over thirty novels, and she has several exciting projects in the works (or at least she thinks they're exciting). Karice lives in the Pacific Northwest with her awesome husband and two cute English Bulldogs. She loves anything to do with snow, and she seeks out the stuff whenever she can, especially if there's a toasty fire to read by.

CONTACT KARICE

Please visit her online at http://www.karicebolton.com or via Twitter/Facebook/Pinterest @KariceBolton.

If you'd like to be included on her mailing list to find out about new releases, go to Karice Bolton's website

Or

you can text KariceBooks to 313131 to receive a message from Karice on Release Days!